D0267728

County Libraries

International County

ACC. No: 03166441

Worst.
Person.
Ever.

Worst.
Person.
Ever.

Douglas Coupland

WILLIAM HEINEMANN: LONDON

Published by William Heinemann 2013

2 4 6 8 10 9 7 5 3 1

Copyright © Douglas Coupland 2013

Douglas Coupland has asserted his right under the Copyright, Designs and
Patents Act, 1988, to be identified as the author of this work.

This book is sold subject to the condition that it shall not, by way of trade
or otherwise, be lent, resold, hired out, or otherwise circulated without
the publisher's prior consent in any form of binding or cover other than
that in which it is published and without a similar condition, including this
condition, being imposed on the subsequent purchaser.

First published in Canada in 2013 by Random House Canada

First published in Great Britain in 2013 by
William Heinemann
Random House, 20 Vauxhall Bridge Road,
London SW1V 2SA

www.randomhouse.co.uk

Addresses for companies within The Random House Group Limited
can be found at: www.randomhouse.co.uk/offices.htm

The Random House Group Limited Reg. No. 954009

A CIP catalogue record for this book
is available from the British Library

ISBN 9780434019908 (Hardback)
ISBN 9780434019915 (Trade Paperback)

The Random House Group Limited supports the Forest Stewardship
Council® (FSC®), the leading international forest-certification organisation.
Our books carrying the FSC label are printed on FSC®-certified paper.
FSC is the only forest-certification scheme supported by the leading
environmental organisations, including Greenpeace.
Our paper procurement policy can be found at:
www.randomhouse.co.uk/environment

Cover and half-title image: JIANG HONGYAN/Shutterstock.com

Printed and bound in Great Britain by Clays Ltd, St Ives PLC

This book began, improbably, as an attempt in *McSweeney's* No. 31 to reinvigorate the biji, a genre in classical Chinese literature. Biji roughly translates as "notebook," and can contain anecdotes, quotations, random musings, philological speculations, literary criticism and anything that the author deems worth recording. The genre first appeared during the Wei and Jin dynasties, and matured during the Tang dynasty. The biji of that period mostly contain the "believe-it-or-not" kind of anecdote, and many of them can be treated as collections of short fictions. My thanks to Graham Weatherly, Darren Franich, Jordan Bass and Dave Eggers. You've made me feel like Cher getting an Oscar.

Worst. Person.

Ever.

01

Dear Reader . . .

Like you, I consider myself a reasonable enough citizen. You know: live life in moderation, enjoy the occasional YouTube clip of frolicking otters and kittens, perhaps overtip a waitress who makes the effort to tart herself up a bit, or maybe just make the effort to try to be nice to the poor—*yay, poor people!*

I suppose, in general, I enjoy travelling through life with a certain Jason Bourne–like dashingness. *Oh no! An assassin is rappelling down the side of the building, armed with a dozen Stanley knives! What are we going to do? It's Raymond Gunt! We're saved!*

That's my name, Raymond Gunt, and welcome to my world. I don't know about you, but I believe that helping others is a way of helping yourself; what goes around comes around—karma and all that guff. So, seeing that I'm such a good soul and all, I really don't know how to explain the most recent month of my life. There I was, at home in West London, just trying to live as best I could—karma, karma, karma, sunshine and lightness!—when, out of nowhere, the universe delivered unto me a searing hot kebab of vasectomy leftovers drizzled in donkey jizz.

Whuzzat?! Hello, universe? It's me, Raymond! What the fuck!

I am left, dear reader, with no other option than to believe that when my world turned to shit last month, it was not, in fact, *me* who had done anything wrong. Rather, it was the *universe*, for I, Raymond Gunt, am a decent chap who always does the right thing.

And as I look back to try to figure out when the universe and I veered away from each other, I think it definitely had to be that ill-starred morning when I made the mistake of visiting my leathery cumdump of an ex-wife, Fiona.

Fi.

It was a blighted Wednesday off Charing Cross Road. After about fifty ignored emails, Fi deigned to allow me to come to her office, in a gleaming steel-and-limestone executive tombstone that straddles one of those tiny streets near Covent Garden. The building's lobby was redeemed by being filled with heaps of that 1990s art about death and fucking—pickled goats, fried eggs and tampons—and there was a faint hissing sound as I passed through it and into the elevator, the sound of my soul being sucked out of me, ever so nicely, thank you.

Behind her desk sat Fiona, elfin, her pixie hair dyed a cruel black. She cocked an eyebrow at me. "Jesus, Raymond, I've seen rhesus monkeys that look hotter than you." She was busy piling caviar atop a Ritz cracker.

"Lovely to see you, too, dear."

Her office was well-oiled leather and chiselled steel,

a fine enough reflection of her method of handling daily life. What was painfully evident was that Fi was minting money with her casting agency. The joke was on me for having suggested that she give the casting gig a try. She's an expert at meeting people and figuring out instantly what their personal style of lying is and how to make it work for them. What else is acting, if not that?

But you do need to know that Fi is a dreadful, dreadful, dreadful person. She is monstrous. She is the Anti-shag. She is an atomic bomb of pain. If you puncture her skin, a million baby spiders will explode from her body and devour you alive, pupating your remains, all the while making little squeaking noises that will taunt you while you die in excruciating agony.

And yet . . .

. . . and yet there is something about Fi's, um, *musk*. I can loathe her at a distance, but up close that scent overrides every other emotion I harbour for the woman: murderous rage, bilious hatred and not a small degree of fear. Fi is the only woman who's ever had this effect on me. All the crap I've put up with just for a whiff of her: all the times she's fucked me over, looted my bank account, stolen my pills and trash-talked me all the way from Heathrow to Stansted. My inability to overcome this most primal of attractions has been the downfall of my life. There is no other way to explain one of nature's most catastrophic and implausible pairings, but I guess that's what any chap says about his wife.

As I entered her office, Proustian recollections of our time together swam in my head. I felt poetic and wistful.

"One moment, Raymond." Fi removed a black onyx stash box of coke from a desk drawer, sprinkled some of it on top of the caviar, and began to demolish her snack, conveniently forgetting to invite me to join in. The noises from her mouth were like randomly typed keys: "*Vbv bdlkfnsld jz slvbds lbfbakl.*"

"Looks delicious, dear."

Suddenly she leaned back in her chair and began coughing out mouthloads of crackers and caviar. "*Vbn. Sfhejwbe cfbiqq fflekh!!!*"

Heimlich: yes or no? "Dear?"

She waved me away and finally shot a cluster of sturgeon eggs out her nostril. "Fucking hell." She used a nearby letter to fan her face. The crisis seemed to have passed. "Ooh. There. Finally it's gone," she said.

"What is?"

"The food trapped in my esophagus. It's in my stomach now."

"Fucking hell, that's disgusting, Fi."

"How is that disgusting, Ray?"

"It's like you've just taken a massive shit inside yourself."

Fi burst into a cackle. "Sometimes I miss your childlike take on the world, Raymond." She smiled at me.

"Fi, look, just give me a fucking shooting assignment. I'm three months behind on my rent."

"Stop throwing your money away on dildos and Asian preteen porn, darling. Then you won't always be broke."

"I don't go to Thailand, dear. Nor am I into goats and gerbils."

"So what did you *really* spend all your money on?"

"Fi, need you be such a raging twat?"

"Coke bill overdue?"

"Coke's a bit out of my league these days." I glanced over

at her door to see a pink silk ascot tied around the knob. "Hmmm. What about you—into autoerotic asphyxiation these days?"

"Oh, don't *mention* autoerotic asphyxiation to me! Fucking entertainers! All these actors and musicians ever want to do is strangle themselves while they're getting off. I can't believe more of them haven't died."

"How does that whole strangling thing work, anyway? I mean, do actors recite a bit of Hamlet, sing a song or two and then suddenly, *Oi! I'm famous and I think I'd better go strangle myself while I come!*?"

"Pretty much. And you'd think they'd hire someone to babysit them while they do it."

"Yes, but that would wreck the fun, wouldn't it? 'Ooh! I can't breathe! Help me! Help me!' Not very sexy at all. Chances are your babysitter would be so repulsed by your lack of commitment she'd let you hang anyway."

"I keep the ascot there to give my clients proper hanging lessons. The DIY sites on the Internet are hopeless, and a dead client is a client who's no longer making me money."

I looked at Fiona's beloved onyx coke box with sad beagle eyes.

"Blow!" said Fi. "Excellent idea." She dived in.

God only knows how badly I was salivating at this impudent display of purchasing clout. She vacuumed two rails, wiped her nostrils and said, "I like to see you grovel *and* be deprived of drugs. Life is good."

"You ball-curdling witch. What is your problem?"

"My problem is *you*, Raymond darling. I don't like having you in the same city as me."

"Can't say I like it much, either."

"Yes, but the thing is that you, darling, are a failure. When people bump into you, they justifiably equate me with you, and you have to imagine how that makes me feel." She put the coke box back into her drawer. "I really can't have that, at least not until a few more years have gone by and all memory of you and your rapidly accelerating downward failure spiral has faded away like a pensioner's capacity for long division."

"I see." I leaned back in my chair. "I seem to remember a much younger version of you making bedroom eyes at me from the floor of the 1992 Daytime BAFTA Awards when (if I may pat myself on the back here) I accepted my trophy for Best Hand-held Camera Work in a cooking or DIY home-improvement show."

"You have to stop living in the past, Raymond." She made her *oh-why-not* face. "How would you like a camera gig in the sun-kissed Pacific, ogling young beauties all day, just you and your shoulder cam?"

I kept silent, awaiting the catch.

"There's no catch, darling."

"What's the catch?"

Fiona sighed. "Paranoia has never looked good on you, Raymond. Here I am offering to rescue you from your prison cell of a life and you make me sound cruel and vindictive."

"What's the catch?"

"I don't know if I'd call it a catch, per se . . ."

"What's the catch?"

"Darling, you would have to work for Americans."

"Jesus fucking Christ."

"Sorry, darling, but take it or leave it. A friend, Sarah,

handles the people for a U.S. network and she owes me a favour."

"Who's this Sarah, then?"

"She's—well, I'm hoping one day she'll become my . . . *special* friend."

Doubtless some filthy labia-chewing swamp raccoon. "For God's sake, you're not still tinkering with lesbianism, are you?"

"If trying to grow as a person is a crime, I stand accused." Fi clasped her hands together on her desk like a schoolgirl. "Sarah, like me, is only trying to expand her world, and I like to think of myself as a nurturing, mentoring woman."

I snickered.

"Take it or leave it, Raymond. At the count of three I rescind the offer. One, two—"

"I'll take it."

"Go talk to Billy."

Her face became all business. It was as if I were no longer in the room as she stared down at her iPad and began browsing through toddlersroastingonaspit.com. She said, "Go on. Billy will arrange your flights and your visa for Kiribati. Lovely place. Whores growing on trees, from what I hear. Coke bushes around every corner."

After a moment she looked up me. "Really, Ray—be a love and fuck off. And as you leave, Billy will offer you a complimentary bottle of water and some sanitizing hand wipes. Cold and flu season."

"It's a wonder Billy hasn't been strangled with a shoelace by one of those man-sluts he arse-rapes nightly out on Hampstead Heath."

From behind me I heard, "Those days are over, Raymond. I have found love and am a reformed man."

Billy appeared, as polished and moisturized as a daffodil salesman at Harrods, but incongruously dressed like a Canadian lumberjack out for a day of chopping down a forest of larches.

"Oh. Hello, Billy."

"Hello, Raymond."

I had no mirth in my heart for Billy, and I remain convinced Billy was part of the chorus saying "Dump the bastard" back during the divorce.

"Going to Kiribati, I hear. Lovely place."

"Let's just do the paperwork."

"Manners, please."

"Or else what?"

"Be rude to me one more time and I'll go online and start a wicked, *wicked* rumour about you."

"Like what?"

"Like . . ." Billy paused a second. "I know: I'll go into an online chat room posing as you."

My interest was piqued: "What kind of chat room?"

"A shit-eating chat room. I'm sure there must be hundreds of them. And once there, I start the rumour that you, Raymond Gunt, are a . . . a *log hog*."

"You *wouldn't*."

"*Wouldn't* I? Or maybe I'd invent some other scarier category . . . I know: you're into *funnel cakes*."

Fi cackled with glee and then her phone rang, a zithering that made my spinal hairs rise. "Both of you—out," she ordered. "That's my Bollywood line. Without the rise of the Indian middle classes and their zest for quality English-language entertainment, I'd still be rolling in the muck like you. Now fuck off, Ray. Really. And enjoy the South Pacific or wherever this Kiribati shithole is."

Not putting a trapdoor opening into a cobra pit past her, I fucked off. Billy followed me into the hall. He said, "FYI, you get to have an assistant with you on this gig."

"An assistant?"

"Yes. All they need is a valid passport and the ability to tolerate you day and night."

I didn't absorb what Billy said next. My brain stopped at the word "assistant"—the joy! On a fly speck of coral dust in the middle of the ocean with no labour laws, no police and most likely no witnesses to whatever punishments I might dole out to my assistant—or rather, my *slave*. A lifelong dream of human ownership was coming true.

"... and so I'll email you shortly. Goodbye, Raymond."

"Right. Yes. Goodbye, Billy."

Down on the street I looked at my BlackBerry: it was a Wednesday, fuck it, always my bad luck day. I then sort of spaced out looking at the phone's screen. *Wednesday* . . . *Wednesday* . . . *Wednesday* . . . what the fuck is a "Wednes"? I mean, for Christ's sake, *think* about it.

....

Wednesday comes from the Middle English *Wednes dei*, which is from Old English *Wōdnesdæg*, meaning the day of the English Woden (Wodan), a god revered in Anglo-Saxon England until about the eighth century. *Wōden*, or *Woden* in Modern English, is the head god in English heathenism.

....

So wait a second . . . this guy, Woden, gets a whole fucking *day* named after him? Do *we* have no say in this matter? Let's rename Wednesday something better, like, say, James Bond. And we can call Thursday Hitler and Saturday Tits and . . . You get the idea.

I looked up and saw that I was once again inside that wretched, unwieldy dump people call the real world. I rode home on a series of buses, and what is a bus but failure crystallized into the form of two storeys of metal, painted red, hurled out into the world to hoover up losers from the streets of London.

Kiribati?

Could be kind of nice. Pretty, even. Who knew . . . maybe my luck had turned.

. . . .

The Republic of Kiribati is an island nation in the central Pacific Ocean. It is comprised of thirty-two atolls and one raised coral island, and is spread over 1.4 million square miles. It straddles the equator and borders the International Date Line on the east. Its former colonial name was the Gilbert and Ellice Islands. The capital and largest city is South Tarawa.

Population: 105,000
GDP: $206 million
Internet top-level domain (TLD): .ki
International calling code: +686

. . . .

02

When I arrived in East Acton, I looked about: nice enough day—but then on Henchman Street some verminous panhandling dole-rat squatting on the sidewalk stuck out a soiled Caffè Nero coffee cup and begged for a few pence, instantly blotting out my good mood. I kicked him on the shin. I mean, for fuck's sake, here he is, the same age as me, but I'm out in the world, work, work, work, making the world a better place for everybody, and this guy? All he does is sit around all day, expecting the world to throw him cash.

"What was that for, mate?"

"Get a fucking job, you lazy shit."

"Job? You want me to get a job, do you?"

He stood up then. He was sunburned, somewhat larger than me, dressed in oily rags arranged in a manner that would have been considered Duran Duran stylish in 1982, but, thirty years later, flecked with feces, discount fag cinders and the spattered remains of meals-in-a-can, constituted a rather terrifying mite-breeding facility. "Say that to my face, mate," he growled. He was wearing a name tag: **NEAL**—like anyone gave a shit what this street-fuck's name was. His left eye was a milky cataract white.

Seeing as I'd kicked a hornet's nest, I decided the best course of action was to flee.

"Come on mate, don't be a coward!"

Just fucking speedwalk out of here, Ray, don't let him smell your fear. Why, look up there—its Wolfstan Street, where you can turn right and never see this unoccupied dickwad ever again.

Whump!

Tackled from behind . . . *fuck*. Two hundred pounds of man stink crunching my face onto a sidewalk papered with lung oysters and chip wrappers gone transparent from oil.

You'd think I'd find a shred of mercy or concern or even interest from the citizens of glamorous West London, but no, they were all so fucking busy with their drug-taking, their lotto-ticket-buying and dole-robbing—assuming they were even fucking English—that seeing a visibly sane man like me being attacked by an obviously violent nutter like Neal elicited not a whiff of protest.

A colon–scented mouth and the one working eye asserted itself in front of my face. "We like ourselves, don't we?"

I shut my eyes.

He twisted my right arm behind my back, "We like ourselves, don't we? So, what's your name, then?"

I twisted around; there was no escape to be had. My eyes opened. *Fucker.*

He smiled at me. "And our name would be . . . ?"

The smell of street grit reminded me of childhood. *I'm not telling this low-life fuck my name.* "I'm not telling a low-life fuck like you my name—*Neal.*"

"Right then." Neal did something I still don't quite understand to this day, but it resulted in a jolt of pain in the shoulder that was a gourmet blend of stubbed-toe-meets-hot-boiling-chip-fat.

"Raymond!" I moaned.

"Whazzat?"

"Raymond! My fucking name is *Raymond!*"

"That so?" Neal rubbed his dreadful, dreadful hair in my face. "My name is Neal, and my hair is called Neal, too. I can give my hair a name because I'm nuts and live on the street and I haven't washed it since Princess Di died. It's my way of letting my love for her live on and on."

"You sick, contaminated fuck, what is wrong with you? Get off before I get fucking superAIDS from your fucking beard."

"Can't do that, mate. I have a lifestyle, and part of me being me is me keeping my style alive."

He is off his fucking rocker. "Are you off your fucking rocker? No one dresses like Duran Duran anymore. The eighties revival came and went. People barely dressed like that back in the fucking *day* and all of those wankers can't change their own fucking diapers anymore. If you have to dress like some haircut band, at least make it Echo and the fucking Bunnymen instead of Duran fucking Duran."

Another profound jolt of pain racked my shoulder. I shrieked.

Grannies with vinyl tartan grocery carts passed by as if Neal and I were tweens sharing a chaste kiss.

"Right," barked Neal. "Echo & the Bunnymen thought they were so cool, but it was just Ian McCulloch acting all fucked up with asymmetrical hairdos so that birds would form a line outside the bus and chain-bang him one by one."

"Well, that's why anyone becomes a musician, Neal. Why the fuck else would you do it?"

The pressure on my shoulder was eased.

"You have a point."

"Neal, I would like you to stop crushing my skull into the pavement. You may like life on the street, but I, myself, am not used to smelling evaporating lapdog piss close-up."

Neal began to croon: "*I was working as a waitress in a cocktail bar!*"

Oh Jesus, the daft fucker was singing eighties pop tunes in the key of hepatitis C.

"I said: *I was working as a waitress in a cocktail bar!*"

Neal shook my neck; a fleck of pigeon shit went up my right nostril. "Raymond," he said, "you have one last chance before this escalates to the theoretical next stage. I repeat: *I was working as a waitress in a cocktail bar!*"

I whimpered my required line: "*That much is true.*"

....

"Don't You Want Me" is a single by British synthpop group The Human League, released on their third album, *Dare*, on November 27, 1981. It is the band's best-known and most commercially successful recording, and hit number one in the UK's Christmas pop chart, selling over 1,400,000 copies, making it the twenty-fifth most successful single in UK Singles Chart history. It topped the Billboard Hot 100 in the U.S. on July 3, 1982, and stayed in the top for three weeks.

The title is frequently misprinted as "Don't You Want Me Baby," which is the first line of the chorus.

Basically, everyone on earth loves this song.

"And? And what comes next, Raymond!?"

Jesus fucking Christ. *"But even then I knew I'd find a much better place, either fucking with or without you."*

"Louder!"

"But even then I knew I'd find a much better place, either with or without you."

"Raymond! You are a man redeemed. Next line!"

"But now I think it's time I live my life on my own, I guess it's just what I must do."

"Louder! All together now . . . One, two three . . ."

In stereo: **"But now I think it's time I live my life on my own, I guess it's just what I must do!"**

"Very good, mate." Neal let me go to sprawl beside him.

We lay there on the street, drunk with song. I looked over my left shoulder to see a pair of pigeons bobbing towards us. I was feeling oddly philosophical. "Neal," I said, "what the fuck is it with pigeons, anyway?"

"What do you mean, Ray?"

"I mean, how many fucking crumbs can there be on this street—or any other given street in the world?"

"Go on, Ray. I'm listening."

"I mean, it's not like there's a mobile croissant-shredding machine that trundles about the city strewing fresh, delicious crumbs all over the place just to feed pigeons." A pigeon ventured close to my face, cooing dementedly. I blew at it and it skittered away. "And yet look at the little monsters everywhere: very plump, likely juicy, too."

"Very roastable indeed."

"Not only are these pigeons plump, Neal, they shit like leaf blowers, and they do all of this on a diet of, essentially, nothing."

"Makes you think, Ray."

"It does, doesn't it, Neal?"

The mood down on the sidewalk was relaxed now. I caught a whiff of piss. "Christ, just smell the piss here. What is wrong with this city? Someone couldn't wait seventeen extra seconds to find a shrub or a loo?"

"You should give urine a chance, Ray. You're reflexively negative about it. Think of all those people in India chugging down bottles of urine every day. Piss is practically a food group over there, it is."

"Neal, there's a reason it's called piss—it's because your body doesn't want it inside you anymore. If we were meant to drink piss, it'd come out of tits. Think about it."

"Good point, Ray."

"Thank you. Just one question, Neal . . ."

"Yes, Ray?"

"A minute ago, when you were talking about giving your hair a name and all that—were you serious?"

"Good God, no. People expect crazy people to ham it up, so I give what I think the audience wants. But I can see you understand me, Ray. I'd never try a stunt like that on you again."

"Thank you for your refreshing candour."

Neal stood up, looming over me on the diseased concrete. "Okay now, Ray, stop being a cunt to the world, and the world will stop being a cunt to you."

And with that, Neal was gone.

Kind of liked him, actually.

03

I got home to my cramped top-floor flat in my building, a forgettable heap with about as much visual magnificence as Margaret Thatcher's morning coffee dump. Unwashed dishes in the sink had gone bacterial and were on the brink of growing fur. Six light bulbs in the room needed replacing. I suppose, were I to wax poetic, the absence of pets or loved ones amplified my sense of aloneness in the universe.

The phone rang: "Hi, Ray. It's Tabitha from Fi's office. She wanted me to prep you for Kiribati."

Tabitha! Tabs! Fi's gofer, a sweet delicate fawn. But the question in my mind about Tabs is: Has, or has not, Fiona tongue-nabbed Tabs in the ladies' room in between her PowerPoint casting suggestions for a Ford Fiesta commercial or the Afghanistan war or God-only-knows what other appalling clients? "Hi, Tabs. What do I need to know?"

"Do you have a valid passport?"

"I do. I never know when an overseas gig might come up." Implicit in this? *Raymond Gunt is a man of the world.*

"Okay, good. Umm. Like, ummm. Well . . ." Typical useless young person, language-wise. "Fi has asked me to drop papers off at your place tonight. Our server's down and you're not far from where I live. Will you be home at seven o'clock?"

Will I? "Yes. Please do drop by."

"See you then."

Fucking hell: my place looked like cat shit in a litter box. The last thing I ever have on my mind is visitors. I began to cull through the worst of it, but I realized a few minutes in that the worst of it was actually a fucking *lot* of it.

I needed to convert my bachelor's dump into a fuck hut, and quick. Who among us hasn't been in this situation?

How to mask the odour of furniture covered in years of rogue jizz blemishes, countless sour-smelling empty wine bottles, a sea of dead remote control batteries and Zantac packaging, a rack of never-used barbells, a Katrina-like swath of take-away food packaging, plus whatever civilization of insects was brave or stupid enough to try to forge a new world within the haphazardly created ecosystem that was my flat?

I lost some of my cleanup speed in the face of all this, but then refocused on why I was doing it: *Tabs*, the milky-skinned naive little doe who would look at a worldly, not-unstudly fellow like me and say, "Please, sir, I need someone to coach me on how to properly perform, as I have almost no experience and would prefer to learn from someone who can obviously teach me thoroughly and with great attention to detail."

In the end it was simply easiest to huck it all out the back window onto the landlady's herb garden. Fucking herbs are indestructible—it's how they got to be herbs in the first place—nature loves nothing more than throwing a species a challenge. Technically, by nature's standards, smothering Mrs. Radley's herb garden was doing it a favour by speeding up evolution. In any event, that bloated pension-sucking hag was away in Penzance at a family funeral. Recent contact with death would likely make her appreciate herbal trauma all the more.

Ding-dong.

Fucking hell, seven already? Christ.

I buzzed the street door, shouting into the speaker, "Tabs, luv, come in."

As I held the door open, I cast a glance behind me at the main room, which was actually looking okay without most of my defenestrated crap. Those monks might be on to something with minimalism and all that meditating and shit, but fuck monks, I was after *pussy.* "Fancy a drink, Tabs?" I said as soon as she was in the door.

"Do you have a white wine spritzer, maybe?"

White wine? Does she think I'm some bender who rises every morning in pursuit of winking boy cherry? "I'm out of white wine. Fancy a lager?"

"Lager? Oh, um . . . sure. I really just need to drop these off and explain one or two things." She was looking at me funny—she was intrigued by me. I could tell. *Hot dang! This might be the night!*

Through the mercy of God I was able to find two actual Pilsner glasses that were clean—this could only add to my Jason Bourne–like air of urban cool. "Here you go, Tabs. *Skol!*" (Toasting: manly.)

"Oh, um . . . *skol!*"

Again, she was eyeing me in a way that meant more than her counting my blackheads. We clinked glasses. *Soon we shall be one.*

"Raymond—"

"Ray."

"*Ray* . . . a bit of info for you. You'll be flying through Los Angeles and passing through immigration, but that should be no problem. From there, you hop to Honolulu and then some other island in order to get to Kiribati. It's a long slog—thirty-seven hours, all told."

"Lovely sunsets there, I bet."

"Huh? Oh, yes, I suppose so. In any event, I checked and you won't require any vaccinations or a visa. The other camerapersons who've worked there suggested that you bring as many topical antifungals with you as possible."

"Tabs, hang on a sec, luv. Exactly what show is it I'm working on?"

She gawped at me. "You don't even know what show you're working on?"

"It's American, so it's bound to be shit. It didn't occur to me to ask."

"It's one of those reality shows where people stuck on a remote island shag each other over the course of a few weeks and then, I don't know, turn into cannibals at the end when they get desperate for food." She sipped her lager. "And then the last person standing gets a big bag of money. Here's some information about the show, as well as your contracts. We'll need to sign them right now." Her forearms were twitching . . . her forearms connected to her shoulders connected to her magnificent rack. She spread out some papers, and I edged closer to her on the sofa to sign them. She smelled so clean, and her perfume was heaven: Fuck Factor Five or whatever overpriced gonk it is they're pushing at office tarts this season.

She smiled at me—the Look! The Look! She was giving me the Look! "And you'll be getting American union rates, which, after two months—"

Good God. "What? Two fucking months in the middle of nowhere?"

"But it'll be so beautiful, and if it works out, it could be a long-running gig. Fiona worked very hard to get you this slot."

"She did, did she?" Not a good sign.

"It's not my place to discuss this, Raymond, but I think she might still be sweet on you."

Dear God. Discussing an ex with a potential conquest? I was seeing my potential shag putting on little wings and flying out the window—no, more like putting on a little noose and attaching it to the rafters.

"Ray?" She was gathering up her things.

Now or never. I edged closer to her on the sofa. "Tabs, stay a bit longer. Finish your lager."

"Umm. Well. Okay."

"I know Fi can be a handful, Tabs."

Her body language was neutral. "Fi's a pretty good boss. She knows what she wants."

That plus-sized Toby mug I once called my wife? "I'm sure she does." I edged in one breath closer.

"Raymond . . ."

"Yes, Tabs?"

"We need to discuss your personal assistant. Billy told you that you get one, right?"

Ah, yes, my ~~slave~~ *assistant*. At this point, I, Raymond Gunt, mentally vacated the room, transported into the air by those magic words—my own personal assistant out in the middle of nowhere, free of any meaningful legal jurisdictions. I formed my own mental montage: clanking manacles, cracking whips and the sound of a key without mercy locking a cage.

"Ray? *Ray?* You there?"

"Sorry, luv. I was lost in thought. How do I choose my assistant?"

"It's your call. You have . . ." she checked her cellphone, ". . . twenty-three hours to find one. The flight is at six o'clock tomorrow. All they need is a valid passport, and as Kiribati has no union restrictions, it's easy-peasy. If you can't find someone, one will be appointed to you."

"Well, I don't want *that*." I scanned my mental Rolodex for potential assistants. A friend? None. Drinking buddies? Manifold but untrustworthy. Female anyone? Not fucking likely. Family members? Don't ask. Passing acquaintances? Few.

"Ray, you'll be flying business class to Honolulu via Los Angeles, and from there you'll be on a corporate jet."

"Would my personal assistant have to be in business class, too?"

"I suppose if you asked for it."

Not fucking likely. Any assistant of mine would have to be the rearmost seat, right beside the lav and the puking Australians.

My mind was caught in a rare but wonderful joy loop. *Fucking brilliant! Someone to legally beat with a stick!* And then, in a burst of dazzling white light, I realized I had just the candidate.

Suddenly Tabs stood up and headed for the door.

"Tabs, wait!"

"I have spin class, Raymond. I have to go. Enjoy your trip."

"Tabs . . ."

She stopped in her tracks and turned back to me, expectantly.

"I—I can't help but think there's maybe something special between us . . ."

"You noticed?" Tabs breathed.

"Well, yes—a man can't avoid being aware of the needs of a beautiful young girl like yourself." I came closer.

"Raymond, it's . . . It's . . ."

"Yes?" Zooming in for the kill.

"Well . . . you look so much like my father."

"Oh?" Okay, not a total setback. Some birds have major father issues.

"It's been so long since I've seen him."

"Really, luv? How long?"

"Eleven years now."

"I'm sorry. How did he . . . *pass*[1]?"

"Oh. He didn't die. He's in prison."

That was a plot twist. "I'm sorry to hear that. What . . . what was his, um, situation?"

"He was a serial molester. The Tinsdale Fondler. Made the cover of the *Daily Mail*."

"Right."

"I'd best be going now, Raymond."

---

1. *A dreadful, hideous modern euphemism for dying.*

"Yes, Tabs. Thank you for everything. Good night."

Fucking hell.

Deprived of coitus, I daydreamed of slave ownership and got as shitfaced as I possibly could on a bottle of single malt I'd stolen from the bar at a Stella McCartney fragrance launch.

....

Survival is a popular reality TV game show produced in many countries throughout the world. On the show, contestants are isolated in the wilderness and compete for cash and other prizes. The format uses a progressive elimination, allowing the contestants to vote one another off one at a time, until only one final contestant remains and wins the title of "The Survivalist."

You're either into this show or you're not. It's binary.

....

04

Tracking down Neal the next morning wasn't hard. I walked into the off-license, held up a banknote and said, "Twenty quid to whoever can help me find my long-lost brother. He's got one good eye, dresses like Duran Duran and stinks of the worst kind of dog shit."

"Oh, that'd be Neal," squeaked a trainer-clad gran buying a stack of (what else) lotto tickets. "Lovely boy and a great singing voice. This week I think he's in a box behind the stationer's on Old Oak Common Lane."

"Thank you very much."

"What about my twenty quid?"

"Only once I find my prey, Sea Hag," I said over my shoulder as I headed out into the brisk fall air. I could practically hear that mummified old soak composing an indignant letter to the *Daily Mail*, beginning *I'm a pensioner and . . .*, at which point a lifelong diet of greasy fish, scotch mints and whimsically flavoured crisps catches up to her and she falls dead at her kitchen table, not to be discovered for weeks.

Neal was indeed inside a Samsung cardboard box, eating a Subway sandwich, when I found him. He squinted up at me. "Right, it's Cunty, it is."

"It's Gunt to you, Neal. These your digs, then?"

"I'll not have you knocking this box. Samsung has emerged as one of the strongest competitors in the Darwinian world of home electronics."

"For fuck's sake, Neal, it's a cardboard box." I kicked the side for emphasis. It emitted a deep bass thump and didn't rupture, which gave me pause. "I have to admit, if you're going to live in a fucking box, this isn't a bad one."

"My point exactly."

"In any event, no boxes for you anymore, mate, I've found you a job."

"For Christ's sake, Ray, why would I want a job? I'm living the life, aren't I?"

"Look, you ungrateful prick, I'm not talking about picking up litter along some wretched motorway or latrine duty at Rikers. I'm talking about a South Pacific lagoon populated with gorgeous, needy sluts, fuelled by an endless supply of rum drinks."

Neal's lone good eye stared into mine. "If you're one of those people who collects hobos so you can take them home and eat their brains or something like that, good on you, but I'd rather keep my brains."

"It's not that at all."

"Sex with you and the missus, then? Afterwards smother me with a dry cleaning bag and toss me into some brambles off the M5?"

"Why are you being so fucking paranoid, you ungrateful walking toilet? I'm on the level."

"Really? So tell me more."

One thought crossed my mind—fuck: "Do you have a passport, Neal?"

"Passport? Fucking right, mate. Have a look." From within his maggoty jacket he produced a valid British passport. "What's the matter? You look surprised."

He handed it to me and I opened it to the photo page, and there he was, milky-eyed, hair all dagged up with shit and mucus, wearing a shirt like he was an extra from *Oliver!* His expression was crazed.

"I always thought one day I'd like to go and see Dollywood, USA. You know, the singer and that. It's a world-class resort destination. An uddersome song-bird she is."

Fuck me ragged with a concrete dildo—this was going to work. "Neal, here is what we're going to do. You are going to gather your few wretched shreds of possessions and we are going to throw them into a trash bin and you will never see them again. After that we are going to walk to my flat, where I will give you a Stanley knife and you will cut as much of your hair off as possible . . ."

"Hold on. I told you, no sexy shit."

"I'm not finished. After you've sheared away that viral beavers' nest, you are going to apply lice cream to your head—no, your whole body—and then shower it off. After this, you will don clean garments supplied to you by me. You will take vitamins, drink a glass of milk and then, at six o'clock from Heathrow, you will be flying along with me to the islands of Kiribati in the South Pacific, where you'll be working as my personal assistant. I've just scored a gig as a cameraman on some dreadful American TV show where real-life people, not celebrities, shag each other for a few weeks and then turn into cannibals in front of my camera."

"One of those survival shows, then?"

Hallelujah. "Exactly."

"Why do you need an assistant?"

"Is it wrong to care about other people, Neal? Is it wrong to want to help?"

"You just want a slave is all."

"There's that, too."

Neal snorted, then removed something foul from his moustache, which reminded me: "Actually, you'll have to completely shave off your disgusting fucking beard and moustache, too. Deal-breaker."

Neal stared around at his Samsung box with evident fondness. He'd drawn cupboards and windows on its inside with a Sharpie. "I'm not quite sold yet, Raymond."

"Two short sweet months, one thousand quid and afterwards Dollywood."

Neal patted the walls of his soon to be former home. "I'll miss you, old box." He stood and I could see invisible wavy stink lines rising upward from his carcass.

"I take it that's a yes."

"It'll be an adventure."

"Good. I'm two blocks away."

"Don't you have to stop and get some of that lice cream first?"

"That's okay, I've got some at home."

Neal froze.

"No, Neal, stocking liberal amounts of anti-nit cream is *not* part of my regular regime of recruiting and eventually murdering vagabonds. A sexually active man simply has to take a few precautions."

Neal snickered. "You? Sexually active? Sorry, Ray, I figure you haven't had proper physical contact with another person's body since *Friends* went off the air."

"Spare me your editorializing. Do you speak any other languages?"

"No."

"Any other skills you're keeping hidden from the world?"

"I can juggle. And do tricks with coins. That's probably it."

"Perfect skill set. You'll do just fine."

We approached my building and went around back. "Your first job as personal assistant, Neal, is to pick all this crap off the ground and bring it upstairs."

"All of it?"

"Not the bottles and take-away food refuse. Just anything resembling clothing. And there's a throw pillow over there. Give it a shake to freshen it up."

"It looks like there's a kickass herb garden underneath all this stuff, Raymond."

"I know. Herbs: what would we do without them? Nature's little survivors."

"If I'd known about this garden, I'd have changed my diet weeks back."

"Rosemary sprigs on your tinned cat food?"

"Look!" said Neal. "Half a pack of uneaten Starbursts!"

"Yes, Neal, that is correct: life is good."

05

I was in the hire car's rear with Fiona en route to the airport, a generous gesture on her part, but a gesture made only because Billy let it slip during a phone call that she was jetting to France at roughly the same time as I was leaving for Los Angeles. In any event, we first had to pick up Neal a few blocks from my place, where he was getting a facial to tidy up his complexion, which hadn't been exposed to sunlight since the Spice Girls ruled the pop charts.

"So Raymond, I hear you managed to rustle up an assistant."

"Only fitting for a man in my position."

"Darling, how on earth did you find someone willing to put up with you?"

"Well, his name is Neal and he has a long track record of living and working in the, um, outdoors."

"You've always wanted a slave, Raymond—and frankly, a slave would be a nice boost to your ego. You're so insecure. No wonder you haven't been properly laid by a non-whore in ages."

When did everyone become an evaluator of my private life?

"By the way," Fi added, "I Googled Kiribati—it's lovely."

A chill came over me. "Fi, you won't actually be physically coming to the Pacific, will you? Not that I wouldn't love to see you and all."

"Darling, you know me better. I'll just sit here and collect fifteen percent of what you make." She paused to stare out the window. "Who is that . . . *fascinating* man up ahead?"

"Who?" The car stopped beside Neal, who sat on the curb staring into another discarded Caffè Nero paper cup as if it contained dancing pixies. His diseased Chewbacca locks gone, and some ghastly white shaved areas contrasting with a decade's worth of windburn, he looked like the sort of relative everyone dreads showing up at a wedding: off his meds, without loyalties and perhaps possessing a bit more insight than is good for him. Some dishtowels repurposed as scarves gave Neal his preferred dash of eighties style.

I was about to call for him, but Fiona shushed me and rolled down her window. Her overture to Neal was preempted just then by two scrumptious schoolgirls, who stopped to bend over him. "Sir," one of them asked, "Are you all right?"

"Me? Oh yes, why thank you, girls. Kind young women like you make my day."

The duo blushed. "Oh, *sir*, anything to help."

"You sweet, sweet girls. Thank you."

The charge in the air was almost pornographic. I swear, if the three of them could have orgied right there on top of the McDonald's litter and a squished Coke Zero can, they would have. A new chill came over me: Neal was one of nature's born studs.

Didn't see that one coming.

I evaluated this new piece of data: was it a plus or a minus for me? I decided to break the mood and yelled out the window, "Neal, load your bag into the boot, you crazed shitpig."

He looked up and smiled.

Fiona said, "That's your slave?"

"It is."

"*He* is sitting next to *me*."

Oh fuck.

I got out so Neal could slide into the middle beside my ex-wife, and we left for Heathrow.

· ·

LHR to LAX = 10 h, 55 m

· ·

06

So I'm standing at the business class check-in counter for the Los Angeles flight when I hear the words, "Mr. Gunt, I'm afraid there's been a mix-up in ticketing."

Reduce the temperature of my blood by twenty degrees. "Oh?"

"I'm afraid your seat has been deleted."

"*Deleted?*" Okay. I'm reasonable. Did I say that I like people? I like people who like people. "What do you mean by . . . *deleted?*"

"The physical seat itself, sir, has been removed from the plane for reconditioning."

"So there is simply no seat there at all?"

"Oh, thank you, sir, I'm glad you understand."

I dropped my eyes to her name tag. **JENELLE**. "Jenelle, is it?"

"Yes, sir." I might add here that Jenelle is a gruesome creature, her sullen jaws most likely sore from chugging her wedding-averse boyfriend's knob for ten long years. "What other seat shall I be seated in?"

"Let me check . . . you're in 67E, Mr. Gunt."

"67E?"

"Yes."

"An E seat—is that an aisle?"

"No, sir. I believe an E seat on that aircraft is the second seat in a row of four."

"*Jenelle*, you do understand that I am in business class."

"Yes, Mr. Gunt."

"Do you have a seat map here at the desk?"

"Yes, sir." Jenelle handed me the map.

"Let me look here. Ah—67E." I pointed to 67E, a centre seat sandwiched between two lavatories.

"It's a full flight, sir. No other seats are available."

Suddenly, from behind me in the coach class international check-in, there came a series of childish screams so horrifying and so loud that even the most sinister baby-hating citizen would worry about the health and sanity of the child, as well as its parents. Jenelle looked up with a smile. I stared at her. "How can you possibly be smiling?"

"Those children, sir. It's heart-warming. They're off to Los Angeles to undergo a new surgical procedure that could save their lives."

I turned around and across the hall saw a telethon's worth of . . . *atypical*-looking children. Okay, tards, actually. Fifteen, maybe twenty of them.

"Jenelle, can you tell me more about these, um, children?"

"They have Buñuel's syndrome."

"Oh?"

"Children with Buñuel's syndrome have no ability to control their emotions. Unfortunately, almost everything they experience is perceived by their brain as a threat, yet the ensuing fear isn't funnelled through the checks and barriers we normal—I'm sorry, *statistically average*—people use to keep a scrim between society and us. So they basically live in a state of perpetual agitation and their voices inform the world of this."

"I see. Might they be on my flight?" I asked.

Jenelle tapped away at her keyboard. "What a coincidence, sir—the Buñuel Children for a New Start party is seated in rows 65, 66 and 67. I can only imagine how thrilled they'll be to have someone as compassionate as you near them in what can only be a long and terrifying flight—possibly the most frightening event most of them have had to endure during their most likely short and sad little lives."

"Yes." *Okay.* "Jenelle, do you have some sort of supervisor or something?"

"That'd be Tracey, sir. Would you like me to page her?"

"Please, yes, let's do that."

A band of Buñuel syndromers and their minders shimmied into *my* business class check-in area like over-entitled cockroaches. Fucking hell, just drug the bastards and show them a *Finding Nemo* DVD for eleven hours or until their bug-eaten frontal cortices cause them to pass out from understimulation.

Across the hall, I noticed Neal's head above the crowd at check-in. Light bulb: whatever seat Neal landed would be mine, and he could sit with the Buñuel children. Thank fucking Christ. Hold on, it was Neal who was drawing a crowd. To wild applause, he began performing some sort of poor people's jig. Oh my dear God, it was the "Come On Eileen" dance from that video by Dexys Midnight

Runners. Words failed me. And then the check-in agents joined in—like a flash mob.

"Mr. *Gunt*." Supervisor Tracey appeared in front of me. "Can I help you, sir?" She resembled a small version of those otherworldly beings that trashed Manhattan in the film *Cloverfield*.

"Tracey, yes, hello. I'm Raymond Gunt."

"How can I help you, Mr. Gunt?"

"I—"

At that moment, Neal came running across the great class divide and threw his arms around me, his breath still reeking of unwashed arses. He backed off and slapped me in the chest, momentarily stunning me. "America beckons and we are going to make the most of it, bro!" He hoisted my bag onto Jenelle's weigh scale.

Bro?

I forgot entirely what I was about to say to supervisor Tracey, who stared me down. "You need to board the flight *now*, sir. Security is that way. If you'll excuse me, I have to go handle passengers with *real* problems."

Jenelle handed me my boarding pass: 67E. "Next!" she called as my bag was swept off to the Crab Nebula by a sluggish black conveyor belt.

Miraculously, security screening was empty. Neal chose one lane; I chose the other, manned by two dim-looking, soul-dead lifers. Then, as if summoned from a rubbed genie's bottle, ten security staff clad in every form of religious headwear imaginable scampered over to confront me. The stupider-looking of the two lifers announced, "This is the training station, sir. Please empty your pockets and put any metals or electronics in a separate bin. Also, please use a bin for your wallet, your shoes, your belt or any other item likely to trigger a metal detector. Do you have a laptop?"

Clad in socks, cargo shorts and a polo shirt, I walked through the screening gate.

Beep.

In the distance, Neal was already gathering his X-ray-screened carry-on bag (a vinyl tote from Tesco). I, meanwhile, watched as every item in my carry-on bag was unpacked, picked at with tweezers, nuzzled with chemical sampling cloths for gunpowder residue, and otherwise examined closely by a group of people who seemingly spoke no English yet had no other language in common. Crows descending on run-over squirrels go at their game with more decorum than shown by this lot.

On my fourth pass through the metal detector, I heard yet another dreaded *beep.*

"Could you please come with us, sir?" said one of the lifers.

Oh Christ, the fucking magic wand. I put my arms up.

"No, sir, could you please come with us into this room?"

"A sleeper cell?"

"I beg your pardon, sir?"

Get a fucking sense of humour. "Nothing."

Inside, a group of five young screeners-in-training stood ready. My screener said, "National security is a vital issue, Mr. . . . ." he looked at my boarding pass, "Gunt." Outside the door I heard the Buñuel crowd whizzing their way towards the gate, sounding like a cluster of ambulances.

My screener said, "If you'll give me one second, Mr. Gunt, I'll remove my flashlight and forceps from the sterilizer."

. . . .

"Come On Eileen" was a single released by Dexys Midnight Runners in 1982. Kevin Rowland, "Big" Jim Paterson and Billy Adams wrote the song; Clive Langer and Alan Winstanley produced it. It also appeared on the album *Too-Rye-Ay*. It was their first number one hit in the United Kingdom since 1980's "Geno." The song won Best British Single at the 1983 Brit Awards. What's weird about this song is that it was so huge at the time and now you listen to it and wonder, what the hell was everyone thinking? Well, that's pop culture for you.

. . . .

07

I was the last passenger on the plane. I walked to 67E, withstanding the angry and accusatory glares of every passenger and each crew member. At the plane's rear, all twelve Buñuel children took one look at me and ignited like smoke alarms.

I forgot to look for Neal. Well, wherever he was, once we were safely in the air, his seat was mine.

Just before we taxied to the end of the runway for takeoff, the captain announced that the entertainment system's software was glitchy and that only one film was available for the flight: "We are proud to present to you the beloved year 2000 family favourite, *The Flintstones in Viva Rock Vegas*, starring Stephen Baldwin and Joan Collins, with a cameo by eighties rocker John Taylor, of Duran Duran."

Liftoff.

The Flintstones in Viva Rock Vegas (2000)
Budget: $58 million (estimated)
Opening wknd: $10.5M (USA)
Gross: $32.5M (USA)
Genre: Family/Comedy
Production co: Universal Pictures

Summary: In this live-action prequel to the 1994 comedy hit, the Flintstones and the Rubbles go on a trip to Rock Vegas, where Wilma is pursued by playboy Chip Rockefeller.

I'm actually not a bad chap.

Really.

I listen to people if they have something to say, as long as they're not too slow or too boring. I leave pennies in the penny jar, and I've been known to double flush in restaurant toilets—courtesy flushes, I believe they're called. But sometimes I am tested by the universe. For example, when I heard the landing gear pull up, I unbuckled and stood up, whereupon a flight attendant screamed at me, "Sir, sit down *immediately*. We are experiencing a pocket of mild turbulence."

Well, okay. I sat down.

Ding!

Good! It was the bell to indicate that it was okay to unfasten our seatbelts and move around, but it set the Buñuel children to expressing themselves with gusto.

Expecting to be reprimanded at any moment, I stood to retrieve my small, chaste Adidas bag from the overhead bin, amid a snowdrift of drool bibs, adult diapers, restraining harnesses and baseball caps reading BUÑUEL CHILDREN ARE PEOPLE TOO, with the intent of finding that cuntfart, Neal.

Just then, the drinks cart emerged from the mid-plane galley to begin a zombie-slow service likely to reach row 67 by the time the plane was over Greenland.

In my mind there existed a duality: I wanted a triple Scotch, but I also wanted to get as far away from the little Buñuel fucks as possible.

Dilemma.

In the end, the triple Scotch won. But when, after seventeen hours, the trolley limped past row 67 and I asked for a triple Scotch, she who told me to sit down during the turbulence said, "I'm sorry, *sir*, but EU regulations prohibit the sale of more than a single drink at a time on all EU carriers, either within or without EU airspace."

"You sound like a computer program."

"I beg your pardon?"

"Nothing. I'll have a single, then."

As the vile, Tabasco-gargling sky-wench grimly slapped a Johnnie Walker and a clear plastic cup with one ice cube onto my tray, she gave me the evil eye. Then she favoured the Buñuel child to my right, who screamed for something incomprehensible, with a cartload of smiles, an infinite glow of love and compassion, plus a juice box featuring the face of a *Toy Story* character whose arrival created a brief interval of merciful silence before the sirens of hell once again flared. How the fuck do humans ever manage to reproduce if *that* is what lies at the end of the coitus/lust/DNA dance of doom?

Having downed my meagre ration, I set off to find Neal.

But you see, the thing was, I was looking for Neal somewhere in coach class. It never occurred to me that the dim fucker could have finagled his way into the business class seat that rightfully ought to have been *mine*. It was only after the third circling of rows 15 to 69 and back again that it dawned on me: *Oh my dear God. No. This isn't happening. No. It just isn't happening . . .*

I walked down the cabin, climbed the staircase into the plane's bubble and there, in 77A, reclining in a pod like something out of a utopian sci-fi movie, was Neal, clinking champagne flutes with Cameron fucking Diaz.

Cameron fucking Diaz?

I loomed over him. "Neal, here you are. Business class? I think not. Come on now, chop-chop. It's time for you to assume your rightful seat, 67E, at the back of the plane. *Now.*"

"Ray, relax. Have a drink with Cam and me."

I was so peeved that Miss Diaz's fame factor didn't register.

"Neal, no. You're my personal assistant and I command you to swap seats with me." Other passengers were staring at us.

"Ray, chill. Cam here is just telling me about various formulas for generating prime numbers. A smart one, she is." The pair made bedroom eyes at each other.

I lost it. "You fecal-scented golem, get out of my fucking seat *now*. What the *fuck* is your problem?"

"Excuse me, sir . . ." Lady Cuntly McRazorpanties, the flight attendant from down below, had followed me up into the bubble.

"Oh, it's *you.*"

"Sir, I have to ask you to leave business class immediately."

"Not bloody likely. I'm staying here, while this git who works for me takes his rightful place in coach."

Lady Cuntly backed off to confer with a hag cohort out by the meal-heating ovens, then came at me again.

"Mr. Gunt . . ."

She knew my name. Bravo!

"Mr. Gunt, Mr. Neal here is a street survivor. We at the airline are honouring the homeless this year, and it was our airline's privilege and delight to offer him the one remaining business class seat as a token of our faith in the triumph of the human spirit over adversity. With the full authority of the EU air system code behind me, I order you back to 67E."

Order me? "Who the hell do you think you—"

Glunkkkk! On went the plastic zap-strap handcuffs from behind and, *ghufghghghg!*, a steward's hand went around my neck and, within a constellation of pain, I was marched back down the bubble's stairs to 67E. I was furious, but it was also (if I'm honest) a bit of fun having everyone I passed looking at me and thinking I was violent and dangerous.

Once I was seated, the steward hissed into my ear, "Mr. Gunt, you can stay there and behave, or we can manacle you to your seat and make an emergency landing in Reykjavík, where you'll be jailed and made to pay a fine that will bankrupt you. Am I clear?"

Dick. "Yes."

"Good. We have approximately nine more hours ahead of us. Behave like an adult and we'll be fine." He removed the zap straps with a small pair of scissors.

"What about my seat up in business class?"

The steward and McRazorpanties eyed each other. "That's not your seat," he said.

"It fucking well is."

"Sir, you're terrifying the children," McRazorpanties chided.

"These tards would be frightened by a paper napkin."

In unison: "Sir!"

"I want my seat!"

"I warned you, Mr. Gunt."

From nowhere came six arms, and *zap, zap, zap, zap*—I was bound onto 67E while a Buñuel child sniffed my hair and began shrieking into my right ear.

I sat there imprisoned, deprived of meal service, unable to comprehend what had just happened, while the Buñuels caterwauled and the drunken yobs voided their bowels in the toilets that sandwiched my ears.

And then Neal came down the aisle towards me. "God, Ray. You must have been pretty out of control."

Words failed me, though I hope bulging forehead veins conveyed what words couldn't.

"Cammie was worried about you and asked me to bring you a flute of champagne, but I thought it might get you in trouble, so I didn't. She's amazing."

Dumbfounded, I stared at Neal.

"Can I get you a pillow or a snack?" he offered.

"Neal, when you were waiting for the car to pick you up, you were sitting on the curb and those two teenage birds came up to you, and I could see that in their minds they wanted to shag you on the spot, and you did, too. I *saw* it. How the fuck did you *do* that? I mean really . . . you look like shit. You smell like shit. You have nothing going for you outwardly . . . and yet you're like Jimi Hendrix with a never-ending rotisserie of pussy circling his dick."

Neal knelt in the aisle beside me. "You know,

Raymond," he said, "I've been homeless for years, but not a week's gone by where I haven't had two or three unique encounters, all of them instigated by women—in their cars, in their offices, in alleyways, once even inside a police van. I just sit there on a curb, like, needing to be fixed, and these ladies come along thinking they know how to fix me."

If pathos and uselessness are somehow erotic, I ought to be the Leonardo DiCaprio of the new era. And yet I end up zap-strapped to seat 67E.

Neal looked at me. "Ray, open your mouth."

"What?"

"Just open your mouth. Trust me."

And so I did, and Neal stuck something in it that felt like a Tic-Tac, and that dissolved on my tongue almost instantly.

"What the fuck was *that*?"

He smiled at me. "Something to make the flight bearable. By the way, John Taylor of Duran Duran is in the inflight movie. Fucking brilliant. See you on the ground in Los Angeles." And with that, he was off.

What the?

When next I opened my eyes, the plane was empty and a team of swarthy-looking people was vacuuming the seats. Grim-faced McRazorpanties walked past carrying a pile of paperwork. "Oh, Mr. Gunt," she said. "You're awake. Good. I think you'll find your party waiting for you at gate two. Have a lovely trip to Honolulu."

Twat.

But a *doable* twat.

08

I had the delight of visiting Los Angeles International Airport in the mid-1980s, when I was beginning my career as a cameraman. The London production company I worked with was treated to a god-like junket: five of us were sent to California to learn about new lines of increasingly digital cameras and new techniques for lighting and sound, as well as to grind our schlongs to the bone on an endless roller coaster of pussy. Enormous meals. The best booze. Women hurling themselves at us. Palm trees. Freeways. Fuck, it was easily the highlight of my young life, and it ended with a farewell shag in the business lounge loo with young Shelley, who worked for Panavision or Kodak or something like that. Returning to London felt like going back to a Dickensian orphanage. Grimness. Clouds. Soot. Diesel fumes. Labour unrest. I mean, it really was an eye-opener to see how Americans lived back then.

The point is that I remember LAX back in the day, and was kind of looking forward to a little dash of that California energy. And as my pretzelled, blood-starved body limped out of the Jetway and into the terminal, I thought that a ghastly mistake had been made. Maybe the plane had landed in Tijuana. The concourse was full of short little munchkins percolating away in Mexican or whatever it is they speak in California these days. A filthy, clapped-out terminal building. Darth Vader Homeland Security warning messages blaring every thirty seconds. Police and K9 search squads imperiously sniffing everything. Greasy fast-food stands. I mean, if they're going to ape Mexico, why not throw in some donkey cock floorshows and a few five-minute hand-job booths? How hard is it to get a titty bar going? Staple-gun a black bedsheet up in a corner, break out a halfway decent flashlight and start minting twenty-dollar bills. Gentlemen, it's not rocket science.

Neal saw me coming and waved me over to our gate. "That was a good flight, Ray. I saw the Flintstones movie four times. That Joan Collins, sure, she may have been driving ambulances in the Korean War, but she's still got something going. And how are you?"

"Fucking Americans."

"I have to agree. I was expecting something a bit fancier, maybe even kind of like that bar scene in *Star Wars*." At that moment half of Peru cut in front of us and clattered away to some distant gate. "The one thing I wasn't expecting was . . ."

"An anthill? Neal, please tell me that our flight to Honolulu is on time and that I have a seat in first class."

"As your personal assistant I'm on it."

Neal talked to the gate agent and confirmed that all was well and that boarding would start in two hours. I quickly found the business lounge—the very one in which I'd banged young Shelley, no less—and even found a vacancy in my old toilet stall, and sat down to have a verklempt little moment while I attempted to relax my churning guts.

When I got back to the lounge, I soon learned that, in LAX, free mini bottles of booze were treasures of yore. In fact, anything alcoholic was behind a bar backed by a trio of shrieking wide-screen TVs carrying that ghastly style of news Americans delight in, where three crawls are going simultaneously and where the stupidest incidents are inflated into cosmic importance by the world's ugliest reporters. Has this country never heard of a casting couch?

> **Frank:** Julie, we've just reached our contact with Homeland Security. Apparently the kitten is still stuck up the tree.
>
> **Julie:** Frank, did Homeland Security say whether this was a politically motivated stranding?
>
> **Frank:** Julie, according to my sources, the kitten went up the tree—and remember, Julie, this isn't official yet—the kitten climbed the tree with no backers or lobbying groups in mind.
>
> **Julie:** Frank, let's go to live cam so that viewers at home can get a look at the kitten. Also, I've just heard from Rick in Atlanta that the kitten has a Facebook page showing some images that some viewers might find disturbing. Rick?
>
> **Rick:** Thanks, Julie, these images aren't for everyone. A visit to the kitten's Facebook page revealed images of not just one, but *several* molested dead birds lying on its owner's front door welcome mat. In the kitten community, we've been told, these sorts of ritualistic murders are called "gifts." Back to you, Julie.

Talk about a culture in free fall. At the bar I asked for a double vodka tonic and received a snitty look from **LACEY**. "I'm sorry, sir, but federal regulations prohibit the sale of any drink containing liquor in excess of one point five ounces."

"Can I order two drinks, then?"

"I've been told to exercise my judgment as to whether I think the purchaser intends to drink them both, and if I think that is the case, I have an obligation to sell that person just the one drink," **LACEY** said.

"Okay, I give up. I'll have a single vodka tonic."

In the absence of any other customers, **LACEY** ever so grudgingly mixed me a vodka tonic that stank of floor cleaning products. "How much do I owe you?"

"Cocktails are complimentary to visitors to the lounge, but customers are not constrained from tipping if they wish to."

"Do you find yourself getting many tips, **LACEY**?"

"I believe in doing a good job."

"So if I don't give you a tip, you'll still think you are doing a good job?"

"I suppose so, yes."

"Must be fun being you." I downed the rest of my vodka and bounced off to rejoin Neal, who, to my joy, sat dejectedly at the gate, surrounded by Peruvians or Nicaraguans or Mexicans. All that was missing were hutches full of angry chickens and the sound of pan flutes.

"Get yourself a drink okay, Ray?"

"Neal, I think this country has changed a great deal." I thought of young **LACEY**, growing old and haggard behind a bar, never having received a tip, her mind full of endless televised pseudonews. **LACEY** would finally give up and put her head in the oven. Her Mexican land-lord would then sweep in and quickly bury her corpse beneath the backyard piñata, and then move his extended family of seventeen into **LACEY**'s apartment, forging a document so they could take over her identity.

We heard the boarding announcement for flight 13 to Honolulu. *For passengers with small children or in need of extra assistance, we ask that you step up to the gate now for pre-boarding. We'd like to also invite our passengers in first class and/or members of our Elite Mileage Club to board now or at their leisure.*

"Ciao, Neal. See you on the ground." I ran to the gate, flashing my boarding pass, feeling young and alive and unencumbered by screaming brats. With a kick in my step, I scampered down the Jetway into the plane. Seat 1K—pretty hard to fuck that one up.

....

LAX to HNL = 5 h, 30 m

....

09

Okay.

So I was the first passenger on board. 1K was a window seat facing north. As I settled in, a gratifying phalanx of the babbling poor began scuttling past, back towards the fartulent rabbit warren of coach. It was all I could do not to stick out my leg and trip these fucking losers, but knowing that I had the power to do so was all it took to make me glow inwardly and refrain. They couldn't close the little blue curtain between them and me quickly enough.

Neal lumbered by. "Enjoying your seat, boss?"

"Oh hello, Neal. What seat are you in?"

"54F, Ray."

"And *I'm* here in 1K. *Adios*, loser."

First class filled up bit by bit. Nice enough looking lot—most likely took a bath before coming to the airport; not on the dole or whatever it's called in the States; haven't yet sold their children to work in thrice-a-day stage showings of burro sex.

The seat beside me stayed empty. Airlines like keeping the first row as empty as they can so that flight crews can deadhead back to their home locations. I was wondering if some delicious, velvety young stew was going to be my flight mate. In my head I was chanting: *humungous fucking tits, humungous fucking tits* . . . which, *I* think, is a reasonable enough chant for any red-blooded male.

The public address system came to life: *Due to a software error, tonight's inflight entertainment system is limited to channel 2. We apologize for any inconvenience this causes.*

I checked the inflight magazine for what was on channel 2 and had a fucking stroke—"The World of Mr. Bean: The complete televised antics of the silently lovable dimwit."

"Jesus fucking Christ, what is wrong with this planet?"

"I beg your pardon, sir?" It was my inflight service director.

"Nothing. Champagne coming soon?"

"No champagne before the flight, sir. The Department of Homeland Security has banned all on-ground beverage service of alcohol. Can I get you water or juice?"

"Right, right. Orange juice, then."

What did she hand me? A fucking *juice box* that didn't even have fucking juice in it: it was a *juicealicious blend of exotic flavours with omega-3 acids added for good health.* Translate: leftover crap swept from the fruit factory floor pulverized into nothingness, heated to three hundred degrees Fahrenheit to eliminate contaminants and mixed with plutonium to kill all the nutrients in order to make the resulting sewage that dribbles down the sluice shippable to everywhere from Antarctica to Death Valley with no need for refrigeration. I'm no fucking nutritionist, but people, how hard is it to not eat shit?

"Thanks, but I'll settle for water." I gave her back the box.

After I buckled up, I glanced behind me and the plane seemed to be full; passengers had stopped coming in from the Jetway. It dawned on me that the seat to my left was still empty. Finally! A fucking break. I'd sprawl out without having to chat up a next-door neighbour, melon-breasted or otherwise.

And then, subtly but unmistakably, I heard a slow, thumping rumble headed my way.

Bwana! Kimba the elephant is approaching from the western side of the rubber plantation . . .

I shut my eyes and tried to imagine what new horror could be coming toward me, and I was rewarded beyond my darkest expectations.

My inflight service director, whose name tag read **TRISH**, said, "Right this way, Mr. Bradley. You're in 1J. It's an aisle seat, so you'll have access to the washroom. On behalf of the entire flight crew, I want you to know that we'll do everything we possibly can to make your trip to Hawaii as wonderful as possible." Trish cracked me an ever so tiny smile.

10

Right.

I think I said earlier that I am a peace-loving man. Nothing would please me more than world peace and a stronger United Nations. You bet! *Hey, all you useless little countries! Banding together will give you the illusion of hope!* I also genuinely like puppies. Although I find it appalling that Chinese people relish them as food, I like to think of myself as open-minded: we miss so much joy in life when we say no to new experiences.

So there I was, calmly ensconced in 1K, when I had that Steven Spielberg moment where my plastic cup of water suddenly developed tiny wavelets . . . what could it be? *Probably just shutting the cargo doors. I am an accomplished flier. Nothing fazes me!*

And then—Christ, there's just no other way to put it—the fattest human being I've ever seen boarded the plane, a man, maybe fifty. Imagine a container of cottage cheese dumped onto a kitchen floor and then sprung to life in human form. This newly created golem had little dollops of fat that resemble squirrel tits hanging from underneath its arms. Its forearms resemble brains, but on the elbows there were rusty patches of eczema that spoke of a life spent dining from vending machines. The only use society might have for a beast like this is to make people feel better about not being him.

The Blob looked at 1J. Yes, that is correct . . .

Trish did what anyone does upon encountering a freak: she fawned all over him. "Hello, Mr. Bradley. So nice to see you again! Welcome to the flight."

Pretty hard to forget someone like Mr. Bradley, who approached 1J like a snail, in a trailing, suctiony manner. Did he bother to say hello? No. Did he apologize for his existence? No. Instead, he rummaged under one of his multiple boob flaps and removed a small packet of orange-coloured processed crisp thingies and filled his mouth in one pass, afterwards wiping his hands on the five visible square inches of his knees.

Trish added an extra strap to Mr. Bradley's seatbelt, and then another. She sweated and grunted as she plunged her now-moist fists into Mr. Bradley's damp cavities in the hope of finding a clasp, and when she finished, she knew she would never be able to unsee or unfeel what she had just experienced.

Something whimsical came over me, just an impish impulse to give back to the world some of the joy it has given me over the years. I said to Mr. Bradley, "Do you enjoy being a member of the plus-sized community?"

He looked at me. *Snuffle; snort; glungh.* "What?"

"I asked whether you greatly enjoy being a member of the plus-sized community."

No reply. So much for chitchat.

At last the plane taxied to the runway and, God help us, even with this diseased neutron star beside me, was able to lift off.

Ding!

Passengers are free to get up and move about the cabin, but FAA regulations require passengers to remain seated with their seatbelt on at all times during the flight.

I said to my neighbour, "What the fuck is that supposed to mean?"

"Huh?"

"How can passengers be free to get up and move about the cabin if their fucking government tells them to remain seated and belted at all times?"

"There's no need to swear."

"Oh, fuck off. Waddle back to coach and eat a fucking baby."

As I teased him, I was very careful to enunciate in such a way that, to eavesdroppers, my words would appear as innocuous as, say, *Can I read that magazine when you're through with it?*

Mr. Bradley's face began empurpling and I felt like a painter working on a successful canvas. I casually opened a copy of some disgraceful codswallop of an American newspaper and pretended to read its investigative paragraphs. I could tell Mr. Bradley had no idea what to do about me.

Then Trish, who had been futzing about in the galley, came through to ask business classers what they'd like from the menu, chicken or beef. This was far too good an opportunity to miss, so I used my highly focused ultra-indoors voice to say to Mr. Bradley, "By the looks of you, you'd best hope they have all of Noah's ark on the menu."

"Excuse me?"

The couple across the aisle glanced our way. I put on my normal person's face.

"May I ask you to please stop insulting me?"

I gave a theatrical shrug. "I've no idea what you're on about." I received a sympathetic glance from my other cabin mates and gleefully returned to the dreadful American newspaper.

When Trish reached our row, she asked the couple across the aisle for their choice, then turned to ask Mr. Bradley, with at least some level of genuine curiosity, "What can I get you tonight, sir—beef or chicken?" It took all of my strength to not bust into full-body laughter.

Instead of shouting, *Give me every piece of fucking food in this plane!*, Mr. Bradley pretended to mull over the question, finally arriving at "Chicken, please."

Trish turned to me. "Mr. Gunt, all we have left is the beef."

"No problem. And look, I'm not that hungry. If Mr. Bradley would like my meal as well, he's certainly welcome to it." I spoke with an air of church-boy sincerity that Trish couldn't help but regard as a genuine expression of human kindness.

More purple from Mr. Bradley. A brief patch of turbulence caused ripples across his gut. He caught me staring and said, "You think I like being this way?"

In a calm, therapeutic manner, I said, "Sir, are you a nervous flier? I used to get nervous too, but my doctor gave me something to take before flights and now flying's a breeze."

"My problem isn't flying, Mr. Gunt." He'd remembered my name! "My problem is your rudeness."

I gave him a wounded look. Then I heard the tinkle of the approaching beverage cart. "Maybe a drink is what you need. Nothing like a drink to ease the nerves." *It'd take a fucking Exxon Valdez–full of booze to get this whopper sozzled.*

Mr. Bradley blurted out to Trish a request for a double Scotch and received that very American reply: "I'm sorry, sir, but the FAA prohibits the sale of alcoholic drinks over one point five ounces. I'll be back to you shortly—beverage service is starting in row 8 tonight."

Purple changed to beet red. *Dear God, this is fun.*

When Trish at last reached row 1, she had his mini bottle ready. "Your Scotch, Mr. Bradley?"

"Thank you."

She poured the contents onto ice and was about to hand the glass to him with a pack of smoked almonds when she paused, put her hand back into the bin and removed two more nut bags. She set all three beside his drink without comment. "Mr. Gunt?"

Trust me, this was the only time in my whole fucking life I'd refused the offer of a drink, but it was just too good an opportunity to waste. "No, thanks—I have to make sure I fit into my swimsuit. Soda water's great, if you have it."

My seatmate was maroon now, and I thought, *Ahh . . . three more hours of fun.*

"I know the feeling, Mr. Gunt," said Trish, patting her minuscule waist with a wink. "Here's some water. Nuts, maybe?"

"No. All those oils are really fatten—" I gently corrected myself. "They tend to linger in the body."

She nodded at me and then rolled the cart into the pantry.

I could sense the quickly spinning hamster wheels of hate in Mr. Bradley's being.

I said and did nothing more until our food came. Instead of a hot meal, dinner was a disposable box containing a croissant stuffed by careless chimps. The bar-coded label on Mr. Bradley's box read: "FIRSTCLASS" CHICKIN CROISANT. Trish offered me one reading: "FIRSTCLASS" BEEFE CROISANT.

Ah, the American education system.

I declined. Trish then asked me at the very least to have a roll with butter, and I graciously said, "Sure, why not?" On the tray was a pack of ketchup. I tore off the tiniest strip from the corner and then used the ketchup to write PIG on the surface of my bun. I waited for the right moment to hold it clearly before me and ask Mr. Bradley in distinct, soothing, broadcaster-like tones audible to all, "Mr. Bradley, are you feeling a bit better now that you've had a drink?"

He looked at me and then at the bun.

He burped.

Whatever he says, it's going to be priceless.

His body started shaking up and down like a hardware store paint-shaker, and *then*, spectacularly, he vomited onto the carpeted bulkhead wall in front of us. He lurched upward in a last cosmic gym crunch, then slumped forward, his head dropping onto his chest. He was still.

Well, fuck him if he can't take a joke.

I shouted, "Flight attendant! Mr. Bradley's in terrible distress!" *And there's the foulest puke you ever smelled all around him, and it is ruining my flight, so please mop it all up.*

I, the hero, then shouted, "Does anyone here know CPR?" Even if they did, they'd have an easier time giving it to a bouncy castle at a children's birthday party than trying to revive Mr. Bradley.

Some losers from coach peeked through the curtain to see what the commotion was about. Trish screamed for them to sit back down. She velcroed the blue curtain closed, then asked over the PA if there was a doctor on board. But even if there was, come on—what could he do? You'd need a forklift to lift the fat bastard out of the seat.

And then Neal poked his head through the curtain. "I used to work as a paramedic, ma'am," he said to Trish.

She practically wept with relief and waved him through.

"You never told me you were a paramedic, Neal. I specifically asked you if you possessed any real world skills, and you said you had none."

"Surprises make life fun, Ray. Here—help me lay him out in the aisle."

Christ, it was like trying to drag a melon wagon up an alpine meadow. "How much does this fucker weigh, do you think, Neal?"

"Maybe twenty, twenty-five stone."

"He took one big puke and then slumped over."

"Probably a heart attack."

Neal, Trish and I finally got Mr. Bradley's corpse into the aisle. All eyes in business class were agog at having so much deadness so close by.

"You never really think of death too much in our culture," said Neal.

"I know. It's unhealthy, really. We need to find the joy and laughter in death as well as the depressing bits."

"Amen, Ray."

Trish was wiping up the puke on the bulkhead wall.

"What happens next?" I asked Neal.

"Put him back in his seat, I suppose."

"You have to be fucking kidding. After what we just went through?"

"We don't want rigor mortis to set in while he's blocking the aisle. It's our last chance to, umm . . . bend him to our will."

And so we wrestled Mr. Bradley back into 1J, where he sat frozen as if in a state of permanent excitement while awaiting a truckload of greasy, heavily salted meals.

"Don't expect me to keep this fat dead fuck company for three and a half more hours. You work for me, Neal, so you can sit beside him for the rest of the flight."

"*Me* in first class?"

"It's your lucky day, Neal."

"I'll say. Hey, is that a croissant I see there at your seat? All we got in coach were snacks that kind of looked like what you'd find under the front seat of a well-used family sedan. Not too appetizing. But you— *you* got a sandwich."

"It's yours if you want it."

"Thanks, Ray, you're the best."

And thus I moved to seat 54F, entertained, relaxed, relieved and happy. The rest of the flight was a dream in spite of collective bleatings of amusement around me at the appalling *Mr. Bean* program.

Fucking *Mr. Bean*.

....

Mr. Bean is a British comedy series of 19 twenty-five-minute episodes written by and starring Rowan Atkinson. The pilot was broadcast on England's ITV on January 1, 1990, and the last episode in late 1995.

The series follows the exploits of Mr. Bean, described by Atkinson as "a child in a grown man's body," as he solves various problems presented by everyday life—often causing mayhem in the process. Bean rarely speaks, thus making the series ideal for global domination in the crowd sedation sector of the TV industry. The show has been sold in 245 territories. It is relentless. It can be enjoyed with equal ease by three-year-olds and Alzheimer's patients. Mirth: the universal language.

....

11

Honolulu was a total donkeyfuck, starting with the ridiculous amount of respect paid to that repulsive corpse Bradley, as if dying on a plane is some big accomplishment. Thirty minutes were wasted while medics came to retrieve his husk, and there weren't even any snacks or drinks while we waited at the gate for them to do their thing.

Finally allowed into the terminal, we passed through immigration, which, its being the middle of the night, was a breeze, but then we couldn't find Sarah, our TV network go-to.

So Neal and I sat and waited in the arrivals area, nighttime warmth nuzzling our travel-weary arms and plumeria scent filling the air like sugar. We imbibed the two dozen or so mini bottles I'd stolen from the drinks wagon during the death kerfuffle and contemplated our next step—locating our charter flight to Kiribati.

Travel had turned Neal into a fucking child: "Wow. *Me* in Hawaii. Whatever next?"

"Look, Neal, Hawaii is not some magical pixie wonderland; it's an American state populated by atomic weapons, a remnant native population and people too stupid to spell their way out of a paper bag. Most of them came here to escape pathetic lives in the forty-nine other states, so in some sense, Hawaii is a scenic cul-de-sac filled with people who want to drink themselves to death without feeling judged."

"Smells nice, though, doesn't it?"

"It certainly does."

"Where's this Sarah woman, then?"

"If she's American, she's most likely playing Scrabble with a chimp and losing."

A jet took off in the background. Ukulele music was playing over the PA. The booze was doing its job, and I did kind of like this place. And then we saw Sarah: late twenties, long brown hair, dressed like women in ad agencies do: V-neck sweater with three-quarter sleeves— distinct upwardly mobile cleavage. I said, "Look at her. *She's* not about to do *anyone* unless it ratchets her up the ladder."

"You sure, Ray? She looks kind enough."

"Neal, I stopped trying to nail that type a decade ago. Birds of her calibre have been getting hit on since they were two years old; by the time they're four, they're already technically out of my league."

As Sarah came closer to us, I realized she was sniffling as if something sad had just occurred.

"Are you . . . Sarah?"

"Yes. Hello." Her body language said *almost too upset to shake hands*.

"Raymond Gunt."

"Neal Crossley," Neal chimed in, then added, "Sarah, hey, what's wrong?"

"It's awful," she said.

"What's awful?"

"Matt Bradley—he's dead!"

Oh dear. I looked at Neal, and he at me, and he said, "Oh?"

I disingenuously asked, "Was Mr. Bradley with the TV network?"

"He was."

I thought about this. "Why on earth wasn't he on a corporate jet?"

"I don't know," Sarah said. "Something about wanting to be with the common folk who made him what he was."

I thought, *Good fucking thing he's dead, the way I treated him.* "What was his role in the show?" I asked.

"He was the brains. The show's soul. He knew the answer to everything, how everything actually *worked*: casting, cameras, human behaviour under stressful conditions." She honked her nose loudly into a tissue. "It's just awful. I don't know who's going to replace him."

It took every molecule of falsity within me to say, "No wonder you're so sad."

"Sad? About Matt Bradley? Good *God*, no. He was awful. I'm thrilled he's gone. I'm just sad because my workload's tripled and I was supposed to go to Fiji with my boyfriend and now I have to fly to Kiribati myself to oversee a bunch of imbeciles who, in turn, oversee our bikini-wearing human lab rats. It's so unfair."

Now this is my kind of woman. I think that was when I first contemplated falling in love. "Join us for a drink? Nothing to mix it with, though."

"What do you have? *Ooh!* Tia Maria!" She grabbed the bottle and tipped it back.

I said, "It really is a terrible fucking thing, Matt Bradley being dead and all."

She held up a hand as Neal twisted the cap off another mini bottle for her. "Please, your language."

"Sarah, what is it with you Americans and swearing?" I asked. "You crow over enhanced interrogation procedures and the current destruction of shitholes like Africa, but I throw in one 'fuck' and you all go nuclear."

Sarah chugged her drink as she looked at me, then tossed her mini bottle in the trash. She was going to say something sanctimonious. *Oh God . . .*

She said, "*Bono* still thinks there's hope for Africa."

I blinked and we passed a moment in total silence.

Then she laughed. "Come on! I'm totally fricking kidding. Look! You've got *me* swearing now! Pass me another Tia Maria."

Phew.

"I was sitting next to Mr. Bradley when it happened, you know," I confessed. (Actually, I was bragging.)

"No!" She was unscrewing the next mini bottle's top.

"Seat 1K. Twelve inches away."

This sank in to Sarah's mind as she guzzled the bottle. "They put *you* in business class?"

"I . . . yes, they did."

"You must have friends in high places. I would have thought they'd put a B-unit cameraman in a cage with the goats."

"Well, that makes me feel great."

"It's a food chain, Raymond. Get used to it. There are a few things you need to know about this show and how it's run."

"Such as?"

"Such as, it's a temple of lies built on fear and cocaine."

"I suspected as much, but hadn't dared hope it was the truth."

She laughed at me. "I'm messing with you! It's actually more like a church or a cult. You can't make any mistakes or it's . . ." She mimicked slicing her throat. I honestly can't think of any other point in my life when I've fallen so hard and so fast for a woman.

She patted my arm then—contact! *Please, dear God, there has to be a broom closet we can use nearby. I don't think I've ever troubled you much; just making a small request here.*

"We've got to be flying to Kiribati soon enough," Neal interjected, wrecking the mood. "Any idea where our plane is?"

"Follow me."

We followed her with pleasure towards an exit surrounded by GIs or commandos or whomever it is the president hurls off to face certain death in whatever goatfuck war his country happens to be waging.

"We have to go to another terminal," Sarah explained, as we stepped out into the tropical night. "And there's our van and driver."

We hopped into a minivan and drove past a bunch of generic airport buildings—pleasantly scented airport buildings, but still, it was an airport. I tried to remember where I was, or what time it was, and just kind of gave up, happy to be like the cartoon character Snoopy, dancing his happy dance atop a cumulus cloud laced with dog bones.

A thought occurred to me. "Why is it Americans are socially permitted to say 'fricking,'" I asked, "when, in fact, everyone knows the word they're actually saying is 'fucking'?"

Neal mulled this over. "That's a real conundrum, Ray."

"I know! I mean, here you have some bland ho-bag telly presenter saying, 'I'm so fricking mad' about whatever, while you, the home viewer, know she's three millimetres away from saying, 'I'm so *fucking* mad.' But instead of being outraged because she basically said 'fucking' on TV, everyone giggles, like she's being cute."

Sarah gave me a contemplative look.

I was on a roll. "And then, later on, when they're masturbating to the mental images of that bland ho-bag—not me, mind you, the public in general—the masturbators get turned on by the tiny fragment of difference between her saying 'fricking' and 'fucking,' like it's a little tiny sliver of porn."

"Right," says Neal. "It's subtle, innit? But it's like ten times worse because the public is thinking, *fucking, fucking, fucking*. They're so full of shame or so socially conditioned that the mental effect of saying the word 'fucking' is technically amplified. By actually saying the word 'fucking' in real life, instead of 'fricking,' you're doing American society a favour."

"Exactly," I said.

At that point, the minivan's driver—some bearded chunk of chewed-up-and-spat-out social debris—pulled to the side of the road, turned around and started screaming at us, "Shut up! Shut up, both of you! I have a nephew in *Iraq*!"

Neal and I genuinely had no idea what on earth was going on.

"Iraq?" Neal said.

"Iraq?" I queried. Then we did it again.

"Iraq?"

"Iraq?"

Was he serious? "Sorry to hear that, sir," I said, "but could we keep on going?"

"No."

"Excuse me?"

"Not until you apologize," the driver said.

For what? "For what?" I wondered.

"For using the F-word."

"What is the connection between me using the F-word and your nephew being in Iraq?" I was baffled.

"Don't make things worse."

"Make *what* worse? I can't apologize for something I don't even know I've done, can I? I just don't get the link."

"Get out of my van!"

"No fucking way. Now you owe *me* an apology."

Neal backed me up, as a good ~~slave~~ assistant should. "As opposed to the apology you want to extract from us, which doesn't make sense no matter how one approaches it."

"Thank you, Neal."

"You're welcome, Ray."

Sarah said, "Driver, there's an extra twenty in it for you if you ignore these pinheads."

"No, ma'am, I'm taking a stand here."

Insanely loud volleys of trucks stuffed with pineapples and bound-and-gagged whores destined for Dubai roared past us, shaking the van.

I said, "Okay, then, so on one hand you have Iraq, which is what it is. And then on the other you have the difference between 'fricking' and 'fucking,' which is basically the difference between the letters 'RI' and 'U'."

Neal added, "You could almost make it a scientific equation, like:

$$Iraq = U - RI$$

"I don't think so, Neal. It would be more like a differential equation:

$$Iraq = {}_U\!\int^{ri}$$

"I see," Neal said. "Much more subtle."

"I rest my case."

By this point, our purple-faced driver (shades of Mr. Bradley) had opened his door, got out, come to the right side door panel, opened it and was screaming for us to leave. Talk about baffling. "Sarah," I asked, "can you tell us what on earth this guy is on about?"

"You said it yourself, Ray. Americans don't like swearing."

"But Iraq? What the *fuck*?"

"It's . . . complicated."

"So there's a relationship between fricking-fucking and Iraq?"

"Perhaps in a theoretical way."

"Neal, close and lock the doors."

"Done, boss."

The driver started pounding on the side of the van.

"Sarah, use your iPhone to capture a few seconds of our driver going apeshit."

"Done."

I hopped into the driver's seat. Before he added two and two, we peeled away. I asked Sarah, "Which way to the hangar?"

"Next exit, three buildings on the left."

"And when we get questioned about why we took off in his van?"

Sarah wore the expression of a child choosing the candy bar she wants. "He kept on saying he wanted to frick me. Like he was obsessed. But I thought, *Sarah, you're a big girl, you can take it.* Then he stopped saying 'fricking' and started saying 'fucking'."

Neal said, "And that's when Ray and I snapped out of our jetlagged sleep. We couldn't believe this nasty piece of work was hitting so explicitly on Sarah." Neal was instantly, deeply, into the story. "'Fricking' is one thing, but 'fucking' is a whole new level."

"Oh, thank heavens I had you two there to rescue me."

"Think you'll be pressing charges, then?"

"I'll certainly discuss the idea publicly."

Ah, when life is good, it's great, isn't it? Cocktails. Laughter. Me looking like an alpha Jason Bourne–like killing machine in front of the woman I now officially loved. Added bonus: a sidekick to torture who also feeds me good lines. I didn't want our minivan ride to end, but it did, at a small satellite terminal for private jets.

We pulled up to the curb. The head of local transportation asked, "Where's Dino?"

I said, "You mean our driver?"

"That's him."

"Sarah?"

Sarah took Dino's dispatcher aside. While she spoke with him, the man nodded gravely and looked suitably outraged. As Sarah came back to us, I heard her say, "For the good of the show—and because right now is more about the memory of Matt Bradley than it is about me—I'm going to let it slide. But you might want to get Dino in for some counselling."

"You're a wise and kind woman, Sarah," I said, and she giggled.

Inside, the hangar lobby resembled the Columbine parking lot, network TV people keeled over and looking miserable in the wake of Mr. Bradley's death.

Sarah vanished while we stood for a few minutes trying to decipher the action. She returned with a cartoonishly handsome executive-type guy. He barely glanced at us, then asked her, "Are these the two B-unit camera guys?"

"It's them. Guys, this is Stuart."

"Great." Stuart proceeded to ignore us, quizzing Sarah. "Did you get a refund of the Fiji tickets?"

"I did."

Shit. This guy was Sarah's boyfriend—my *competition.*

Sarah turned to us. "Fellas, we're going to be a little while organizing a thing or two. Go grab a bite from the vending machines." She gave each of us a pile of U.S. dollar bills and a chaste kiss on the cheek. "Thank you for rescuing me back there."

I said, "Our pleasure, ma'am. I didn't know Matt Bradley for long, but I know he would have done the same thing."

She giggled a big satisfying giggle and went off to wherever. But Stuart didn't follow her. Instead, he came up to me. "Okay, *fella,*" he rumbled. "I can see you mind-raping my Sarah, so I'll ask you to stop right now. If I ever get even the slightest inkling that something is happening, I'll sweep down from the sun with one thousand of my best ninjas and carve you into hamburger. Am I clear?"

"Uh . . ."

"Am I clear?"

"Right. Loud and clear."

"When are we leaving for Kiribati?" Neal asked him, trying to break the tension.

"No idea. Screw off, the both of you." Stuart stalked away.

12

Maybe you have a Stuart McDoucheworthy in your life. *Look at me, I'm Stuart. When I check myself out in the mirror, I think I'm better-looking than even, say, Matt Damon. I coast on my good looks.*

"A right dickhead," Neal observed.

"No, he can't be a dick, Neal, because he's a twat." At least Matt Damon has the talent to play Jason Bourne. Without his looks, Stuart would be nothing more than, well—he would be nothing more than *me.* Except *I* am a well-rounded bloke seasoned by a life of adventure; it kills me to think of all the attention Stuart gets just because he has a fucking *chin.* I seriously wish that Stuart had spent his entire childhood being serially arse-raped by teachers, scoutmasters, members of the clergy, relatives, policemen, doctors, door-to-door salesmen and all registered sex offenders within a 500-mile radius of his unprotected bedroom.

Neal said, "This certainly mixes up your mating strategy, doesn't it, Ray?"

"What on *earth* are you talking about?"

"It's pretty obvious you want to bonk Sarah till her skull pops. Even that clueless American twat noticed that. Shall we hit the vending machines while we're hanging about, Raymond?"

"Might as well."

* * *

Okay.

I'm not a celebrity chef. I like to think of myself as a giving, caring person who really does think about the modern world—someone who tries to improve the planet, even though it seems pretty much doomed. As a consequence, maybe I'm not fully qualified to pass judgment on the diet of most Americans. But as I stood there staring at the shit-coated guano logs and repulsive cans of room-temperature weasel piss in the airport vending machines, I was appalled. "Come on, America, you're living creatures, not science experiments."

"Scary, isn't it, Ray."

"How on fucking *earth* do Americans expect to ensure that weaker countries stay weak when all they eat are overpackaged chemical goatfuckings manufactured in the same factories that make dildos and pesticides?"

"Ray, I don't think there's anything in there we could actually put in our bodies."

Still we scanned the grids of toxins wrapped in bright paper and the cans of sugary blight.

"Look!" Neal was pointing, with a heartbreaking note of hope in his voice. "Look at that bar there—it's got peanuts in it. That's food."

"Probably tastes like a pocket calculator garnished with dried herpes juice flakes."

"That's quite a word picture, Ray."

"I try." I was reflective for a moment, "Neal, back home in your Samsung telly cardboard box, what do you eat?"

"I like to think I eat very well—that I'm discriminating, actually. Always try to eat vegetables and the like. I find the women who work in the better class of restaurant enjoy feeding me properly out the back door. They like to take me on as a personal project. I can't count the number of them I've shagged, too, in the back alleys after closing time."

The fucking hobo lives like a king. "God, there have to be more options for breakfast in this place."

"Let me look around the corner."

Neal went scouting and returned a few minutes later. "Ray, you have to come see this."

He led me down a hallway and into what had been maybe a hip and trendy waiting lounge back in the days of Led Zeppelin's 1973 North American tour, but was now a putty-coloured, soul-crushing dump with a groovy tattered orange stripe around the ceiling. Seated in the lounge's cracked leather chairs were twenty-four men and women who were . . . who were . . . awfully . . .

"Ray," Neal whispered, "that is one highly fuckable group of people."

"*Fuckable. That* is the word I was looking for."

We scanned the crowd: cheerleader, MILF, yoga teacher, schoolgirl—every fetish category imaginable, a true buffet. And while I'm not gay, I could swear the guys had something going for them, too.

"This is no accident, Ray."

"How do you mean?"

"To gather a group as fuckable as this one would take a trained professional weeks." He took a few steps forward and asked a "farm gal" who they were.

"We're this year's *Survival* contestants."

"Ah! That's terrific. I'm Neal. I'm working on your show."

I came over to ogle her chest. "Hello-hello."

"Raymond here is a cameraman on the show and I'm his personal assistant."

She smiled but didn't get up to take Neal's extended hand. "Sorry. We're all pooped. They're pre-starving us for the show, and we're actually not allowed to speak to crew. They said our meals would be here soon, but that was eight hours ago, and we can't leave the lounge to go find something to eat because our flight could be leaving at any moment. It's awful."

"We're looking around for something to eat too," said Neal. "If we have any luck, we'll bring you back something."

"God bless you."

As we walked away, I was shagging all twelve of the girls in my head. "Holy Christ, Neal, two months with that lot? We'll be living like gods."

Down a few corridors, we saw a thirteen-year-old driving a golf cart. In the back seat were twenty-four packaged meals. I flagged the boy down. "I'm Raymond, and you are . . . ?"

"Todd."

"Todd, right. Stuart told me to bring the meals to the contestants, so if you'll get out of the driver's seat, I'll take over."

"But I was supposed to—"

"Never mind that. I'm much older than you and I'm taking over. We don't want to have Stuart angry at us, do we?"

"No!"

"Okay, then, Todd, just fuck off now."

Todd got out and Neal and I hopped in.

"Well, that was easy," I said as we whirred away.

"Sure was."

The contestants were to the right, but we turned left and, before a glorious panorama of Pearl Harbor, stopped to inspect the succulent contents of the contestants' clamshell containers.

"Excellent-looking chicken tikka masala, Ray. Want to try some?"

"We need forks. Where's the cutlery?"

Neal fished around in a bag, removed something and handed it to me. It was a forky thing, but with a round depression.

"What the fuck is this?"

"It's a spork."

....

A **spork**, or a **foon**, is hybrid cutlery having a spoon-like scoop at one end with three or four fork tines. Spork-type utensils have been in use since the late nineteenth century. Patents for spork-like designs date back to 1874, when the word "spork" was registered as a trademark in the U.S. Sporks are used by fast-food restaurants, schools, the military and prisons.

....

"A *spork*? Who the fuck would eat food with a thing called a spork?"

"Look," said Neal. "You can see a forky bit on the

edge of the spoony bit." Neal dug into his chicken. His sporkwork was surprisingly dexterous.

"Jesus, Neal, watching you eat with a spork is like seeing Helen Keller at a ladies' afternoon tea."

"Sporks are the wave of the future, Ray. Oh—pass me some of that ravioli."

"Will do."

I took two sporks and began using them to down some of the smashingly good pasta.

Neal said, "Wait, a second, Ray—you don't need two sporks. The whole point of a spork is that you only need the one utensil."

"Neal, I'll use two sporks if I fucking well want to."

"But it's defeating the whole spirit of the spork."

"*Spork spirit?*" It's hard to get mad at Neal, because he suffers from a medical condition called total fucking stupidity.

"Ray, don't get mad just because I say yes to life. I like to keep myself available to the universe, because it brings me wisdom. Maybe you just don't want me to soar."

"It's a goddamn fucking *spork*, Neal. It is the embodiment of everything that is wrong with the fucking Western universe."

"Ray, just eat."

"I can't. I'm upset." It's true. When I get exercised about something, the adrenaline kills my hunger. Fight or flight.

"But you're going to sugar-crash, Ray, and then where'll you be? It'll take you days to rejigger your system back to normal."

Neal, confound him, had a point.

"Here," he said. "You have to eat something. Start with these."

"What are they?"

"Mixed nuts."

"What's this weird-looking one?"

"A macadamia nut."

13

When a movie is made of this entire soul-fart of an experience, this will be the point where we cut to a scene in which our hero opens his eyes to find himself in bed with an IV in his right arm, while in the background comes the sound of hooting, hollering and the loathsome Neal, singing and most likely dancing his own version of the 1984 Tears for Fears classic, "Shout."

What the fuck?

As our hero regains consciousness, he will realize he is in a six-bed hospital ward shared with five nut-brown Samoan wrestlers, all disintegrating as a result of heart disease or diabetes garnered from a lifetime of fatty, sugary snacks purchased through welfare fraud.

The music will stop and our hero will hear clapping and laughter, and then his faithful ~~slave~~ friend Neal's footsteps approaching.

"Ray! You're awake!"

"What the fucking hell is going on here?"

"You had an allergic reaction, Ray. That macadamia

nut you ate. You swelled up like one of these fellows here—you almost died."

I shuddered and a wave of hunger went through me. "Neal, how long have I been in here?"

"Two days, Ray, but I knew you had *Survival* spirit and would make it through."

"*Survival* spirit? I have no such fucking thing. What is wrong with you, Neal?"

"It's a good thing I have some paramedic training. Your eyeballs were about to pop out of your skull like Ping-Pong balls."

At that very moment, I heard a voice that made my gonads retreat into my groin.

"Darling! You're alive! All the whores along the International Date Line must be rejoicing at the news."

Fiona? What was *she* doing here?

"Hello, darling. I can see your brush with death has made you contemplative and given your soul complexity and depth."

"Fi, what in God's name are you doing in . . ." I looked at Neal.

"Honolulu General."

"What the *fuck* are you doing in Honolulu General?"

"Well, for starters, I'm feasting on your tears. To me they taste of joy. Second, as you know, I was in southern France. I was having a strawberry lubricant-scented frolic with a gifted young thing who was, um, auditioning for a part in a global beverage campaign, when suddenly, just as I was about to withdraw the long string of beads from . . ." She paused, noting that the five belugas in the room were listening, completely rapt.

"Go on," said Neal, also enthralled. "Tell us more. You were talking about beads."

"Very well, I will, although before I was using beads, I was using a handful of those Babybel cheeses that come in the red vinyl mesh—just the right amount of satisfying texture and shape. And my young crumpet! Her name was Gwyn. So naive, yet so eager to learn. Skin like a peach. And so respectful of authority."

There was total silence. Fiona looked around, clearly pleased with our reaction.

"To cut a long story short, I was in the midst of naughty, sexy, lubricated fun when the phone rang with the news."

"News? You came all the way here because you heard I had an allergic reaction?" I was touched.

Fiona snorted and Neal leapt in. "Bad news, Ray," he said. "That load of contestants that was about to take off when you ate the macadamia nut?" With his right hand, he made the international sign for a nose-diving corporate jet. "All gone."

I thought about this. "Well, at least they went to their graves hungry."

Fiona nodded. "Them and the entire casting team. So, thanks to contractual obligations, *I* have been dragged in to recast the show."

Shit. I *knew* I shouldn't have been so hard on Mr. Bradley. And then a chill went through me. "Wait— was Sarah on the flight?"

Fiona's unholy left lizard brow arched upward. "Someone has a crush, do they?"

Neal said, "No, Sarah wasn't on the flight."

"Did someone say my name?" Sarah appeared at the door with a magnificent spray of cellophaned pink orchids, which she tossed to Fiona. She came to my bedside, sat down on the edge and smooched my cheeks while every other man in the room began to mentally schedule his next wank. "Ray, your *Survival* spirit saved you!"

We all stared at her.

"I'm kidding!" she said. "Fortunately, your ex here has come to help us." She looked fondly at Fiona. "And even though Fiona was extremely busy, I thought it would be a nice gesture if she came to visit you."

Fiona rolled her eyes.

"How do you two know each other?" I asked.

Fiona looked at me cagily; Sarah was nothing but sweetness and light. She said, "Fi and I have been helping each other with all sorts of casting calls over the years. We see each other at industry events all the time."

Fi said, "Sarah gives the best backrub in the business."

Sarah blushed. "I just don't like seeing people tense."

"She's coming back to my hotel room after this to give me one," Fi said. "I can't tell you how badly I need it. I've been living on planes the past few days, and recasting a show from scratch is a Herculean task. We can't find any of Bradley's casting notes."

It was funny, but right then I had a tiny out-of-body experience—one of those rare moments where you step outside of yourself and see the human condition whole. You experience a warm glow, and you get the big picture and realize what's important in life and what isn't. "What about me?" I asked.

"You have to stay in the hospital a bit longer," said Neal.

"It's that bad?"

"No," said Fiona. "It's just easier to keep you here instead of booking you into a hotel. Besides," she looked around, "you have so many new friends." She glanced at her iPad. "Whoops! Backrub time!"

"You bet!" said Sarah. "It'll be the most amazing one you've ever had. I'll make sure every inch of you is thoroughly de-stressed—anything to ensure that this season *is* the best season ever."

Everybody laughed except me.

Sarah kissed me goodbye, while Fiona shook her purse like a maraca.

"What's in there?" I asked.

"About a thousand OxyContins I swiped from the dispensary during the fire drill an hour ago."

My posse left, and I fell asleep to the sounds of my roommates discreetly pleasuring themselves to their memories of Sarah.

....

OxyContin is the brand name of a time-release formula of oxycodone produced by the pharmaceutical company Purdue Pharma. It was approved by the U.S. Food and Drug Administration in 1995 and first introduced to the U.S. market in 1996. By 2001, OxyContin was the bestselling non-generic narcotic pain reliever in the U.S.; 2008 sales in the U.S. totalled $2.5 billion. An analysis of data from the U.S. Drug Enforcement Agency found that retail sales of oxycodone "jumped nearly six-fold between 1997 and 2005."

In 2001, Purdue Pharma permanently suspended distribution of 160 mg tablets in the U.S. It is speculated that the DEA had requested Purdue to discontinue manufacturing them.

Nobody ever mentions the good side of OxyContin: it makes you feel like Jesus fucking a horse.

When I came to again, I found a note from Neal on my bedside table, penned on the frayed corner of the cover of a five-year-old copy of *Us Weekly* magazine. I looked at its central photo: an off-the-rails starlet whose twat must, by this point in her career cycle, be dangling between her legs like Luciano Pavarotti's tonsils.

> *Ray! Off to a 4G with the nurses on night duty.*
> *Meet you at the airport.*

Airport?

Just then, Fiona, clad in jodhpurs, entered my room once more, looking annoyingly relaxed.

I was polite. "Had a lovely time pussy-boxing with Sarah?"

"Yes, indeed. Our bodies sang."

"I'm sure."

"Her flesh—so velvety yet muscular—*soooo* pliable. I suppose I shouldn't tell tales out of school, but she blows off heat like a cheap baseboard radiator."

My tallowy Polynesian roommates snapped to attention.

"Am I allowed out of this wretched hospital or what?"

"You are. In addition, out of the warmth of my heart, you're coming to the airport in my limo. We're on the same flight. Lucky us."

"Lucky us, indeed. Wait—why did you come up to the room to fetch me instead of sending an assistant?"

She rattled her purse, newly refilled with Oxy, and smiled. "Tabitha is downstairs waiting for us."

"*Tabs* is here?"

"You're not the only one who wants a slave, Raymond." Fiona burst out laughing, and two of my Samoan cohabitants threw soiled garments of some sort at me. I got out of bed. "That's our cue to leave, dear."

....

Haole, in the Hawaiian language, is generally used to refer to an individual who fits one (or more) of the following categories: "White person, American, Englishman, Caucasian, any foreigner." Its use historically has ranged from a sociological description to racist epithet. Anyone who's spent time in the Hawaiian public school system knows it is almost exclusively used as a racist epithet.

....

14

The limo was waiting for us out front. Tabs stood beside it, chewing gum and smiling as a trade wind blew up her schoolgirl-style skirt to reveal the cleanest, whitest, softest panties in the western hemisphere.

"Ray! I was so worried about you!" She gave me a smashing hug and we clambered into the car.

"You know me, Tabs. Living life to the max. I—"

Fiona cut me off. "Raymond, you could no more live life 'to the max' than you could doggy-paddle to the fucking moon. Your voyage through time is like the journey of a small piece of cat shit passing through a human colon, where it squeaks and slithers until one day it drops into a toilet called the grave."

I gave Tabs a brave smile. "Poor, poor Fiona, always wearing the mask of wit to cover her withered interior world."

My thinking on Tabs was that, although I was in love with Sarah, nailing Tabs would be a commitment-free treat, like finding a ten-quid note on the sidewalk.

The limo careened forward, and we headed off to the airport. "So, Fi, where's Billy in all of this?"

"He's on a flight from LA. We'll see him later."

Tabs continued to sneak glances at me. I still had no idea whether looking like her father, Mr. Molesty, was a good or bad omen in the screw department. Only time could tell.

The car slowed to a stop and Fi snapped, "Fucking hell, it's an eight-lane freeway on a tiny island in the middle of nowhere in the middle of the day and it's a fucking traffic jam."

From her tone of voice, I could tell she was entering one of her dreaded hate warps.

She threw perhaps five hundred male headshots at Tabs. "We're looking for the top twenty most fuckable. Here's a Sharpie. Start rating them one to ten now."

I stared at Fiona. She looked back at me. "No, Raymond, I am not going to give you the female candidates. Your taste in women is useless."

"Fi, I'm bored out of my mind. I have to have *something* to do."

"Then hand these photos to the driver and ask *him* to decide which ones are the most fuckable."

I asked, "Why don't you just use your own judgment, dear?"

"Because I am toying with *lesbianism*, Raymond, and I'll just end up choosing the women who look like the guys who show up to grout my new kitchen back-splash tile. The driver looks like an average guy with centre-of-the-bell-curve taste. I trust his judgment more than yours. Or mine. Driver!"

"Yes, ma'am?"

"My assistant, Raymond, is going to show you a pile of photos of models. I want you to rate their fuckability on a scale of one to ten."

"Yes, ma'am."

And that is how I ended up spending an hour of my life gridlocked on the 801 showing headshots of dick bait to HARLAN, who truly had pedestrian taste. Example: "I could do her. She's like that actress you never see anymore, Julia Roberts. Yeah. I could do her *good. Yeah.*"

When I was through penning his ratings on the photos, Fiona screeched, "Raymond, shut Harlan's window so he can wank in private."

I shut his little window, and perhaps he did, indeed, have a boxer fiesta. We still weren't going anywhere. Fiona and Tabs, for their part, judged mounds of headshots in the same tone of voice they might use to order Chinese take-away.

"Fuckable?"

"Nose is too weird."

"This one?"

"Looks like he undertips in restaurants."

"Him?"

"Pepperoni nipples."

"Him?"

"Kind of poofy."

I interjected, "Fi, maybe I could be of assis—"

"Raymond, you are really getting on my nerves. If you bother me one more time, I am going to start looking into how it was that Matt Bradley died on that plane, because I know, Raymond, in my heart of hearts, that you are somehow responsible. If I decide to investigate, your deed will be exposed and you will spend the rest of your life as pubic bling within the California penal system. Do you understand me?"

I shut up and looked at the traffic.

"Okay, Tabitha, now we have to divide the fuckables into the twelve standard reality TV categories. Make piles. Here goes: blond stud . . . brunette stud . . . hillbilly . . . gay guy . . . useless black guy . . . semi-fuckable nerd . . . token ugly-but-hot guy . . . fiftysomething guy . . . average Joe . . . and former pro-athlete-or-astronaut. Remember, they all have to be fuckable except for the semi-fuckable nerd. He's like a poodle thrown into the centre of a pit bull fight to get things warmed up."

"Righty-o."

And that, dear reader, is how you get on the show.

15

When traffic finally evaporated, we roared to the airport in what felt like seventeen seconds. Our trusty private jet awaited us and, in a wonderfully pre-9/11 way, we were up its mobile stairway in a flash.

Neal was already onboard. He had loaded our bags and was looking annoyingly relaxed. "Ray, ever tried enemas? Right hot if administered by a real nurse. Oh, look—bottles of free chilled Chardonnay here in the side console!"

The doors closed and the jet began moving. "Wait—it's just the four of us on this flight? Really?" I asked.

"It is. Move your butt," Fiona said. "We have to lay out female candidate headshots."

"What time do we land in Kiribati?"

"Kiribati?" said Fiona. "We're going back to Los Angeles."

"What the fuck?"

"I can't cast a show in the middle of the ocean. We have to actually *see* these people first-hand before I choose. I do have standards."

Fucking hell. But I have to hand it to Fi: nobody works harder once she sets her mind to it.

"Neal," said Fiona. "I want you to go through our choice of top fifty females. Select twenty using your internal fuckometer."

"Are there any character categories we need?"

Fiona beamed as though she'd discovered Willy Wonka's gold ticket. "Yes! Finally someone in this absurd carnival we call life who properly understands the show's dynamic!" Fiona shook a finger at me. "Ray, you'd better look out or I'll make Neal *my* personal assistant." This was an actual warning, not an attempt at humour or flattery.

Neal swelled under her attention. "So we'd best get the highly fertile blondes and brunettes picked first."

I watched Diamond Head vanish behind us out the window.

Fiona dumped a stack of headshots onto the seat beside her. "Yes, and you can also separate the brunettes into either aggressive or under-the-radar. The under-the-radars win more often than not. Blondes have targets on them. It's nature's way."

"We also need a Spanish-speaking brunette with an absurdly English first name," added Tabs. "It means the parents were ambitious for their children, and it will broaden the show's viewership into the Latino market."

Fiona said, "God bless Jennifer Lopez's mother for opening that door back in the 1960s."

"Here," said Tabs, waving a fan of photos. "I've narrowed it down to the most brazenly ambitious: 1) Persimmon de la Cal Empanada Delgado; 2) Gwendolyn Rodríguez-con-Pollo; and 3) Daisy Fernández."

Fiona scrutinized a photo of Daisy Fernández's knockers. "Wouldn't want to get stuck eating those puppies. You'd die of vinyl poisoning before you reached for the dental floss. I say we choose Persimmon de la Cal Empanada Delgado and be done with the rest." She held Persimmon's photo up for Neal to see. "You like?"

"I like."

"Then we're agreed."

"Absolutely."

So Neal was suddenly a confident industry insider, while I, Raymond Gunt, accomplished videographer and connoisseur of womanly charm, was frozen out? "Fiona, I resent not being included in the casting process. You'd think that—"

She cut me off. "Take a *Penthouse* into the loo and finger-bang yourself. We're working." She returned to her stacks. "Now we have to find a hot mom. That's tricky because she has to look like anyone's mother but your own. It's a real casting challenge."

"Is that the same as a MILF?" asked Neal.

"Good question, but no. A MILF can be any female anywhere on planet Earth who is past her prime yet still exhibits some dimension of fuckability."

"Good to be clear on that."

Out the window lay five hours of featureless ocean. I opened a bottle of Chardonnay and glugged away while the unholy trio performed a task that was rightfully mine. *Threatening, slightly crazy black woman. Female hillbilly. Possible lesbian. Afghan war hero. Brainy Asian.*

I closed my eyes and before I knew it the wheels were touching down. I'd slept through most of the flight.

On the ground, a car was waiting just off the tarmac.

The four of us hobbled to the vehicle while underlings lugged our bags to the boot. At the car door, Fiona said, "Raymond, I'm sorry if I've been a twat. You can't imagine the pressure on me."

"That's sweet of you, Fi."

"Could you do me a favour and run and get my Hermès scarf? I left it on my seat. Pretty please with a cherry on top?"

For Fiona to apologize for anything was newsworthy, and I found that my usual defences had dropped. "Sure," I said. I went back into the plane to search. Nada. I glanced out the window only to see the limo drive off. *That malignant clit.* I picked up a pile of unchosen head-shots and kicked them out of the plane into an uncaring world. "Fucking losers!" I shouted as they fluttered onto the tarmac.

"Mr. Gunt?"

I looked down the stairway and saw a pimpled Todd-like geek. "Yes."

"I'm Walter, your hospitality ambassador."

"My what?"

"I have instructions to offer you as much enjoyment as is possible at LAX. I'm here to take you to our ultra-exclusive VIP lounge."

16

I hopped onto Walter's little electric cart and we headed to one of the terminal buildings. We parked and he escorted me up a red carpetway to a pair of ornate golden Shangri-La doors. *Please, dear God, let there be needy sluts in bunny costumes on the other side.*

Walter opened the door to expose a bar that looked somehow familiar. And then I saw her, the dreaded **LACEY**. She looked up at me. "Can I get you a drink, sir? Wait a moment—it's you."

I turned right around, but saw, through a now-closed-and-alarmed security door, young Walter driving off in his goddamn cart. I touched my left front pocket: my phone was in my carry-on in the limo, and my passport, too. Fucking hell. I turned around to hear **LACEY** say, "May I see your boarding pass, sir?"

"Boarding pass? What the hell are you on about?"

"You came in through the VIP exit. I'm required to ask all VIPs to show me a boarding pass."

"I'm on a private jet, thank you."

"Your passport?"

"It's in the limo."

"Then I'm afraid I can't serve you alcoholic *or* non-alcoholic beverages." She pushed a button that buzzed. "Garcia will be here shortly."

"Your gardener?"

Sour face. "Your racial stereotyping is dehumanizing. Garcia happens to be the head of security in this terminal."

"Why call security?"

"Between you and me, it's because you didn't tip me last time. This is my revenge."

I was speechless.

"And as there are no microphones recording this conversation, and we're the only two people in the lounge, Garcia bangs me twice a week in the men's room. So he's in my palm. He won't listen to a word you say."

I remained mute.

"Would you like some corn nuts? The airline catering company grows half the corn in Nebraska, so I'm allowed to offer them even to people who enter this lounge without authorization. There are some napkins here, and if you feel like cutlery, please enjoy a complimentary spork from the cutlery bin. Oh, look—here's Garcia now."

A swarthy hobbit entered the lounge. "**LACEY**, do we have an incident here?"

"I'm not sure, Garcia. This gentleman arrived through the VIP doors without a boarding pass or passport. You know, with the war on terror, you can never be too careful."

Garcia stared at me. "Do you have any form of documentation on you, sir?"

"No. It's all in the fucking limo."

"Watch your language, sir. You're in the United States. People here don't appreciate profanity."

"This man here swore quite a bit at me, too, Garcia. Does that count as terror in your terror handbook?"

Garcia gave me the steely eye. "You were swearing at **LACEY**?"

"What the fuck is wrong with you people?" I said.

"This is the last warning I'm giving you sir. No profanity."

Trying to configure sentences without swearing caused my brain to seize up. I knew there and then exactly how a stroke feels when it strips you of the ability to speak. I began to make sound effects instead: ". . . #$((>@ ***. . ."

"Garcia, listen to his speech patterns. I bet you anything he's high on some form of illegal drug."

"What flight did you come here on today, sir?"

"In a private ffff . . . In a private jet, thank you."

"From where?"

"Hawaii."

"We're going to have to do a sweep of that jet, pronto." He removed a walkie-talkie from his breast pocket and made a show of finding the plane on the tarmac. While he did this, **LACEY** offered me more corn nuts.

"Sir," said the hobbit, "I'm going to have to ask you to come with me."

"What the fuck?"

"That's it, sir." Garcia ran towards me with a pair of zap-strap handcuffs he produced as if from nowhere.

LACEY smiled.

Zzzzzap! Thirty seconds later I was being frog-marched down the concourse, which looked even more like Mexico than on my first stop. I'd hoped to make a friendly joke about Garcia's mother fellating bored donkeys out behind the Cinnabon, but the cuffs stung too much and made it difficult to be witty.

....

Cinnabon is a chain of American baked-goods stores and kiosks normally found in high-traffic areas such as malls and airports. The company's signature item is a large cinnamon roll. As of July 2009, over 750 Cinnabon bakeries are in operation in over thirty countries around the world. Its headquarters are in Sandy Springs, Georgia. For many people, the odour of a Cinnabon quickly alerts the reptile cortex that one is in the middle of an unpleasant travel experience. Curiously, scent scientists have done multiple analyses of airport environments and came up with an interesting observation, published in the March 2013 issue of *Boarding Pass* magazine: if one were to take one bottle of all the perfumes and colognes on earth and mix them together, the resulting odour would be exactly that of a duty-free shop.

....

Garcia marched me through a door emblazoned with a janitor's icon, which, in fact, opened into a corridor in LAX's massive underground security system. Were Neal there with me, he'd have said something charmingly childish along the lines of, "*Oi!* It's like entering the Matrix! I wonder if we'll meet enchanted animals who speak Jacobean English!"

Not me, however. My extensive life experience had prepared me for being hurled into a room filled with innocent middle-class people, all of them face down on rectal probe tables while burka-clad TSA agents used hot-dog forks to dig in deeper and deeper, ferreting out smuggled nail clippers, Bic lighters and containers of shampoo larger than 1.5 ounces.

I was partially correct. I ended up in a cell with old-fashioned steel bars and a chrome toilet, like in a seventies cop show. My cellmates were two cold-sored Venezuelans detained, they told me, for smuggling fertilized parakeet eggs, along with a Mrs. Peggy Nielson of Kendallville, Indiana, who, through some form of accidental keystroke in a system somewhere on the planet, had landed on the no-fly list with a level red warning attached to her.

Peggy, God bless her, wouldn't stop yammering on about how, instead of returning with her family to her numbingly dull cornfields after a Disneyland holiday, she was being whisked off to Guantánamo Bay without legal recourse.

I was in a foul mood, even for me. "Listen, Mrs. Nielson. You might as well get used to a life of gang rape and prayers five times a day. It's a nasty, shitty world. How do we even know you're really who you say you are? You could be a very good little actress, for all I know."

She began to cry. "Disneyland was so amazing—and now *this*. Why are they doing this to me? My life is boring. I'm no terrorist."

"Are you sure about that?"

"What is wrong with you? Why are you being so mean to me?"

"What's wrong with *me*? What's wrong with *you* . . . Peggy *bin Laden*? Your mom-pants and that poorly styled meerkat on your head don't fool me for one second. The more you snivel, the more I question your supposed identity."

More boohoos and even more snivelling. A merciful spirit swept over me. "Mrs. Nielson, for God's sake, look at life for what it is—a repulsive waste of self-important protein molecules. It's not you who did something wrong. It's *life*."

"That's so negative. You're so *negative*!"

Well, I *had* tried to be nice. "Peggy, you're wearing out my patience. What sort of place is Kendallville, anyway? A hub for the manufacturing of crybabies?"

"I hate you."

"But I don't hate you. I, actually, in some hard-to-describe way, like you."

"Really?"

"I do. But you have to tough this out, Peggy. What comes around goes around. I prefer to think I lead a fine and upstanding life. When things turn to rat shit—as they invariably do—I never think it's me who's done something wrong; it's the fucking universe having a bad day, and I just happened to be there."

"That's a new way of looking at things, Mr. . . . ."

"Gunt. Raymond Gunt."

Miracle of miracles, she stopped snivelling.

The Venezuelans regarded both of us with disdain, and I stared right back. "Look here, you two. Go fuck dead goats or whatever it is you do in your taco factories back home." I turned to Peggy. "Venezuela. Dreadful country. Nothing but cocaine and Miss Universe contestants."

"Nothing but grief."

"See there, Peggy? You really can turn that frown upside down."

"Thank you, Raymond Gunt. Tell me, where were you headed before you ended up here?"

"Kiribati. I'm a cameraman on that TV show *Survival*, and if I ever get out of this hole, that's where I'm headed, on one of the posh private jets the TV network uses to fly me around."

"I have to admit, I love *Survival*."

Oh, crap.

"What's it like being on a shoot? Where do crew members sleep when the contestants are in their camps?"

"Well, you know, Peggy . . ." *Christ, get me out of here now.* I stared around the cell and suddenly had a brainwave about how to escape. One of my Venezuelan cellmates was idly snacking on fragments from a Hawaiian Airlines snack pack he'd dug out of his pocket.

I walked over to him. "Share?"

"*¿Qué?*"

I snatched his snack bag, dug inside and found what I wanted: one macadamia nut. I ate it.

....

Tree nut allergy is a hypersensitivity to tree nuts that causes an overreaction of the immune system, which may lead to severe physical symptoms. Tree nuts include Brazil nuts, cashews, chestnuts, hazelnuts, macadamia nuts, pecans, pine nuts, pistachios and walnuts. The severity of sensitivity can vary from person to person. Those diagnosed with ana-phylaxis will have a more immediate mast cell reaction and must avoid all exposure to any allergen-containing products or by-products, regardless of processing.

Tree nut allergy is distinct from peanut allergy. Peanuts are legumes, whereas a tree nut is the hard-shelled fruit of certain plants. A person with a peanut allergy may not necessarily also be allergic to tree nuts, and vice versa.

Many people feign nut allergies as a means of establishing an often pathetically small amount of control in a social or dining situation. In a recent and highly gratifying airline deci-sion, a passenger who alerts airlines of a nut allergy after having obtained a boarding pass must be removed from a flight and forced to wait until a different plane, certified to have no contact with nuts, appears, a process that can some-times take days. This process is irreversible, even if the pas-senger immediately admits he or she is a lying needy tard.

17

Next thing I knew, I was staring up into Neal's face—and yet it wasn't Neal. This person had a proper haircut and shave, moisturized skin, a silk tattersall button-down shirt and radioactive-looking American-white teeth.

"Wakey-wakey, Ray. Good to see you up and alert."

"Who the fuck *are* you?"

"It's me, Ray, your buddy, Neal."

"Why am I not in that airport shithole?"

"You ate a macadamia nut, you sly devil. Your one-way ticket out of the Homeland Security system. We're on a jet to Kiribati."

"My brain feels like a caged circus animal. What the hell happened to you?"

"I got myself a makeover. Ever had one? You go in looking seedy and feeling like a failure—and then all these smashing hot birds and enthusiastic gay guys run their hands all over you and you walk out looking like a pop star. I had to do *something* while you were stuck in Homeland Security's intensive-care pavilion. A few of the girls from Fi's casting session took me on as their project, so to speak."

"But what the fuck happened to your *teeth*?"

"There was nothing wrong with my teeth, Ray—at least, nothing Zoom laser-whitening couldn't zap away in seconds."

I looked around me. "And why am I not in some American prison?"

"Oh *that*. Fiona brokered your release. She's a smart woman, Ray."

I instantly needed to know what my exact trade value was on the open market. Three defecting Chechen spies? Five political dissidents with a cache of industrial data? A phalanx of Chinese terracotta warriors? "What did she trade me for?"

"I believe Fiona was able to get you released for a pair of matinée tickets to *Billy Elliot, the Musical* at a Los Angeles dinner theatre. Pretty good seats."

"*Matinée* tickets? She didn't even have the decency to trade me for evening tickets?"

"Ray, tickets to evening shows are hard to come by. You could get seats in the balcony, but you wouldn't really enjoy the magic of it all."

I spat out, "The *magic* of it all? It's *Billy* fucking *Elliot, the* fucking *Musical*."

"Exactly, Ray. I hear it's a pretty good show, but I don't know if I hold with having an adult dressed up as a wee boy dancing on stage. A bit like mutton dressed as lamb, if you ask me."

I breathed deeply and decided to get a better grip on my physical situation. The jet was similar to the one we flew to LA in, and I was in a gurney, facing forward.

Neal removed the IV drip from my right hand. "As I keep saying, Ray, good thing I was once a paramedic.

Otherwise, you'd be stuck in one of those hospitals for crack babies like they have all over the U.S. I've read them about in the *Daily Mail*."

"Where is that ball-chopping witch, my ex-wife?"

"She's following in another plane with Sarah and your friend Stuart."

Safe for the time being.

I hobbled out of bed and sat in a leather seat, too tired even to bother scoping out a source of booze. "Neal, how long have we been in transit from London?"

"Several weeks at least, Ray."

"At the moment I feel like we're some form of sock puppets who exist solely to amuse some cruel cosmic manipulator whose hand is up my arse."

"I know what you mean, Ray. We haven't even crossed the equator. Maybe our journey was meant to be different from what we thought."

I looked at Neal. "Don't be such a fucking simp. Of *course* things are different from what we expected. It's called life."

"Maybe you should get a makeover, Ray. It'd perk you up."

"I don't need a fucking makeover, Neal. I'm quite happy with how nature made me."

Neal said, "I would never wish to imply that you were anything less than movie star material, Ray. But . . . you know . . . an apricot facial scrub and some flesh-tinted crème to cover your gin blossoms might make a big difference."

"*Gin blossoms?*" I was outraged.

"Well, perhaps it's just all the fresh air and exercise you get that makes your nose and cheeks shine just ever so slightly red."

"I do not have *gin blossoms*."

"See, Ray, a makeover would get rid of all that nega-tive energy. I'm just pointing it out, is all."

"Neal, less than a week ago, your entire physical being resembled a dag hanging from a sheep's arsehole."

"Indeed it did, Ray. I'm lucky to have a friend like you to help me pull myself up by my bootstraps and make something of my life."

"Finally, a whiff of gratitude." I looked over to where he was sitting. On a polished walnut table in front of him was a snifter of cognac and what appeared to be a script. "Found something to read for the journey?"

"It's the script for the TV show. Bloody brilliant."

"Who else is on this plane?"

"Just us for now. They're sending it to pick up a group of network executives."

I looked out the window: ocean. My stomach cramped . . . food! "Neal, I haven't eaten since I don't even remember. Get me some food."

"Right, Ray." Neal lifted one hand, and the sleekest, most kitten-like flight attendant I'd ever seen appeared. She had a velvety smooth, unravaged face, and a name tag reading **ELSPETH**. She scurried to me with a tray of dainty little triangle-shaped sandwiches, no crusts, each triangle a different flavour—just the ticket. "Here, some nice posh sandwiches for me favourite patient. Fancy a moistened tow'lette, luv?"

I grabbed the whole tray of sandwiches and set it on my lap. Elspeth made ever so tiny a flicker of a face at Neal, then scurried away to fetch some tea. It hit me: "Neal, you've already banged Elspeth, haven't you?"

"Well, you know, Ray, what with you being here in

the cabin laid out like a corpse—it made young Elspeth and me want to do something to celebrate life rather than be overpowered by the stench of death. You were wheezing something awful the first hour, too, and it terrified her. So to lighten things up, we made love and we also made an iPhone film of what we thought was your death rattle and posted it online. Amazing smoking hot Wi-Fi this jet has. Let me show you . . ."

Neal picked up an iPad, typed COMICAL GEEZER DEATH RATTLE into a search box and held it up to show the results. "Look at that!" he said. "Your death rattle clip is already the number four comical GIF on the *West London Morning Shopper*'s website! You're a star, Ray!"

"Give me that fucking thing." I looked, and there I was, death warmed over on the gurney. "Make it go away."

"Too late, Ray. Don't get angry. Enjoy the moment. I'll ask Elspeth to make you a steak Diane or something fancy."

On cue, Elspeth arrived with my tea. "Elspeth, guess what?" Neal said. "Our clip of Raymond's death rattle is the number four comical GIF on the *West London Morning Shopper*'s website."

Elspeth squealed with delight. "I'll have to email me mum. She's getting a gastric band put 'round her stomach next week. News like this'll give her a lift. Poor thing. The council agent had to jackhammer her out of the bedroom. So humiliating. Hasn't set foot downstairs since before Simon Cowell started on TV and brought so much sunshine into our lives. How rich d'you think that Cowell is, you reckon?"

Elspeth's council estate accent was like three raccoons trapped in a Dumpster. I was trying to tune them both out when our jet made a sudden downward lurch. Elspeth squealed anew and ran to the cockpit for information.

Neal looked out a window and said, "Ray! Look out the window—you can see the Pacific Trash Vortex!"

"The *what*?"

"The Pacific Trash Vortex—that continent of plastic trash you've been reading about for decades. Good Lord, it's big, isn't it? Travels clockwise. The largest manmade object on the planet. Makes you proud and disgusted about being human, all at the same time."

"I'm not going to look out the window at garbage, Neal." But, of course, how could I resist, especially as the jet keeled westward. I actually couldn't have turned my head away if I'd wanted to.

Against the g-force, Elspeth shunted back into the main cabin. "We've been ordered to land."

"Land? Land *where*? There *is* no fucking land to *land* on." Was I squealing? Maybe.

"Wake Island."

"*Where?*"

....

Wake Island is a coral atoll with a 12-mile coastline in the North Pacific, located 2,300 miles west of Honolulu, and roughly two-thirds of the way to Guam. It is an unincorporated territory of the United States, and all island activities are managed by the United States Air Force. Access is restricted. Wake Island also contains a missile facility operated by the United States Army and features a 9,800-foot runway.

....

I asked, "Who has the authority to make a plane land in the middle of nowhere?"

"The U.S. government," said Elspeth.

"Fucking Americans." I craned my neck to try and see it. "Where is it?"

"About ninety minutes away."

....

LAX to AWK = 9h, 5m

....

The **Great Pacific Garbage Patch**, also called the **Pacific Trash Vortex**, is a gyre of marine litter in the central North Pacific Ocean. It is characterized by high concentrations of pelagic plastics, chemical sludge and other debris that has been trapped by the current of the North Pacific Gyre.

Reports have estimated that the patch extends over an area larger than the continental U.S., but recent research sponsored by the National Science Foundation suggests the affected area may be twice the size of Texas; a recent study concluded that the patch might be even smaller. Data collected from Pacific albatross populations suggest there may be two distinct zones of concentrated debris in the Pacific.

Despite its size and density, the patch is not visible from space because it consists primarily of suspended particulates in the upper water column. Since plastics eventually break down to smaller polymers, concentrations of submerged particles are not visible from space, nor do they appear as a continuous debris field. Instead, the patch is defined as an area in which the mass of plastic debris in the upper water column is significantly higher than average.

Most people are horrified to learn of the vortex's existence, but at the same time, it's kind of awesome to discover there's a whole new continent on the planet you never knew about before. Life: it's magnificent!

18

Now, I'm obviously a sensitive man who enjoys the fine things in life: food, wine and art—yay art! Art everywhere! Art for everyone, even for useless people! But this love of art notwithstanding, I do wish I were more of a poet. That way, I could properly describe the fiery sunset over the Pacific Trash Vortex—a vision that made my soul frolic like a wee lamb in a meadow. How's that for poetry?

"More lamb, Mr. Gunt?"

"Great idea, Elspeth."

Elspeth replenished my ceramic tray with sumptuous lamb curry, and I tucked right in as the trash vortex turned from amber to orange and then to crimson before vanishing from sight. The night sky that then descended had that bright blue light one only sees flying over oceans—daylight with a strong camera filter—and soon we heard a *ding!* and Elspeth told us to get ready for landing. Neal was blithering on about there being something eerily familiar about the shape of Wake Island—he just couldn't figure out what it was. I assumed his street person's psyche was reasserting itself after having spent

a week away from gutter puke and angry confronta-
tional yobs armed with shoplifted carpet knives.

The captain came over the PA to ask us to lower our
blinds as we approached the island.

"Lower my blind? Whatever for? I'm not lowering
my fucking blind."

"Come on, Ray. They wouldn't ask us to do it if it
weren't for a good reason. The air force runs this
place."

Neal obediently lowered his blind while Elspeth
lowered the others. I, however, decided to make a stand.
"I am going to do whatever I want with my blind.
Look—I'm going to Morse code a message to the Wake
Islanders." I began to open and close my blind.

"You know Morse code?" Neal was amazed.

"I do," I said. "My uncle was an amateur ham radio
geek." I continued to send my message to the world:

$- / .-. / -.-- / .- / -. / -.. / -- / .- / -.- / . / .-- / -. / . / .-.. / --- / .-- / . / . / .-. /$
$-- / -.-- / -. . . / . / .-.. / .. / . / -. / -.. / . . . / -.-- / --- / ..- / .-. / .. / -.. / -. / -.- /$
$.. / -. / -.-. / .- / -- / . / . / .-. / .. / . / -.-. / . / -. / -.-. / ..- / -. / . / - / . . .^2$

After we landed, we taxied to a disintegrating concrete building under a glorious full moon. We popped
open the cabin door—*ahhhh*, the *woosh* of tropical air,
so fresh and good for the soul. As Neal and I inhaled this
salty Micronesian syrup, a military Jeep roared up to the
plane and slammed on the brakes. Two MPs hopped out,
bounded up the stairway and yanked me to the ground,

---

2. *t r y a n d m a k e m e l o w e r m y b l i n d s y o u f u c k i n g
a m e r i c a n c u n t s*

where they slapped me in handcuffs. This was getting all too familiar.

Neal shouted, "You should have lowered your blind, Ray. You don't want to mess with these folks."

While I was being brutally thrown snout first into the Jeep's back seat, its driver carried a plastic shopping bag over to Neal and Elspeth. He removed fragrant jasmine leis from it, draped them over their heads and said, "Welcome to Wake Island."

Another Jeep pulled up. Although my head was upside down and a seatbelt buckle was digging into my right nostril, there was no ambiguity about the identity of this new arrival.

"Mr. Gunt," said Mrs. Peggy Nielson of Kendallville, Indiana, who was now wearing a lieutenant's uniform. "Maybe next time you'll lower your blinds."

19

Okay. We're all adults here, and we've all been in situations beyond our control. Hell, it's what gives life its spice: you miss a bus, the hot water stops working, a 767 slams into your office tower. When things go sideways, I try to make lemonade out of lemons, as it were. So from my awkward face-into-the-upholstery enforced yoga position in the rear seat, I greeted Mrs. Nielson civilly as she stood outside the Jeep. "Oh. Hello, Peggy."

"Hello, Raymond. Here I'm addressed as Lieutenant Healey, *Jennifer* Healey."

"How surprising."

"Was it really so hard for you to lower your blind before landing? Your behaviour could be construed as very compromising. We have high-res, high-speed digital film of you on the plane admitting that your uncle was a ham radio geek."

"What the fuck?"

"Language, Mr. Gunt. We lip-read everything you said."

"To be clear, Lieutenant, I was being insubordinate deliberately as a protest against your government's ridiculous fucking stance on global politics, which tried to force me to close my tiny little blind on a lovely Pacific night."

"I see."

"I'm sure you do."

Neal and Elspeth, in the meantime, seemed genuinely shocked that the two of us knew each other.

Peggy—excuse me, *Lieutenant Jennifer Healey*—replied, "In my twenty-one years with the service, Mr. Gunt, you are the worst human being I've ever met. The. Worst. Person. Ever."

"Um, Lieutenant, is there any way for your staff to change my yoga position here in the back seat? It's hard to open my windpipe to reply to you."

"Not yet, Mr. Gunt. We're still assessing your threat level to staff here on the island."

"Okay. Could you at least tell me what you were doing in my prison cell in LAX dressed like a soccer mom with a dead meerkat glued to your head?"

"Those cellmates of ours, Mr. Gunt, were the two most powerful narcoterrorists in the western hemisphere, only posing as parakeet egg smugglers."

"Really?"

"Yes, really."

"Well, regardless, you wouldn't want to French kiss those two, would you? Cold sores like raw hamburger patties all over their mouths. Come on, Peggy, have a laugh. You've got to admit, that is an unappetizing thought."

She exhaled a large breath. "In a weird way, I owe you, Raymond. Once your body was carried away, the three of us were able to bond over how awful you'd been—which in turn led them to slip up and give me some information

I needed. I may run this island full-time, but those two have been in my gunsight for two decades, ever since I started working for the government. Nabbing them was personal to me, and they'll be locked up for the next few hundred years."

"So I actually helped society."

"You might say that."

"I even helped you fulfill your dream."

She eyed me warily.

Neal volunteered, "Raymond wants a better world for all of us. You know—children singing in fields full of flowers—ebony and ivory and all that Michael Jackson stuff, minus the pervy bits."

From my upside-down position, I looked around me at the cheerless architectural boneyard of crumbling buildings. Time had stopped somewhere in 1971, when Richard Nixon stopped here to take a dump on his way to Guam.

Peggy—*Jennifer*—finally spoke. "The war on terror and the war on drugs are the same thing to me, Raymond. Actually, I'm at war with everything—it makes mental bookkeeping easier."

"I imagine so."

"Boys, pick Mr. Gunt up. I want him standing to attention."

The MPs hauled me out of the Jeep and stood me up. My legs and arms tingled as blood circulation returned.

"If you change your attitude, Raymond, I might tell you more about what we here on Wake Island are doing. I promise, it's fascinating."

"Blimey," said Neal, as if trapped inside a Beano cartoon. "A secret mission!"

Trucks were roaring about in the background. It was nighttime, but it was also hopping. I sensed something big going on.

I said, "I'm honoured you'd consider trusting me so much, Peggy. Now, could you please uncuff me?"

"Not yet." She called to the MPs. "Boys, toss him into the slammer!" Then she giggled. "I've always wanted to say that." She put on her aviator glasses, which, under moonlight, gave her a Mexican Day of the Dead kind of look. "Lock Mr. Gunt in Sector D."

20

So I was thrown into yet another prison cell. I was actually feeling okay about this most recent incarceration and was planning to catch some shut-eye. But when I sat on my bunk, I found a DVD of *Billy Elliot* and a remote control. Outside the cell's bars was a 55-inch plasma TV. Inside the DVD case was a note from Peggy:

Greetings, Raymond Gunt.

The DVD is cued to "The Angry Dance" from this most beloved of motion pictures. Perform it tomorrow at lunch in the mess for everyone and you will be allowed to leave the island. Raymond, it has to look like you are trying, really <u>trying</u>. If I don't think you are trying hard enough, your plane and your friends fly on without you, while you stay here indefinitely to pay for your willfully disobedient violation of the Homeland Security Act. Get cracking, Raymond! Lunch is at noon, sharp.

Love, "Peggy Nielson"

Fuck.

http://www.youtube.com/watch?v=UOGBTFFxOpY

Imagine being locked in a cage and not only having to watch *Billy Elliot*, but being ordered to replicate some sort of dance routine—I mean, honestly . . .

"*Hello*, Raymond."

I turned around and saw Peggy on the other side of the bars. She looked softer and had makeup on, as well as civilian clothing—one of those muscle dresses favoured by Mrs. Obama.

"I see you got my note," she said.

"What the fuck is going on here?"

"Raymond, Raymond, Raymond. You don't honestly think Homeland Security would swap a possible threat to national security like yourself for a pair of theatre tickets?" Peggy's crisp, unironic tone reminded me of being on hold with United Airlines. She began twirling her hair. I didn't like where this seemed to be going.

"But I must say, your ex-wife is a terrific bargainer. I wanted tickets for the evening performance, but she drew the line at a matinée."

"Did she?"

"Fortunately, back in the cell at LAX, you confided to me where you were going. The moment I heard that, I knew you were mine. There was no way I was going to let your plane pass by my island empire here."

"You grounded our flight just for me?"

"Is that so wrong?" She licked an index finger and then trailed it down her cleavage, and I felt as if someone were walking over my grave. "Don't be coy, Raymond. You know there's something between us."

Here's the thing: Peggy Nielson—or rather, Jennifer Healey—is the first nubile woman I've encountered since puberty whom I haven't repeatedly mind-boffed, or even considered mind-boffing. I fought for time and said, "Tell me more."

She looked both ways and then came closer to the bars. "In all my undercover years, nobody has ever seen through my Peggy Nielson persona, not one person. Only *you*."

"You can't be serious."

"But I am. You get me like nobody else ever has."

My brain went into Jason Bourne car-chase mode: *Reverse the BMW into the taxi queue? Plough forward at triple speed? Haul arse the wrong way on a busy Moscow thoroughfare? Am I willing to mow down a few pedestrians?*

Peggy—no, Jennifer—reached for my shoulder through the bars and caressed it. "I thought we might watch *Billy Elliot . . . together*."

Christ, this woman really had a massive pulsating lady-boner for me. I needed to start thinking of her as fuckable or I was never going to get out of here. But she had as much sexual allure for me as Mr. Bean. Why, oh why, did she leave me cold when, to be honest, I've even mind-shagged Margaret Thatcher—well, come on, let's be totally honest here, who *hasn't*? All you need is the right lighting, a nice bottle of Italian red, shovel-loads of ketamine and maybe one of those autoerotic asphyxiation getups Fiona's clients are always dying in. I mean, I've mind-shagged female restroom logos all around the planet. I've mind-shagged the boot at the southern tip of Italy on Google Maps. So to not be able to contemplate getting it up for Peggy/Jennifer was cruelty beyond measure, especially as I was technically now her love slave— and who out there hasn't wanted to be a love slave at some point or other? But failure to perform carried potentially life-threatening consequences.

"Have you ever seen *Billy Elliot*, Ray?" Her fingers, still inserted through the bars, were now rubbing my neck.

"Um, yes, I watched it—or part of it—on a Singapore Airlines flight back in '04."

"Singapore?"

"They were revising their chewing gum laws, and the BBC wanted arrest footage."

"You're a fascinating man, Raymond Gunt." Her hand slid down towards my gentleman's region. "My, *my* . . . you're so tense."

"It's been a week of airports and hospital beds."

"Go on. Tell me what you thought of *Billy Elliot*, then." I could smell her breath: Listerine.

"Well, to me it all boils down to whether Billy is a poofter or not. I mean, if he were a flat-out flamer, there'd have been no movie. He simply would have looked at his small town, said, 'Right then,' moved to London, entered the sex trade and gone to dancing class at night, but where's the uplifting story in that? I think viewers are really thinking, *What if Billy's a poofter, even though he says he isn't?* But because he's underage, you're not allowed to mention sex, so instead you have to say how heartwarming it all is and be inspired. And the thing is, in real life, a small-town Billy Elliot would most likely lure you out into the bramble hedge for a good tussle, save some DNA from the crime scene, and then black-mail the bejeezus out of you to pay for his dancing les-sons, until you justifiably went out and slit his throat."

Jennifer looked at me with eyes that beamed with admiration. "Raymond, you have such *imagination.*" She pulled me closer by the belt and started to fondle my gentleman's bits, which were about as aroused as a small bag of sun-dried apricots.

She said, "Raymond?"

Gulp. "Yes?" I shut my eyes.

She let me go, but then I heard her key inside the cell's lock. I swallowed, hard.

Suddenly a harsh alarm began to clang. Jennifer screamed, "*Shit!* Why do the engineers need me now, of all times?"

Blowing a kiss and mouthing, "Later," she left me.

In gratitude to the gods, I hit PLAY on the DVD and began to practise my brains out.

....

The chewing gum ban in Singapore was enacted in 1992 and really does ban the import and sale of chewing gum. The offense is punishable by caning.

When first introduced, the ban caused open defiance, but offenders were publicly "named and shamed" by the govern-ment to deter other would-be smugglers.

Origins: In his memoirs, former Singaporean prime minis-ter Lee Kuan Yew recounted that as early as 1983, chewing gum was causing serious maintenance problems in high-rise public housing. Vandals had been disposing of spent gum in mailboxes, inside keyholes and on elevator buttons. Chewing gum left on floors, stairways, buses and pavements in public areas increased the cost of cleaning and damaged cleaning equipment. However, Lee thought that a ban would be too drastic and did not take action.

In 1987, vandals stuck chewing gum on the door sensors in a new $5 billion metro system. The doors malfunctioned, causing disruption of train services.

In January 1992, Prime Minister Goh Chok Tong decided on a flat-out ban. The import of chewing gum was immediately halted, but a reasonable transition period was given to allow shops to clear their existing stocks.

Yes, this really happened.

....

21

Morning came. Fucking hell. My feet were cheese-gratered and bloody from a night spent rehearsing the appalling routine in which little Billy lugs his twinkle-toes up and down the bricks of some failure-filled housing estate, which is, in the film, conveniently devoid of crack ampoules, used condoms and surgically licked-clean crisp packets.

I involuntarily dozed off at 11:30 a.m., only to be woken at noon by a gorilla of an MP. "Got orders to take you over to the canteen for your matinée performance." The word "matinée" filled me with foreboding. Was this all somehow being engineered by Fiona?

I caught sight of myself in a mirror en route to the venue. Not my Bourne-iest moment. I was highly unshaven and putty grey—I mean, how can that even *happen*, skin turning grey? Blood is *red*. How hard is it not to even be pink? I asked the gorilla if I might stop to shave, and of course the answer was no. Fucking Americans.

I hobbled after him for maybe a quarter-mile to a small building housing the canteen. The sun was directly overhead; I had no shadow. The exterior humidity was like a proverbial wet towel, and I was soon drenched in sweat.

Now, I like to give life a go. I like family dinners. I like to see elderly people trying their hand at painting even though they couldn't possibly have a career ahead of them because they'll soon be dead. But in spite of my positive disposition, I was at a low point as I entered what for me could only be a dome of shame, the mess hall. Two stainless steel doors opened inward and . . .

Brrrrrrrr! Air conditioning! Extreme American air conditioning, one of the few things they're good for! *Thank fucking God*.

Inside the mess, the tables were arranged in some sort of pecking order, not unlike at private schools: head table; peons; losers; victims; thugs; the doomed; the hopeless. Enter a room like this and you might as well not bother being born in the first place. And, of course, there at the head table, along with Elspeth, Neal and the flight crew, sat Miss Lieutenant, glowing with B vitamins and sunshine and whatever anthraxy sludge the U.S. government forcibly injects into its military's bloodstream.

Some idiot up before me was juggling hatchets. The good thing, though, was the room's atmosphere of . . . cheer . . . *bonhomie*, even!

I thought, *You know, Raymond, how bad could this possibly be? This could be a lighthearted episode in your life's journey.* If I spun it properly, I could even turn it into a fundraiser for some dismal charity like Alzheimer's or AIDS or poor people.

That's when Neal saw me. He flew across the room, shouting, "Ray! You won't fucking believe this! I know this whole island inside out!"

Okay, Neal's a street nutter and all, but he totally lost me. "Come again?"

"Wake Island! I've been here a million times before in the video game *Battlefield 1943*! Except I was playing the Russian version, where it's called *Forceps 13*, you know, in those backwards upside-down letters communists like." Neal was wearing an ensemble of expensive resort wear and, unlike mine, his skin had colour.

"Neal, you lived inside a cardboard box slathered in human feces on the streets of West London. Where on earth did you play a complex video game requiring an expensive console and a place to play it?"

"Those birds at the Russian massage parlour on Gunnersbury Avenue."

"Kum Guzzling Traktor Sluts?"

"You know the place?"

"Only to walk by it, Neal. Frankly, I find the flyer cello-taped to their front doorway's glass offensive to women and people of taste and refinement everywhere, not just West London."

"Oh, Raymond, you're the king of the purchased wank, so you're the last person who should be judgmental. And those girls on Gunnersbury—so new to democracy and freedom and its ways—were so kind. They were always willing to feed me and take care of me when life on the streets got too rough. But forget all of that. Last night, once I realized where I was, I couldn't sleep. So some of the lads took me out in the Jeep—full moon!—and we visited the strategic points of *Battlefield 1943*, like connoisseurs discussing brandy, stopping in all the best spots. We got to waste a whopping good bundle of ordnance out by the rusting Jap tank in the lagoon *and* we got to blow shit up, including the remains of the Pan Am Clipper dock! Funny, but these airmen all feel like brothers to me now. A band of brothers is what we are." A tear ran down Neal's cheek.

"Neal, fucking hell. Remember who you are."

"Sorry, mate. I'm just sentimental is all. We've been through some things together, you, my brothers and me."

Oh. My. God. Neal was confusing reality with his video game experiences. "Neal! Kum Guzzling Traktor Sluts!" I slapped him, and some semblance of sanity returned to his face.

"Sorry, Ray."

We heard polite applause for the hatchet juggler. I looked over at my tormentor, the flawlessly uniformed witch. She saw me staring her way, smiled and grabbed her soup spoon. She stood up and tinged her glass, and the room—maybe two hundred enlisted folk—went quiet. "Timothy," she said to the previous act, "thank you for your juggling magic, and thanks to all the other participants in today's end-of-project Celebration of Excellence fun." She cleared her throat. "Gang, today's a big day for all of us, and I don't need to say why. We've worked hard as a team to fulfill our Wake Island mission, and in a few short hours we'll have some results— photos and data—and we're all excited about that."

What the fuck?

"It can be a tough life working here: hot days followed by nights that somehow feel hotter. Weeks that go by without a breeze, and then suddenly we get a typhoon. One thing for certain is that we're never at a loss for extremes on Wake Island.

"But one extreme we don't get enough of here is the

extreme of talent. I took piano lessons. Maybe you did, too. Or clarinet or electric guitar. We're all old enough to know that talent is something either you're born with or you aren't. So imagine my pleasure to learn that we have a celebrity visitor here on the island who's going to help us kick off our great day of days . . ."

Mumbles of expectation.

"Today I present to you the beloved well-kept-secret English entertainment treasure, Mr. Raymond Gunt."

22

Up front, a set of packing crates was stacked in a formation replicating the estate housing from the previous evening's DVD. I tried putting myself into some kind of stoked mindset, but really, if they were going to do council housing, why not take some bags of flour and throw them around to represent recently raped unwed mums left for dead? Or at least bundles of palm husks to signify pensioners stabbed for the postage stamps in their purses and also left for dead?

A faint drumbeat began to emerge in stereo from speakers on either side of the crates. Lieutenant Nielson continued: "So let's all get ready to enjoy a sweet treat from the land of tea and hard-to-digest food. Craig and Justine from the radiological data interpretation team have helped assemble today's sound system. Thanks, guys!"

Crap! She wasn't going to give me a chance to introduce myself and turn the dance event into a fundraiser for the world's useless people. How dare that sociopathic gorgon deprive me of my right to help the planet! I mean, was it wrong to want to bring even a whiff of joy to someone with a shit life? It wasn't *my* problem they had no money or some disease. What mattered was that *I* cared about helping humanity.

I realized that, in my head, I was sounding like some lefty feel-good brochure entitled "Self-Esteem," which you find untouched in a Boots pharmacy waiting area, right beside the pamphlet titled, "So Your Urethra Is Starting to Burn."

Lieutenant Jennifer was winding up. "And now, Wake Island, put your hands together for the dance stylings of Raymond Gunt, a man who only wants to bring joy and magic to all our lives—but not scary magic, because that would be contrary to Christian beliefs. Take it away, Raymond, with your interpretation of 'The Angry Dance' from the beloved film *Billy Elliot*!"

Boomp boomp boomp . . .

I jumped onto the first crate to mild applause. And to my own astonishment, I found myself doing Billy's moves.

You have to remember that the last time I danced to any song whatsoever was to "Like a Virgin" in an Ibiza nightclub when I was riding a cosmic wave of some IQ-killing party drug in an attempt to land this girl from Liverpool with scientifically unaltered tits like musk melons and wearing a bright yellow dress. But it all went wrong because she passed out and I had to carry her into the chill room—which you'd think might have led to a cheerful grope of some sort, had it not been for the skinhead muff-snacker in charge. "You, Mr. Fuckingperve, get your fucking hands off that girl or I'll personally come and slice off your testicles with the opening tab from this can of lager."

Ah, memories.
Wake Island.
Crates.
Demented cunts.
Check, check and check.
Showtime!

* * *

Now, I suppose we've all had a dream at some point in our lives about kacking our trousers in public. It must surely be universal. So imagine you're having that kacking-your-pants dream, except instead of shitting yourself, you're dancing in front of two hundred barbaric airmen in the middle of the Pacific Ocean and you have no idea how to dance, but there's no waking up here, and you're light-headed from lack of sleep and bad diet, and you're realizing that being an actor/dancer/performer is hard work. It really is. Hats off to every bender who's ever trudged his way through *Swan Lake* or a production of *Lord of the Dance*, and even to those heartbreakingly deformed little Oompah-Loompahs in *Willy Wonka*. Tough line of work, dancing.

At first, there was little audience reaction. Maybe the people in the back rows couldn't quite see me, I thought, so I hopped up onto a third crate, arching my feet and making some kind of go of it.

And then I had a moment of pure bliss when I realized I really didn't give a fuck whether I ended up locked away in a forgotten prison until global warming drowned me.

. . . And then I was hit on the head with a grape.

I snapped back to reality: they were booing. Not good.

Another grape.

And then increased booing.

Well, what else was I expecting, up on the fifth crate, shuffling my body around like a tard?

Suddenly, cheering broke out. *¿Qué?*

I looked down to see *Neal*, fuck him, stealing my limelight. He was already on the second crate, doing a flawless "Angry Dance" for an audience of baboons who had at least stopped throwing food at me, and who were showing distinct signs of feeling genuinely entertained.

Shuffle-shuffle. Neal leaped up onto my crate. Tempted as I was to shove him off, an instinct for survival got the better of me. I thought, *Oh Christ . . . I'm going to have to be comic relief. Well, worse things have happened.*

The crowd, of course, had completely fallen in love with Neal. I could see the women in the front row holding up their hands, trying to guess the size of his member. Heterosexual men behind them were figuring out ways of adding him to their sports teams. Moreover, in the midst of his truly accomplished dancing, Neal was somehow managing to mock me the way mimes mimic passersby: he caught my slumping posture, my grimacing facial expression and my doomed efforts at dancing to the beat perfectly. Even I had to smile.

Then, at last, it was over.

Thunderous applause.

Waves of love.

Thank fucking Christ.

As Neal took deep bows, I scuttled off the bottom crate, crab-like, over to a buffet table now devoid of food save for saltine crackers in little cello wrappers. I pocketed as many as I could, then turned around to find the canteen almost empty; the audience had fled. Neal was standing with Jennifer, who was all smiles for me: "Raymond! I had no idea you and Neal were planning such a sensational performance. I underestimated you."

"Well, you know, uh . . ." Finally, I'd caught a fucking break. I changed the subject. "Neal, where did you get the new clothes?"

"Jenny here gave them to me. They belonged to some French bloke."

Jenny?

She cut in. "Arnaud du Puis, the world's leading radio telemetry expert until last Bastille Day, when he jumped off the dock directly onto a Portuguese man-of war the size of a child's wading pool."

Neal added, "One of the lads told me last night that a clump of poor Arnaud's lymph nodes washed into the lagoon, but an albatross ate them before they could be landed in a net."

"Neal is the same size as Arnaud," Jennifer volunteered, "so fortunately the clothes won't go to waste."

Pinching his jacket material, Neal said, "Everything's made by Paul Smith. The fabric breathes."

"Linen!" said Jennifer. "Don't talk to me about linen—the wrinkles! Gentlemen, as a token of our thanks, you'll be riding as my guests on today's mission."

"Today's *mission?*" I asked.

The **Portuguese man-of-war** is a jellyfish-like marine invertebrate whose name is borrowed from the man-of-war, a fifteenth-century English warship.

The man-of-war is not a true jellyfish but a siphonophore, which differs from a jellyfish in that it is not actually a single creature but a colonial organism, made up of many minute individuals called zooids.

The man-of-war is found floating on the surface of warm seas, its air bladder keeping it afloat and acting as a sail while the rest of the organism hangs below the surface. It has no means of self-propulsion and is entirely dependent on winds, currents and tides.

The stinging venom-filled nematocysts in the tentacles of the Portuguese man-of-war can paralyze small fish and other prey. Detached tentacles and dead specimens (including those that wash up on shore) can sting just as painfully as the live creature in the water, and may remain potent for hours or even days after the death of the creature or the detachment of the tentacle.

Stings usually cause excruciating pain to humans—not unlike the effect of globules of molten steel or lava burning through the skin. The stings leave hideously disfiguring red welts that normally last for weeks and that people on the bus stare at and then quickly turn their heads away from.

23

Jennifer and Neal wouldn't tell me what the day's operation was to be, only that "we" were going to be taking some photos. An hour after the performance, we walked up aluminum stairs into a massive beast of a plane with no windows, save for a few up front, where we were to sit.

"What's in the back?" I asked.

Neal, for some reason, seemed to be clued into what was going on. "It's a surprise, Ray. Just rekindle your sense of childlike wonder and go with the day's flow."

Jennifer hopped in and took the main passenger seat in front of us. "Ready, boys?"

"Yes, ma'am!" said Neal. Me, I coughed up a loogey that was not unlike a sea creature. I flicked it out the closing door, where it landed on someone's shoulder. I suppose it was very good luck for him, like being shat on by a gull.

The engines started. Over the roar, I asked, "Can you at least tell me how long we'll be flying for?"

"Forty-five minutes there, one hour on location and then home."

"What do you mean by '*on location*'?"

Her reply was cut off by the atrocious noise of the plane's engines. Neal and I put on heavy-duty protective earmuffs. We taxied and took off, then headed southeast amidst glorious whipped-cream clouds. Neal had a window on his right; I had one on my left. Couldn't ask for a better view, really.

About forty-three minutes into the flight, high above the Pacific, Jennifer turned around and gave us each a pair of goggles with dark glass lenses.

"What are these for?" I asked.

"Put them on, Ray," said Neal. "You'd better, really."

"Why the fuck do I want to wear some stupid glasses, Neal?"

"Ray, in one minute we're dropping an atomic bomb."

"We're *whatttttttttttt!!!!!????*"

The lieutenant pointed something out to the pilot. She then turned around and smiled at me reassuringly. "It's a new tactic, Ray. We're using leftover Cold War nuclear warheads to vaporize the Pacific Trash Vortex!"

"It's a genius idea, it is, Jenny," shouted Neal.

I screamed, "Are you demented cunts out of your fucking minds!"

"Showtime!" shouted Jennifer.

Behind us, bay doors opened and something dropped from the plane.

* * *

Now.

Oh dear.

This is awkward.

You see . . . I *know* nuclear warheads have a bum rap in our culture—radiation, nuclear winter, massive extinction, sad little doll heads lying in the gutter covered with bits of black muck. But to watch one exploding in real life is insanely fucking awesome. Yes. It is true. I wouldn't have believed it if I hadn't seen it myself, snacking on saltines and drinking Arrowhead bottled water while our plane circled a heaving, pulsating, smoking-hot 15-kiloton explosion, with Neal pointing out little sparkling patches on the ocean where extra-dense bits of plastic trash were blipping into a green eco-friendly solution for a better tomorrow.

Yes, yes, I know, I know. Atomic weapons. Charred little kittens. Nuns vaporizing. The economy in shambles. But still . . . what a fucking sight!

I had to knuckle-bump both Neal and Jennifer for so skillfully keeping it a surprise for me. My hostess loaned me her iPhone and I took some smashing "Me and my good buddy Mushroom Cloud" photos, which she promised she'd send me once her workload lightened.

"Bombs are one thing, Raymond, but *caramba*, the paperwork involved in dropping one! There'd be less paperwork involved making the entire country switch over to metric."

I had seriously underestimated this woman.

She caught the new, appraising look in my eye. "Too late, Raymond. The mood's gone. You and your pals are on your way tonight."

Fucking hell.

And then the plane cartwheeled, and that's when I actually shat my pants. No dream.

24

Let me tell you, the first thing you do when you shit your pants for real is tell nobody. *Nobody.*

And then you try to deal with the fact that your plane just cartwheeled over a lake of fire, as the pilot declares, "That was easy," followed by the lieutenant laughing giddily and Neal shouting, "Blimey! Let's do that again!"

And you sit there trying to figure out how you're going to get back to a clean, dry room on Wake Island with a hose to rinse yourself off and fresh undergarments and a fresh pair of trousers identical to the ones you've just kacked—as well as a rubbish can large enough to bury the soiled pants in.

"Ray!" Neal called out. "To think just one week ago I was frittering away my life in a cardboard Samsung telly box—and here I am living large!"

Sadly, the condition of my pants made it impossible to continue to enjoy the nuclear fireworks. Neal mistook my new highly focused and somewhat unhappy facial expression to be some sort of politically correct judgment on the bombing.

"Don't be such a sourpuss, Ray! Think of all that plastic, gone forever—fluffy little dolphins now able to romp through lagoons free of plastic six-pack yokes. Seahorses cantering about, snacking on little bits of seahorse food. It's a Disney movie down there now, like *Finding Nemo*. It's world peace. Our Jenny here is a planetary hero."

"You're making me blush, Neal," said Jennifer. Then she stared at me and her brow furrowed. "Raymond— are you . . . *leaking*?"

Neal looked down at my seat. "Oh, now you've done it, Ray . . ."

"Done what?" asked Jennifer.

I said, "Look, both of you, it's nothing . . ."

"Raymond's shat his pants."

"Raymond!" Jennifer sounded really shocked.

"Christ, the plane did a fucking cartwheel overtop a nuclear explosion."

"Changing the subject," Neal chided. "Common behaviour for someone experiencing fecal remorse."

Jennifer flipped into problem-solving mode. "Raymond, once we're on the ground, I can have someone come meet us with a hazmat suit. I'll call for one right now." She clicked a button on the dash and began barking into her headset: "Alpha nine, alpha nine, we've had a Code-Mocha bowel evacuation—"

"No, really, I—" But there was no stopping her.

Neal, meanwhile, looked me over with a father's sad, judgmental eyes.

I said, "Come on, Neal, I think what happened was a perfectly normal response given the situation."

"I would never judge you, Ray."

"Thank you, Neal."

"Bye the way, Ray, Sarah sent me a text to relay to you."

"What the *fuck?* Neal, since when do *you* have a cell-phone?"

"Poor Arnaud du Puis never cancelled his account with Orange France, so I took the initiative and started adding to his contact list the numbers of people connected to the show. That Sarah is one hard worker, mate. I think she has a thing for you. In fact, I'm sure she does."

She does? "I'm listening, Neal."

"She said, 'Give my Ray-Ray a big hug and tell him I can't wait to introduce him to the alluring ways of the tropics.'"

"Show me."

Neal showed me the text; he was word for word. "I think she could be The One, Ray, I really do," he said.

I thought of her spooning me back to health in Honolulu, her cheerful manner, her milkmaid freshness—her absolutely perfect pair of baps.

The flight back was as airy and hopeful as the infinite shaving-cream clouds above us and caterwauling flocks of sea birds below. The cockpit was somewhat chilly with the altitude, and I felt like I was sitting atop a tub of melted gelato, but I didn't care.

Once on the ground, we were greeted by perhaps fifty goons, all of them clapping wildly for the lieutenant. Jennifer took a bow, smiled for the cameras, gave a small speech and then said, "But before I disembark, we have a small medical issue to attend to." She stood away from the door, saying, "Raymond, the medics will take good care of you. They really will. All of us here in your Wake

Island family just want you to get clean again. And watch your left leg. You're dripping on the hatch."

The crowd went silent as it watched me walk down the aluminum stairway, where I was met by a ginger-haired medic—whom I recognized as being the one on whom my good-luck loogey had landed earlier. He came at me with a huge Spielbergy Tyvek jumpsuit, bellowing, "Mandatory for potential bowel-related contamination scenarios! Can I ask you, Mr. Gunt, if you have any history of hepatitis A, B or C, cholera or superbugs?"

"Fuck off."

"No need to swear, sir. There are ladies present."

Fucking Americans.

The silence continued as everyone watched me don my hazmat suit. I gave up trying to maintain dignity. I'd be out of this fucking sun-kissed dump soon enough. Also, I had just witnessed the first Pacific detonation since 1962.

25

Instead of taking me to a nice clean clinic furnished with a functioning shower, Ginger the medic led me behind the Quonset hut beside the canteen, where three of his pals stood ready and armed with firehoses.

"Look, boys! It's Billy Elliot!"

"Let the dance of pain begin!"

Bloody hell.

But when you're caked in your own leavings, you really don't mind being hit with brutally hard jets of water. Truth be told, it just gets the crap off sooner, though it does hurt like all get out. When the water hits a large enough flap of trouser fabric, liftoff is easily achieved, and more than once I was hurled into one of the canteen Dumpsters, crammed, no doubt, with saltine packaging and empty Pepsi bottles.

And, of course, there was much festive heckling. "Come on, Billy! Eat hose water, you po-faced Limey bitch!"

"Aim for his teeth, guys! Maybe we can ship his teeth to wherever it was his chin went."

But then I removed my kacked pants and turned away

from them. I bent over to let their warm, brackish water rinse away the last of my self-marinade. The tone soon changed when they realized they weren't so much torturing me as they were administering a fairly efficient enema whenever I unclenched my rusty bullet hole. They soon turned off their hoses and walked away in disgust, Ginger tossing a pair of clean sailor's trousers to the ground. I togged up.

* * *

Right.

The jet. Time to leave.

Just then Neal roared up in a Jeep driven by one of his video-gaming friends, with two more in the rear seat, all of them holding foaming half-full Oktoberfest mugs of beer. "Rejoice, Ray!" Neal shouted. "The trash vortex will soon be gone."

"Christ, Neal. You're wasted. Let's just get to the fucking plane."

"Not until you have a beer with us, my friend. Everyone on the island is celebrating a new era of hope for mankind."

"Yes, yes, whatever. We're the worst thing that ever happened to the planet. But a pint of lager right now *would* be just the ticket."

A back-seat goon turned a spigot on an aluminum canister and . . . voila! A cold, frosty, surprisingly delicious mug of lager appeared. I became drunk with the first swig. "All hail the atomic bomb!"

"To the bomb! The bomb! The bomb!"

It was a matey moment that cancelled out the horror of my cleansing. I climbed in beside Neal and we began driving on the runway, carving donuts and weaving in between other Jeeps filled with soused airmen. The whole island had erupted into an orgy of stress release.

"Makes you feel good, doesn't it, Ray?"

"Just hand me another fucking beer." *Finally*, a bit of light-heartedness after seventy-two hours of total shit.

Neal found an eighties radio channel on the Jeep's satellite set, and the afternoon turned into a blur of hair-band ballads and puddles of vomited saltines. Around sunset, to the waning sound of Haysi Fantayzee's hit "Shiny Shiny" from the departing Jeep's sound system, I found myself utterly cunted and lying in a heap on the ground at the foot of the stairs leading up to the jet. Neal was Angry Dancing his way upward. I crawled after him. Once on board, I heaved my old aluminum medical gurney out the door. It bit the concrete with an aching clang. Elspeth closed the port and, finally, Wake Island was history.

....

Haysi Fantayzee was a British New Wave band of the early 1980s. Their single "Shiny Shiny" was released in 1983. It's fun.

....

26

I can't remember the last time I've been so thrilled to hear the landing gear pull up. Neal, Elspeth and I feasted on Advil and microwave luxury meals as we tried to process the biggest twenty-four-hour travel kludge in history.

"I telephoned me mum when I was down there," said Elspeth. "I told her where I was and she said her brother, Olly, went through Wake Island back in the late 1970s on a transpac boat when he was shipping off to Yokohama."

"Where's Olly now?"

"He runs a Dungeons & Dragons shop in Hull. He never really was the same after he'd spent time training dolphins to wear video cameras on their foreheads. I think those little buggers stole his mind."

"You're fucking kidding me."

"Laugh if you will, but Olly served the Queen very well." Elspeth wiped tomato sauce from her lips. "And now he throws rocks at you if you go too near his council flat door. Fucking dolphins."

"They think they're actually going to fix the trash vortex with bombs," I exclaimed. "These fucking Americans are like *children*."

Neal, being one of nature's mimics, said, "Imagine John F. Kennedy and Marilyn Monroe riding in a bomber above a nuclear blast. 'Ooh, Mr. Kennedy, that H-bomb is so scary.' 'Don't you worry, Marilyn. Just cover up your diseased minge with this lead-lined X-ray-proof garment I stole from Jackie's hope chest.'"

"John Kennedy," said Elspeth. "Is he the one who had a lot of sex and the retro hairdo?"

"Dear God," I said. "What year were you born?"

"I'm old enough to be a flight attendant is how old I am. Just like Prince William's mum-in-law."

We became reflective then and took a pause from eating. Overtop the dusty whoosh of sleek jet engines I put forth a question. "Neal, let me ask you this: do you think camel toes are, in any way, you know . . . *hot?*"

"That's an excellent question, Ray."

"Oh God," said Elspeth. "I'm going to be sick."

Neal said, "Come along, Elspeth, think of this as an interfaith symposium, with you representing just one of several points of view. But I do want to say that simply because a woman's got camel toe, it in no way indicates she's a slag."

I said, "Thank you, Neal. I, too, believe women are the future—yay, women! Yay, tampons and all that! But it's the camel toe part about women that's the topic here."

Neal reached for brandy. "It's hard to really get in the mood when there's a badly packed kebab three and a half feet away from your eyes. It's all about the packaging."

"Agreed," I said, "Part of the charm of the quim is that it's on the inside, not the outside."

"And," added Neal with authority, "just because there's something big on the outside doesn't always mean a bird's got a clown's pocket on the inside. Perhaps the contrary. And it's a slippery slope, too. One day you're fine with having a camel toe, and the next day you're out behind the chip shop with your knickers yo-yoing up and down, servicing strangers for the price of a pack of fags. Not helping society much that way, are you?"

Elspeth rebelled. "Will you two *stop* blabbing on about camel toes! I would like to enjoy my chicken piccata in peace."

So much for the consolation of philosophy.

I looked over at a pile of apparently blank CDs on a seat beside me. "Neal, for fuck's sake, who the hell uses CDs these days?"

"Oh, them. They're bootleg Harry Potter movies I promised someone in LA I'd take to his friend in Kiribati." Neal threw a Sharpie my way. "Do me a favour, Ray, and write 'Harry Potter' on them so they don't end up in the rubbish."

"Will do, mate."

....

Sharpie was the first permanent ink pen-style marker, launched in 1964 by the Sanford Ink Company. In 1992, Sharpie was acquired by Newell Rubbermaid. The Sharpie created an entirely new category: a rigid felt-tip with minor give to allow for characterfullness. There's something fun about Sharpies that's really hard to articulate. They are to handwriting what Play-Doh is to sculpting.

Bonriki International Airport is the only international airport in Kiribati and serves as the main gateway to the country. It is located in the capital, South Tarawa, a group of islets in the atoll of Tarawa in the Gilbert Islands.

· ·

AWK to TRW = 8 h, 30 m

· ·

27

Stuart Greene.

What a total fucking dick.

But let me back up a bit.

We finally landed in Kiribati in the fiery coral dawn. Christ, could these people have found a place on earth more remote? Excuse me, but were the Kerguelen Islands all booked up? Was Pitcairn Island shut down for an extended religious holiday? Try Google-Mapping this place; it's a dogfart.

On a practical level, since cartwheeling over the atomic blast, I'd been down to a borrowed pair of sailor pants. Before we landed, Neal gave me one of Arnaud du Puis's linen outfits.

"Ooh," cooed Elspeth after I changed, "you're dressed just like Ewan McGregor." She brushed some dust off the lapel.

Neal added, "And your lobster-like sunburn from our afternoon beerfest gives you a previously missing out-doorsy air. We should go drunk-driving around Wake Island a lot more."

Wake Island *had* left me a bit tender red on the scalp and face. Still, standing on the Bonriki tarmac, I was feeling pretty darn good about myself, and felt even better when I spotted Sarah, with a clipboard, overseeing some staffers while something was being unloaded from an aging prop plane. She smiled and waved at me, and my heart swooned. And then a pickup truck approached and came to a stop. Stuart got out of the passenger seat. He looked at me and said, "Oh, great. It's *you*."

"Hello, Stuart."

"Jesus, you look like Rock Hudson with late-stage AIDS. What the fuck happened to you since Hawaii?"

"Well—"

"Like I could care. Which one of you is Neal?"

"That's me." Neal raised a hand.

"You've got some Harry Potter CDs for me."

"Brilliant! So you're Stu Greene." Neal reached into his jacket pocket and removed the CDs I'd labelled. He handed them to Stuart, who looked at them and froze.

"Everything okay?" asked Neal.

"Neal, who labelled these CDs?"

"Um, Raymond here. What's up?"

"It's just that *Raymond* spelled 'Harry' with an 'e' instead of an 'a'." He held it up for Neal to check out.

Neal looked and said, "H-E-R-R-Y. Huh. Don't see that every day now, do you?"

....

Harry is a male given name, the Middle English form of Henry. It is also sometimes used as a diminutive form of Harold or Henry. It is never, ever, ever spelled with an 'e'.

Now, I like to think of myself as an educated bloke. I wasn't head boy or Stephen fucking Hawking or anything, but Stuart—what a dick.

"Jesus, Gunt, how the *fuck* could anyone be stupid enough to spell Harry with an 'e'?"

"It's not as bad as you're making it out to be."

"Not as bad? How did a useless imbecile end up on *my* payroll?"

"That's deeply unfair, Stuart. I was a bit drunk at the time."

"Drunk? Gunt, even if my brain had been raped by a gallon of tequila, I'd still have the fucking wits to spell 'Harry' properly."

At that moment, a rusty, windowless van used for hauling medium-sized groups about the airport was approaching. On its sun-rotted leather seats lounged a spent-looking array of executives, plus a handful of stocky types who could only be cameramen—hod carriers in any other period in history—torsos lopsided from decades of tramping across deserts and mountains and battlefields and swamps with a Sony always over the right shoulder, their livelihood also betrayed by their nylon cargo pants, capable of conveying a nineteenth-century hunt's worth of crap from airport to airport to airport, fully washable and dryable in any hotel room on earth in under three hours.

Stuart whistled for the driver to stop, then bellowed, "You! Bus people! Come over here!"

Neal studied the passengers more closely as they disembarked. "*They're* looking a bit wasted."

Stuart agreed. "They're all of them drunk and pissed off. There's been an international incident that's utterly

screwed up our supply shipments. Some dipshits somewhere let off a bomb. Airports are shut down all over."

"Bombs go off all the time," Neal protested.

"An *atomic* bomb."

Neal and I looked at each other. "Well, that's different, isn't it?" Neal said. "Where'd they drop it, Stuart?"

"No one's saying. Rumour is Hawaii. Anyhow, this
bunch here has been drinking away the boredom all
night while we wait for word about supplies and tech
support staff."

Neal asked about the luxurious TV network yacht.

"It was en route from Hawaii, but now it's delayed
because there's an exclusion zone for all boats."

"Probably stuck in the trash vortex," I said.

Stuart had no time to reply, as twenty of my new
co-workers, at the tail end of a long drunken night, stag-
gered towards him from the rusting wagon. And then
one more figure came bouncing along. Oh good fucking
Christ: *Fiona.*

"Raymond? Raymond! Could that really be you? You
look like Rock Hudson with late-stage AIDS."

Stuart smirked.

An executive beside Fiona said, "Who's that, then?"

She replied, "*That's* Raymond Gunt. You'll be working with him. He's a dreadful human being."

"People!" shouted Stuart, holding up the offending
CDs. "I ask you, would any of you, even at the end of
a five-day meth binge, *ever* be stupid enough to spell
'Harry Potter' with an 'e'?"

Someone said, "Why are you asking us?"

"Because your new co-worker here, Patient Zero,
actually did."

"Thank you, Stuart," I said. "Might I add in my defence that I was cunted out of my brains on booze?"

Someone near the front said, "I still don't know, mate. Pretty fucking stupid if you ask me."

"Who died and made *you* Alex fucking Trebek?"

"Watch your language!" shouted Stuart. "There are ladies present."

"But you swear yourself!"

Ignored.

Everyone melted away to various destinations. Fiona left too, scurrying to a nearby private jet. *Joy to the world!* I did watch her closely, however, and because of this I saw her hand the pilot a bag of money. How do I know it was a bag of money? Because I know Fiona. When we were together, we purchased truck-loads of blow all the time, and she has a *very* specific way of handling money; her body language changes when she's in contact with cash. She keeps her hands close to her stomach and then passes the wad to its recipient in a direct line from her belly button. Of course, she might only be scoring coke from the pilot, but it was a pretty big bag, so . . . I made a mental note and left it at that.

Sarah, meanwhile, peeked out from behind Stuart, looking fresh as the dawn, her breasts as insistent as rising dough. "Looks like I'm missing out on some fun here." She gave me a kiss on the cheek. "Raymond, you poor thing, you're sunburned! Let me go get some lotion from the medic. I'll warm it up to just above body temperature so that it feels nice when I put it on you."

From behind, Neal jabbed me in the ribs with his index finger.

Sarah went off to get some lotion, and Stuart said, "Gunt. Stop brain-raping Sarah. I am *on* to you, buddy." He looked at his watch and cursed as he got back into his pickup truck, muttering, *"Fucking atomic bombs."* He peeled away from us.

Me, Neal and Elspeth remained on the tarmac. Fiona's jet was just taking off.

"Ooh," said Elspeth, pointing at Sarah, now far down the tarmac in pursuit of lotion. "Play your cards right and you'll be stonkering her something quick. Watch out for that Stuart fellow, though."

"So what do we do now?" Neal asked.

"While I await my lotion, why not investigate . . ." I looked at a sign, ". . . Bonriki International Airport."

28

Welcome to Bonriki International Airport!
Gateway to the city of Bairiki. Whether you're
passing through or staying for a while, be happy
and enjoy our fine island hospitality!

•

Miss Phibbs's Restaurant and Foot Clinic now
open after tsunami repairs. Perhaps enjoy a delicious
meal of octopus, coconut, tinned luncheon meat
and hen's eggs. Or maybe excellent entertainment
on a colour television set.
"Satellite dish since 1994."

•

Bridge to North Island is now out of commission
due to salt corrosion. Truck access now only
at lowest tide.

•

Remember: condoms promote licentiousness,
so reconsider before using.

•

Coral is pretty, but it cuts you easily and then
infection will set in and you will die.
Remember sand shoes when visiting reefs.

•

Kiribati is a full voting member of the United Nations.

....

Kiribati has few natural resources. Commercially viable phosphate deposits were exhausted by 1979, when it gained its independence from England. Copra and fish now represent the bulk of production and exports. Tourism provides more than one-fifth of the country's GDP. It's a very, very dull place.

....

Dear al Qaeda,

If you ever feel like putting some of your young lads on planes again, I have just the place for you. Snuggled in the warm waters of the central Pacific, Bonriki Airport has about as much protection as a leftover plate of spaghetti in the fridge covered with a layer of cling film. The facility's security team is composed of mange-ridden, malnourished stray dogs whom the natives take great relish in taunting with hurled coral chunks. And I wouldn't worry too much about CCTV cameras or the like. Chances are greater than not that the power is out. Honestly, you could stuff 200 pounds of Semtex up your gary in this place and no one would ever notice your payload. These people are massive.

Yours,
Raymond Gunt

29

"Sarah, we just passed our hotel." (The hotel, I might add, resembled a detention facility in a cruel post-architectural world of cinder blocks and corrugated zinc sheeting. Dumpiness notwithstanding, I very much wanted to be there.)

Sarah was rubbing my head with PABA lotion. "We're going into town for supplies."

"Why now? Shouldn't we at least check in first?"

"No. I think it's best to go now."

The last thing I wanted was to displease Sarah, so I shut up.

Sarah, Neal, Elspeth and I were in a fifteen-seater Toyota van driven by a local. Owing to the escalating global nuclear situation, the private jet that brought us here was forbidden to leave. Elspeth had now joined us as a prisoner of Bonriki until things cooled down. Most everyone was waiting for the heli-evacuation unit to take us to the island so, nuclear crisis or not, we could start shooting our dreadful, dreadful, dreadful TV show.

Kiribati was basically Wake Island covered with palm trees, grey, highly flammable-looking thatched roofing, feral dogs, rusty trash barrels and thousands of poor people smiling, though God knows why.

Neal said, "Supposedly, Kiribati will be the first country on earth to vanish with global warming. Saw that on the telly last year."

"I can just imagine the ripple effect that news must be having at the United Nations," I said. "Kenya and Kuwait will have to sit beside each other. Sparks will fly." Sarah's hands on my scalp felt heavenly, particularly when she worked the base of my skull—such tenderness. It almost made me forget the X-ray sunlight and the stop-and-go jerking of the van on a road that suddenly became blocked by goats.

I yelled a command to the driver. "Fucking hell. Just throw rocks at them."

"No, we must let goats do their thing." Our driver, apparently, found goats sacred.

Sarah stopped her scalp rub and turned to Elspeth. "Why don't you help me out with my shopping list. I can't wait to see the delicious local treats this magic island has to offer."

I was horrified. "No! My head isn't fully lotioned!"

"Oh, Raymond! I'll finish working on you later. Come on, Elspeth. My paper and stuff is at the back of the bus."

Elspeth was excited. "I wonder if they sell bikinis here, though I'd have to shave me lady bits first. Looking a bit like a barber shop floor at the moment."

As the women sat in the rearmost seats and bonded over shopping, Neal and I stared at the goats. "Neal," I asked, "have you ever, you know, wondered what it might be like with, well, *not a person?*"

"You mean a goat, Ray?"

"Neal, those are *your* words not mine, and I'm appalled that that's the first place your mind went—but a goat is as good a place to start as any."

"So you *are*, then, thinking about goats?"

"No, no, I don't want to fuck a goat, Neal."

"Sheep, then?"

"Don't be coarse. I'm trying to have an elevated conversation here."

"So you're wondering in a scientific sense about the physical sensation of the act?"

"Well, sort of."

"Technically, a sheep would be better than a goat."

"Why is that, then?"

"A sheep'd take instructions from you."

I let that sink in.

Neal asked, "Ray, you *are* talking about a female sheep, right?"

"No, Neal, there's nothing wrong with fucking a male sheep, because if I did find something wrong with it, that would mean I was insensitive to the needs of the gay sheep community, and, of course, I believe in equality and peace and freedom for everybody—Oi! Benders forever! But for the purposes of this discussion, yes, female sheep. Definitely. And definitely not lambs. Because that would be wrong."

"Well, you couldn't really just hop the fence and go at it. You'd have to establish some level of trust first."

"Neal, I really think taking a ewe on a date is too much effort for too little payoff."

"Like she might change her mind at the end—and then you're out ten quid for a plate full of clover and a zinc bucket of lager."

"Neal. Stop right now."

"You're right. Probably all you'd need is a pile of alfalfa to keep the front end busy, and maybe a leash to make sure it doesn't bolt when you get to the good part."

"That sounds about right."

"I feel like I'm on the Discovery Channel, decoding animal intelligence like this. You bring out the best in me, Ray."

"I'm touched, but back to our sheep. You've got past the first hurdles and now you're, well, ready to make the big move."

"Wait, Ray—condom or unprotected? I don't want to get mad cow or anything."

"Neal, I think you should be more worried about your date. She's only been grazing in a meadow for a few years, whereas *you've* basically been the clogged bacterial centrifuge of West London since the days of Adam Ant."

"Slight change of subject, Ray. What about all the daggy bits around the sheep's arse? Kind of a turnoff, I'd say."

"I hadn't thought of that."

At this point our driver lurched around to stare at us, purple of face, then screamed at us to get out of his van. *Déjà vu.*

"Sorry, mate, what are you talking about here?"

"You are unholy. I cannot have you in my van. Leave right now."

"What is he talking about?" Sarah called from behind us.

I was the picture of innocence. "No idea. We were

just talking about our love of animals, and—boom! He's lunging at Neal and me, asking us to leave his van."

Our driver escalated his screaming and began making threatening gestures at us. But Neal, with his dancer's grace, seized the man and pushed him out the door in a flash, then leaped out after him. On the littered road's edge, he put a chokehold on the incensed driver to the point where the man's eyes bulged, his mouth frothed and his oxygen supply was depleted enough to make him less of a threat. "Looks to me like we're at a standstill," said Neal, whereupon a motorcycle, sounding like an amplified coffee grinder, zoomed up from behind us at some insane speed and ploughed directly into our driver, hurling him like a Muppet off into a taro shrub. The biker stopped—a young Australian hostel-goer.

"Fuck me! He's not dead, is he?"

We all stared at the body, which seemed utterly still.

"Looks like a goner," said Elspeth.

"No, he's breathing," said Sarah.

"Neal, you're a former paramedic," I said. "What should we do here?"

Neal crouched to do an assessment. "He's definitely not dead. Doesn't seem to be anything broken. Let's call the police when we get into town."

Our Aussie friend was relieved. "You guys are the best."

"Always happy to help a fellow traveller."

"Good on ya. Here's four hits of Ecstasy, and if you get desperate, there's exactly one flush toilet on this island that works. It's in the Mormon high school building. If you act all serious and pretend to like God, you're in, and there's five minutes of heaven awaiting you. Cheers!"

And our fellow traveller was off.

30

We looked at the pills in their Ziploc baggie. I was about
to tuck them into my pocket when Neal said, "You know,
Ray, why not give these pills a try right now?"

I considered this for a moment. "Hmmmm . . . You
know, Neal, I like your attitude. Indeed, let's say 'yes!'
to life."

We each popped one; they tasted bitter, sort of metal-
lic. Sarah and Elspeth declined, and we got back into
the van, Neal at the wheel. He asked, "Sarah, why do we
have to buy groceries? Someone in your position shouldn't
be doing scoutwork like that."

"Because of the nuclear crisis, all food shipments to
the island from Australia and Fiji have been stopped
indefinitely. The locals don't know this yet—we have
a one-hour head start to secure all we need for the shoot.
We have to clean the stores out before word spreads and
looting begins. Let's just go in, max out our credit cards
and exit without leaving a ripple in the water."

The goats before us had cleared to make way for our
van. Fortune was smiling on us.

....

Gilbertese, or **Kiribati**, is a language from the Austronesian family. The word *"Kiribati"* is just the modern rendition of "Gilberts," after Captain Thomas Gilbert, who happened upon the Gilbert Islands in 1788. Unlike many languages in the Pacific region, Kiribati is far from extinct, and most speakers use it daily. About thirty percent of Kiribati speakers are fully bilingual, also speaking English.

FUN FACT: One early difficulty in translating books into Kiribati was references to features such as "mountain," a geographical phenomenon unknown to the people of the islands of Kiribati (heard only in the myths from Samoa). Such adjustments are common to all languages. For example, the Gilbertese word for "airplane" is *te wanikiba*—"the canoe that flies."

About 107,500 people speak Gilbertese, as follows:

In Kiribati: 98,000
In Fiji: 5,300
In Nauru: 1,700
In Solomon Islands: 1,230
In Tuvalu: 870
In Vanuatu: 370
In Ooga Booga: 13

....

Okay . . .

I'm not proud of what happened next, but history demands a full account.

I remember beginning to giggle as we pulled into an appalling slum. "A slum?" says I. "How can there be a slum in the middle of the tropical Pacific? What the hell?"

Neal was agog. "Ray, this is Betio! The magic slum of the Pacific! I saw it on BBC4 at the Russian Kum Guzzling Traktor Sluts' lounge when they were giving me a pedicure. All the islanders living here were relocated from their old coral atolls because of the nuclear testing. But there's fuck all for anybody to do here, so they sit in squalor for a living. Is that a verb . . . to, uh . . . *squalor?*"

The Ecstasy was kicking in. I ventured, "I'm squalling. These islanders *sont* squalling. *Nous nous squallons.*"

Neal pulled up to a cinder-block grocery store and parked. Sarah and Elspeth vanished inside, while we sat there transfixed by a shiny piece of red plastic hanging from the store's eaves. It turned sort of rainbow colours the longer we stared at it. Then it started to make faint chiming sounds. A wind chime was our initial musing.

"Neal, that piece of plastic is fucking amazing."

"It is magnificent. It wouldn't be out of place in a New York art gallery."

We got out of the car to better appreciate the plastic. Its magnificence blossomed ever outward, fractally, and I felt connected to all life—not just my own, but also the lives of all human beings on the planet, and possibly the universe.

Neal said, "Ray, we're just grains of sand in the scheme of things."

"Neal, you are so right."

"All we are is dust in the wind."

"Look, it's turning blue—laser beam blue."

We stood there gawping until a fly landed in my mouth and I horked it out, laughing. It was terribly funny. It just was. Neal thought so too, and we both laughed to the point where our stomachs dry-heaved. Small children with sticks stopped and stared at us, while stray dogs avoided us, rightly fearing our magnificent grasp of the true fabric of the universe.

We were shitfuck stoned.

"I must own that piece of plastic, Neal."

"To the victors belong the spoils."

"Give me a leg up."

"Sure thing, Ray."

Neal kneeled and offered me his cupped hands. I stuck a foot in and he lifted me up to make a swipe at our piece of sacred plastic, but I overreached and fell onto my butt, my elbow landing in, of all things, an octopus somebody had abandoned, goopy and smegmacious. I shrieked like a wee girl. Neal found this utterly hilarious—it wasn't. I frantically removed the fine linen shirt that had once belonged to poor, doomed Arnaud du Puis, while Neal sat doubled over atop some plastic milk crates from Australia until he could catch his breath. As I scraped the worst of the octopular sludge from my arms, Neal hopped on one of the crates and grabbed the piece of sacred red plastic from its string, placing it in his dapper linen jacket's inside pocket.

"Neal, that's *my* piece of red plastic."

"Sorry, Ray. Fate gave you one chance to grab the brass ring, and you missed. Then fate gave me a chance, and the sacred talisman is mine."

"You thieving bastard."

"Sorry, Ray. Law of the seas."

"It's no such thing."

"Ray, I'll let you look at the plastic every so often, but fair's fair."

One thought went through my head: *Neal must die.* As he turned to walk back to the van, I jumped him from behind. To this, he said, "Oh Christ. Ray, just cool down. Maybe they have some ice cream in the store. Let's go get some."

"*Die*, you smarmy bastard." I tried strangling him.

"Okay, Ray, but I'm telling you, this'll hurt you more than it does me." He effortlessly unclamped my arms and hurled me into the ashen remains of what must have once been a sizable pile of snack cake wrappers and fishbones.

I coughed salty dust and watched Neal enter the Island Mart. Suddenly, feelings of love and brotherhood welled up in me for my ~~slave~~ friend. "Neal! Brother! I love you!" But Neal was already inside. I followed, shouting, "Neal! I love you! You're my brother! I'm sorry I tried to kill you," as I pushed through the door.

Neal was staring at a pile of tinned goods at the end of an aisle. Elspeth approached me with a cart full of tinned meats and whispered, *"Raymond, for fuck sake, get your shit together. Stop shouting, we're trying to fly under the radar."*

Sarah was speaking with the manager. She turned to look at me: shirtless, raving, enslimed and sugar-frosted with ashes of trash. I waved at her. A glint in her eyes told me she had a plan afoot, and that I'd better not interfere. In a voice loud enough for the ten other customers in the store to overhear, Sarah explained, "That's Raymond. He's in the final stage of AIDS. Just look how red his head is. The TV network volunteered to take him to a hospice in Brisbane, but, as you can see, the virus has gone to his brain. Poor thing. It's the fantastically contagious strain of the disease, too. I have no idea why he's not wearing a shirt, but I think that goo on his arms might be leakage from suppurating lymph nodes."

Elspeth parked her shopping cart next to Sarah. "And that person staring at the tinned luncheon meats is Neal,

Raymond's fuckbuddy. It's a modern, liberated term that bespeaks the proud man love of those two brave souls. They're political, those two are. It's inspiring the way they still go at it, even in Raymond's final, sad, wildly infectious days."

The man running the store now looked so stressed out I could practically hear his own T-cells suiciding.

Sarah went on, "It's hard to believe Raymond escaped his bio-containment stall at Bonriki Airport—a lovely airport, by the way. But don't worry, we'll have him out of your store in a jiffy, just as soon as we can pay for the multiple carts of groceries required by our crew. Our silly supply ship got marooned in the trash vortex. They called it propeller fatigue. The ocean basically turned into white glue around it."

Elspeth added, "Such a tragedy that vortex is. I hope humanity one day finds a way of making things right with Mother Nature." She paused and added, "Go green!"

The store manager was drenched in sweat and vibrating with worry. Sarah dragged him to the till, saying, "Do you have any jams, jellies or preserves? They make such lovely souvenirs."

"Look!" shrieked Elspeth. "Thong bikinis for sale!"

By this time, the store had totally cleared out.

I heard Neal calling me and found him in aisle 3: Tinned Luncheon Meats.

"Holy *shit*!"

"It's Spam, Ray, an entire aisle of Spam—or, rather, a whole aisle of products highly similar to Spam, yet not really Spam!"

It was almost holy the way the store's sole functioning fluorescent tube lit aisle 3's primary-coloured grids of rectangular tins from all over the planet—although mostly they seemed to be from China.

"Neal, most of these cans are from fucking *China*."

Neal was crestfallen. "I may be snackered on Ecstasy, Ray, but no way in a million years could you make me eat what's inside any of these tins. Christ only knows what's in them."

Drywall

Melamine

Hitchhikers

Nurses

Diseased sheep lungs

Crisps

Cat food too scary for cats

Jellied donkey piss

Yoga mats

Vinyl pool toys

Venereal ovaries

Braided gerbil urethras

Shredded car parts

Dolphins

Neon tetras

Tetra Pak boxes

Broken dreams

Kittens with mittens

Mutton leavings

Silicon chips

Pregnant fetal pigs

Unsold Shrek DVDs

That bucket of blood from Carrie

Angioplasty scrapings

Wank tissues

Biopsy leftovers

Sentient colon polyps

I sat down on the floor and opened a sample can of God's Meat with its little key. Its clear jelly bits soaked up a ray of sun coming through a plastic roof vent. Fucking *marvellous*: like the beginning of the universe, really. Subtle beige chunks of tallow surrounded by pinkish grey mystery tissue: fine Roman marble! Fuck that piece of red plastic Neal stole from me!

I scooped into the can, gorging like a seagull on bites of its holy contents. *Here* was the answer to the mysteries of life. *Here* I found truth. *Here* I found something to live for. *Here* I . . . here I blacked out.

....

Potted meat food product, or **potted meat**, is made of cooked meat product, often creamed, minced or ground, which is poured into cans, sealed and heat-processed. Beef, pork, chicken and turkey are used, as well as non-skeletal meats. What is a non-skeletal meat, you ask? You may regret having asked. Non-skeletal meats include organs and glands, as well as extremities such as feet and tails or retinas or eyelids or udders.

The canning produces a homogeneous texture and flavour, but lower-cost ingredients can also affect quality. For example, mechanically separated chicken or turkey is a paste-like product made by forcing crushed bone and tissue through a sieve to separate bone from tissue. In the United States, mechanically separated poultry has been used in poultry products since 1969. But the real question here is, *What do the Chinese use in their potted meats?* Insert nightmare here.

....

From *The Happy Isles of Oceania* by Paul Theroux (1992)

"It was a theory of mine that former cannibals of Oceania now feasted on Spam because Spam came the nearest to approximating the porky taste of human flesh. 'Long plg,' as they called a cooked human being in much of Melanesia. It was a fact that the people-eaters of the Pacific had all evolved, or perhaps degenerated, into Spam-eaters. And in the absence of Spam they settled for corned beef, which also had a corpsy flavor."

....

31

Okay.

We've all of us gone overboard once or twice in our time and perhaps had a lager or two too many. Or perhaps a flute of champagne past the 0.08 limit. I mean, life is short! Rejoice! And who among us could judge?

When I came to, I found myself on a bamboo deck of some sort, walled on three sides with woven panels made of palm fronds and pandanus leaves, but with no wall in front of me, just the vision of an aquamarine lagoon with gently whooshing waves filled with gumdrops and cartoon characters. My pillow was soft and cool, and the single thin sheet over me was heaven on my skin. I could smell flowers. Okay now, *this* was the Pacific I'd dreamed of.

I looked to my right to see a firm, milky leg—Sarah's!— and I was seized with gratitude to God for having delivered me unto Eden after so many days of total goatfucks. My eyes followed the line of her thigh up to her torso, and a wash of regret passed over me: I had no memory whatsoever of what must have been the absolute best drug-fuelled fuck of a lifetime. *What is wrong with the universe? Just let me have this one fucking memory, is that too much to ask?*

Well, old Ray, maybe the memory will come back to you. Relax. And think of it: there will be other killer shags. The planes are grounded worldwide. No one's going anywhere. You must surely have enough tinned meats to last a decade. The sky and ocean are beautiful. Life is good.

I reached over and traced Sarah's creamy leg. What a perfect fucking ten. What a woman in a million.

My fingers travelled farther upward. I gently brushed the almost invisible hairs that ran from her biff up her crab ladder to her navel. Then I finger-walked over her remarkable knockers up her throat to her . . .

Holy fucking godless mother of fucking hell!

She turned towards me, smiled, let out a small coo and said, "Well, bunny-wunny, I knew one day you'd be mine."

I looked back in frozen horror: **LACEY**.

How do things like this happen? How many of the gods have to be taking a sick day for me to black out and wake up with the hospitality gorgon of LAX? How did she even *get* here? How did *I* get here? Last thing I remember I was . . . high and with Neal looking at tinned meats.

"Ray, don't fret. You were great."

"Where is everybody? Where am I? How the fuck did *you* get here? And why are you calling me 'bunny-wunny'?"

"Ray, we have plenty of time for talking later." She shimmied closer to me, pressing her remarkable breasts (how did I miss *them* first time around?) into my flank.

I shuddered. I had just a bit too much history with

young **LACEY** to ever go that route. Now that I was conscious, you might as well ask me to bang a Ford Cortina. "Where's Neal? Where's Elspeth? Where's *Sarah?*"

"They're out on the yacht."

"*The yacht?!*"

"The TV network banquet should be starting just about . . ." She looked at her watch. ". . . now."

"Oh, fucking hell." Standing up, I slipped on Arnaud du Puis's pants. I looked for a shirt, and all I could find was a vintage Cure T-shirt.

The Cure is an English rock band formed in Crawley, West Sussex, in 1976. The band has experienced several line-up changes, with front man, vocalist, guitarist and principal songwriter Robert Smith being the only constant member, best recognized as the band member with the crazy red mushy lipstick, and you can't believe he's been doing it for all these years, and you sort of wonder if you'd recognize him at the mall if he walked past you without lipstick on.

I left her in bed and climbed down a small rattan staircase onto the beach, which was loaded with . . . thousands of bin bags? Oh, dear God, thousands of trash bags full of the foulest sorts of fish heads, rotting paper towels, rusting cans and fermenting dead whores, and—my nose twitched—everywhere I looked, the sand was peppered with human shit, miles and miles of it, kissed by the loving surf.

LACEY called out, "The locals don't believe in our Western sense of personal hygiene. They just walk into the water, go to the bathroom and come back onto land. So free, and so liberated. You said as much yourself earlier today as we went to the bathroom together out in the lagoon." I turned back to stare in further horror at her as she reached for a nylon sack. "If you're hungry, I brought a duffle bag filled with packets of corn nuts from Los Angeles, and I have half a bottle of water from the drive here in the Jeep."

"Jeep?"

"Yes. Your friend Stuart dropped us off. And your ex-wife. She's nice."

Aneurysm.

"Stuart said he wouldn't disturb us for at least twenty-four hours. I'm so glad I'm not working at the airport bar anymore. Garcia was starting to get too possessive, and the thrill was gone. And after I met you, he could tell things were no longer the same between us."

Stroke.

"Oh, come on now, Raymond. The electricity between us—especially that first time, when you didn't tip me—it was magic."

Throw up inside my mouth.

"Oh look." She had come to the top of the stairs and was pointing at the sea. "I think I can see the yacht out beyond the reef. Imagine the fun they're having: amazing food, the best music, socializing and having a blast. But not nearly the blast you and I have been having all afternoon, my hunny-bunny-wunny."

Cardiac arrest.

"What exactly happened with us here . . . **LACEY**?"

"Happened?"

"Uh, I mean, how long have we been in our magic pad?"

"Eight hours."

My body flinched as though massaged by a stun wand.

"But time has certainly flown. You may be three-eighths of an inch longer than Garcia, but it feels like three whole inches. Though you talk too much. Come back and do me over and over again and again."

Epileptic seizure.

Out in the lagoon, a 500-pounder with octuple beer tits was dumping the natural way. Christ, he could derail a train. Hate to imagine how much Spam went into making him.

I asked **LACEY** "But how did you even find me?"

"I asked Garcia to make some inquiries with Homeland Security. Lieutenant Jennifer Healey was more than happy to tell me where you were, and she even let me fly here free on a bomber headed to Guam that stopped at Bonriki Airport to refuel. I can't say I'm very happy about the global nuclear crisis, except that it's all the more reason to be marooned here with you, you, you and *only* you, possibly for the rest of our lives. Isn't that romantic, Ray**CEY**?"

"Ray**CEY**?"

"That's my couple's name for us. Half Raymond, half **LACEY**."

"Uh-huh. Do you have a phone?"

"A cellphone on Kiribati? Oh, you're just trying to be funny. Undertippers are always such bad jokers."

I had to escape. But how? And to where?

"Did Stuart happen to say which way the hotel was back out on the road?"

"You're not leaving me, are you?"

Good Christ, yes.

"Why would I leave a number like you?" Yet again, more cruel fate: point for point, **LACEY**'s body was hotter than Sarah's, and yet to me, in my right mind, she was utterly unfuckable. I can see what historians mean when they tell us to learn the lessons of the past and how memory can haunt the single or the collective soul.

Wait . . .

Wait . . .

. . . Nuclear crisis.

Nuclear crisis!

"Tell me more about this nuclear crisis."

"It kind of came out of nowhere, really. Just after we took off for Guam, they closed LAX. The bomber flight crew that brought me here was really busy, but they told me a few things. There was a nuclear detonation in the Pacific, not far from Hawaii."

It was thousands of miles away, you chimp.

"And now North Korea's ten minutes from bombing South Korea. You haven't heard about any of this? It's a mess. The Americans say it was part of an idiotic scheme to get rid of the Pacific Trash Vortex, but nobody's buying it. And then a small bomb went off in the Azores, of all places. It's like the Hawaii of the Atlantic, but they think it might have been a Russian nuke headed for South America that got detonated because a deal to sell it went sideways."

Mrs. Peggy Nielson of Kendallville, Indiana, you certainly earned your paycheque this week. "Go on."

"So then Europe got paranoid because a nuclear reactor in Karlsruhe, Germany, melted down—a coincidence? Nobody thinks so. And the Middle East won't let anyone in or out and, well, nobody's going anywhere until this thing cools down. It's like 9/11, except more James Bondy." She tried to look alluring by fluttering her eyelashes while going down on a corn nut.

I shuddered.

"It feels like fate," she said. "It feels like the universe conspired to get Ray**CEY** together in the end."

....

Name-meshing: Two proper names can be used to create a portmanteau word in reference to a couple, especially in cases where both persons are well known, such as "Billary," referring to former U.S. president Bill Clinton and his wife, Hillary.

An early and well-known example was supercouple "Bennifer," referring to film stars Ben Affleck and Jennifer Lopez. Other examples include "Brangelina" (Brad Pitt and Angelina Jolie) and "TomKat" (the now split Tom Cruise and Katie Holmes).

Meshing a name says, "I am you and you are me," noted Denise Winterman in the August 3, 2006, issue of *BBC News Magazine*.

In 2009, the twins John and Edward Grimes followed the growing trend for celebrity portmanteau names when they entered the sixth series of *The X-Factor* (UK) under the name, "Jedward."

The whole thing is just stupid.

....

32

Sometimes a person needs some time alone. While **LACEY** reclined in the *merde*-cloaked Melanesian fuck pad—a pad that rested, I noticed, atop six rusting Mobil oil drums, onto one of which was tethered a ferocious black pig that came alive only when I tripped over a nearby yellow nylon fishing net embedded in the sand and landed right in front of him.

Fuck you, you oinking, amber-tusked chunk of doomed cannibal bacon, I am a free man in Paris, and I am now breaking free of this malarial cumdump. Ha!

I scrambled like a crazy man for the road. Finding it was easy enough, as the island is barely 50 feet wide. On the other side of the road/island lay another coral lagoon that glowed with health. Upon closer inspection, it turned out to be flecked with empty Pepsi cans, plastic water bottles and the cardboard remains of Swanson TV dinners. More artery-clogging shit American food.

I could see the ghetto of Betio to the west, maybe a mile away.

I remembered Neal blathering earlier that the island

was basically 25 miles of nodules linked by a long, thin path that at times became road-like. Well, at least I wasn't in handcuffs and/or a prison cell. Small blessings. I was, however, at least 20 miles away from the hotel.

Two stray dogs growled at me amid the swath of roadside litter. I growled back. They growled louder. Fucking hell, all I needed now was to be attacked by dogs. I decided to ignore them and, thank Christ, they decided the same.

My sunburned scalp was stinging like mad. I removed my Cure T-shirt, put it over my head and tied its corners together into a square that fit snugly on my cranium. Yes, I looked just like a Gumby from *Monty Python*, but the sun was like X-rays.

....

Gumbys are recurring characters in *Monty Python's Flying Circus.* They have toothbrush moustaches and wear hand-kerchiefs knotted at the corners on their heads, wire-rimmed spectacles, braces, Fair Isle knitted sweater vests, a shirt rolled up to the elbows, missing its detachable collar, trousers rolled up above their knees and Wellington boots. They usu-ally hold their arms in an ape-like position, speak loudly and slowly, and pronounce words syllable by syllable. A popular Gumby catchphrase is "My brain hurts!"

....

Where next? The hotel. Right. Two teenage girls approached carrying bundles of laundry.

I decided to lay on some Gunt charm. "Loves, can you tell me where I might find the main hotel around here?"

They stared at me in shock and began to shriek, "*Vakubati! Vakubati!*" They ran away from me.

Vakubati? What the fuck?

"Hey, come on—all I want is directions to the fucking hotel," I yelled, but they were gone.

From the direction of the pig, I heard **LACEY** calling, "Ray**CEY**! Ray**CEY**? Where are you, hunny-bunny?"

What would Jason Bourne do?

He would steal a car.

Where is a car to steal?

A car approached.

It was a 1986 Chrysler LeBaron, more oxide than metal, with its rear seat removed to make room for chicken hutches. Its front vinyl seats were, like most plastics on this island, disintegrating in the relentlessly destructive sun.

I waved frantically and the car pulled over. I began talking to the driver as I opened the door. "Hello. I just need a lift to my hotel. If you like, I can pay you, but I really can't stay here much longer. I'm being followed by a woman with Buñuel's syndrome." By then, I was seated. "Chop-chop. Let's go," I said, then noticed the man behind the wheel: the driver we had left for dead. Mother of fucking God.

* * *

Dear The Gods,

What the fuck is wrong with you?

Yours,
Raymond Gunt

* * *

I launched a charm offensive. "Why, hello, good sir! It's you! How are you feeling?"

"Okay, mon. I'm good."

"It seems people on these delightful islands have a culture of forgiveness and peace," I responded awkwardly.

"Whatever you say. Next hotel is one hour away. I don't charge you, but instead you buy one of my fine hens."

"Delightful idea. Let's get going."

"Delicious hens. Nuclear fallout makes them extra-delicious."

"Doesn't it, though!"

As the driver stepped on the gas, I caught a glimpse in the side mirror of **LACEY** emerging from a cluster of sea grape leaves with a puzzled expression on her face. She was clutching her plastic tote bag of corn nuts.

"So," I said, "I take it you're feeling better after this morning's tiny bump?"

"Bump? I no get bump. I pass out in shrub from drinking too much ceremonial tak-tak. Not really remember much before that. I need to limit the amount of tak-tak I drink these days."

"Well, don't we all, don't we all!"

* * *

Dear The Gods,

I take all that back.

Yours,
Raymond Gunt

* * *

We drove for a few miles or so. Lagoons. Litter. Stray dogs. Chickens in the back seat trying to peck my kidneys. I struggled to remember the name of the hotel Sarah had mentioned. The Douchewater? The Double-Anal? The Deet?

"Say, driver, have you heard of a hotel called the DEET?"

"Ah. The Deet. Nice place. Deet a proud part of island heritage. Hotel named to honour the mighty Deet."

"Really now!" I expected to hear lurid tales of Marilyn Monroe circa 1958 shagging pretty much everyone alive in a popper-scented sling room in a rear bungalow. Or, maybe an international peace armistice signed behind the shed where they slaughter goats.

"DEET be a good chemical. It kills insects fast."

What is he babbling about?

"No more mosquitoes and many fewer flies. DEET be the chemical of progress."

Oh . . . he meant *DDT*.

"Children on island no so bright as before we use DEET, but they no die from malaria. You want snack cake?" He held out a vile, crumbling yellow rhomboid on which a fly was actively laying eggs.

I was starving, and calculated that fly eggs must contain at least a bit of protein. "Actually, yes."

We drove for miles while I digested his tasty offering. I became chatty. "Quite a thing, this nuclear war, isn't it?"

"We used to nuclear war here in Kiribati. Nuclear war invented on our gracious islands."

Uh-oh. I felt a politically correct moment coming on—you know, having to make the empathetic face and show solidarity for these Spam-eating bozos kicked out of their grass huts when the Yanks or the Frogs did their H-bomb tests in the fifties. "Oh, really?"

"Yes. Most of the people on this island are atomic refugees of some sort."

Borrrrrrrrrrrrrrring.

"Our home islands too full of green glow to go back to."

I hate political correctness. One moment you're at the pub making a few biff jokes with some mates, and next thing you know, you're on trial for throwing an empty lager can at the village lesbian.

"We live a simple life here."

Will this bloke's plea for pity ever end?

"Rice. Delicious tinned food from Fiji and Australia. Satellite television. I like Detroit Pistons basketball team."

"Say, driver, there's a local word I'm wondering the meaning of. Maybe you can help me."

"My English be shit."

"Not to worry. The word is *vakubati*. *Vakubati*. Does that ring a bell?"

He slammed on the brakes and began screaming. Plum-faced, he lunged out of the driver's seat and pointed at me, screaming, *"Vakubati! Get out of car, vakubati!"*

"Fuck you, Tonto. I have a hotel to get to."

I scootched over, put the still-running car in gear and peeled off, chickens and all. How dare he try to leave me marooned on some needle-thin chicken path when I, Raymond Gunt, had a job to get to. My mission—well, escaping **LACEY**, for one. And then my actual job as a cameraman: to document twenty-four soul-dead Americans fucking each other's brains out before they descended into cannibalism, all for some tiny sliver of crap money they'd only piss away within a few weeks of winning. The saving grace was that this absurd contest would be happening on an island semi-distant from **LACEY** with absolutely no police, no military and no legal oversight. It was one of those once-in-a-lifetime gifts bestowed upon us by the gods to whom I recently wrote a thank-you letter.

DDT (dichlorodiphenyltrichloroethane) is one of the best-known synthetic insecticides. It was used with great success in the second half of World War II to control malaria and typhus among civilians and troops in tropical zones. The Swiss chemist Paul Hermann Müller was awarded the Nobel Prize in 1948 "for his discovery of the high efficiency of DDT as a contact poison against several arthropods." Its production and use skyrocketed in the fifties and sixties. However, it was banned in the U.S. in 1972 because once it is in an ecosystem, anything larger than a mosquito is totally fucked. If one thing can be said to rape an ecosystem, DDT would be it, and yet for decades people were crazy for the stuff. We are a wacky species, we humans.

The Pacific Proving Grounds is the name of a number of sites in the Pacific Ocean used by the United States to conduct nuclear testing between 1946 and 1962. In July 1947, after the first atomic weapons testing at the Bikini Atoll—yes, that's where the word "bikini" comes from—the U.S. entered into an agreement with the United Nations to govern the "Trust Territory of the Pacific Islands as a strategic trusteeship territory."

Right.

Let's remember that the United Nations at one point existed largely to serve the needs of the U.S. and the West, whereas now it's a free-for-all of pork and smokescreens. That's several metaphors in one sentence. Fun fact: The United Nations building in New York City is the only place in all of North America where smoking is still permitted indoors.

Anyway, the Trust Territory is composed of two thousand islands spread over 3 million square miles of the Pacific Ocean.

One hundred and five above-ground nuclear tests were conducted there, many of which were of extremely high yield. The largest was the 15-megaton Castle Bravo shot of 1954.

....

33

Turns out the Hotel Deet was a mere half-mile off. A sign pointing away from the chicken path read, THE DEET WELCOMES YOU.

Fucking brilliant.

I turned off and drove along a thin strip of coral dust up to a two-storey cinder-block building that looked like a Soviet gulag from the 1960s, except this one was covered in dead air conditioners and drying laundry, with yet another crazed and snorting tethered pig in the front yard.

As I got out of the car, I heard a familiar voice. "Ray! There you are! How did your epic fuckfest with **LACEY** go?"

Christ, did everyone and his dog know about **LACEY**? I turned around and saw Neal, nut brown, in another of Arnaud du Puis's Paul Smith linen suits. His pant legs were rolled up, he was carrying a pair of five-hundred-quid loafers and he looked, for all the world, like a blue chip film star who didn't do drugs and who had invested wisely in real estate, and who now was taking a bit of time out to do a series of prestige ad campaigns for American Express cards, Tissot-Omega watches and a fundraiser for some ghastly disease mercifully confined to Africa.

"So, why aren't you on the yacht?"

"I was, Ray, but then I got sleepy and a Zodiac kindly ferried me back. Forget about me, though. Tell me more about **LACEY**! Everyone's dying to know how it went. It was Fi's idea to give you two a sex holiday."

Aneurysm II: Return of the First Aneurysm.

"Neal, to be honest, I don't remember anything about the past eight hours. Last thing I remember is reading Spam labels with you in the supermarket. Has anyone blown up New York or London yet?"

"I don't think so. But Atlanta is being evacuated. A lot of the satellites have gone down, and most of the major optical cables have been chopped."

"Fucking hell."

....

Southern Cross Cables to NZ, Hawaii, Fiji and U.S. Mainland
Australia-Japan Cable
Indonesian Sea-Me-We 3 and Jasaurus links
Papua New Guinea APNG-2 link
PPC-1 and Sanchar Nigam links into Guam
Hawaiian Telstra links
Gondwana link from New Caledonia to Australia
Intelsat
Inmarsat
SingTel Optus Earth stations

....

....

Zodiac Marine & Pool is a French company known for their widely used small inflatable boats. The word "ZODIAC" is a registered trademark for rigid-hulled inflatable boats.

We found a patch of shade. "Is this our hotel, then?"

"Best the island has to offer. Not really any worse than a few of the cardboard boxes I've lived in."

"Neal, how can anybody possibly have standards lower than yours?"

"Don't be so quick to judge, Ray. I happen to know that *Monocle* magazine rated the food in the Deet's restaurant as among the world's best Polynesian cuisine."

"Since when the fuck do *you* read *Monocle*, Neal? When you were in Brussels attending a Eurocurrency crisis meeting?"

"*Monocle* is a taste-making forum for global elites. No harm in a common man like me dreaming of one day living inside a stainless steel meat locker furnished with classic Eames chairs. And instead of being fussy and negative, Ray, why don't we go inside and give the food a try?"

We started towards the gulag tower. A thick brown hand inserted a piece of cardboard into a window on the lowest level, reading: RESTAURANT BE OPEN.

"Din-din is served!" Neil announced.

As we headed towards the door, I threw a stick at yet another menacing, feral, tethered pig that, no doubt, considering my sunburned skin, saw me as a walking block of Spam. Something about the Pacific always turns one's thinking to cannibalism in the end.

"Neal," I said as I opened the door, "people here have been calling me *vakubati* and then promptly flipping out and screaming and fleeing my presence. Any idea what that's all about?"

Neal said, "Raymond, *you're* the *vakubati*."

"Please explain."

"*Vakubati* is the Kiribati word for fuckbuddy."

"Since when do *you* know the Kiribati language?"

"Everyone in South Tarawa knows about the *vakubati*, locals and visitors alike. News spread like wildfire."

"How the fuck did I become the fuckbuddy-slash-*vakubati*, or whatever the hell it is?"

"When we were tripping out in the Spam store, Sarah told everyone in the store that you and I were fuckbuddies—cheeky sense of humour that bird's got."

"Go on."

"So the thing is, Neal, the Kiribati blame the world's potential nuclear war on you."

"So then, what—I'm the boogeyman to these people? Why not you, too?"

"Well, Ray, look at the facts: you're bright red, you're a bit on the thin side, you haven't had a shave in a while and, at the moment, you're wearing no shirt and a Gumby hat. It doesn't take too many brains to connect those dots, it doesn't."

"They think *I* started the nuclear fucking war."

"It's human nature to blame someone."

By now we were entering the Deet's dining area: folding aluminum tables and white plastic stacking chairs supplied courtesy of the trash vortex. As there was no staff in view, we sat down and looked at our menus, printed out in Comic Sans font and, to judge by the stains and wrinkles and scuffing, laminated some time back in the Thatcher years.

Tuna Schnitzel
Tuna steak kissed by breadcrumbs,
served with Australian-made potato chips
and cucumber slice.

Tuna Salad
Raw tuna fish with onions in a spicy sauce,
served with crusty bread.

Tuna Tartar
Raw tuna fish minced
with hot spices,
spread onto an inviting garlic bread.

As seen in *Monocle* magazine.
"Globalization is glamorous and good."

34

When no one showed up to take our order, we poked around. The kitchen consisted of a dozen plastic buckets, a small gas stove and shelves holding boxed and tinned items: cocktail sausages, Weetabix, irradiated milk from New Zealand.

"Pass me that opener, Neal. Fancy a few cocktail sausages?"

"Indeed."

We began emptying tins. "Best we wash it down with this canned milk."

"I don't know about milk that's been irradiated, Ray. Doesn't seem right."

"But selling milk in a tin *does* seem right?"

"Good point."

We guzzled the milk supply. Finally I was feeling lucid and in good spirits. "Nothing like having your elevenses at sundown."

"Couldn't agree with you more, Ray."

I touched my head. "Christ, I'm still wearing this fucking Gumby hat."

"I didn't want to editorialize on your style, Ray, but yes, you are."

I removed the Gumby hat and shook it back into the T-shirt it was. Neal stared at it, his eyes goggling as would those of a kitten shown dangling yarn for the first time.

"Ray! That's a Cure T-shirt!"

"Yes, I guess it is."

"Where did you get it?"

"It was in the fuck hut."

"I must have that shirt."

Ahhhh, how interesting to have something Neal really wanted. "No, Neal, no. You can't have this shirt, because it is *mine*." I slipped it on for emphasis, and also to cover my sunburned abdomen.

"The Cure changed my life. I remember that shirt. I almost bought one at their July 1993 outdoor concert in Finsbury Park. It's been one of the great regrets of my life that I didn't buy it. And now, decades later, fate has given me another chance."

"Fate has done no such thing. This is my Cure T-shirt, and you can't have it."

"I remember the complete song list that day: 'Shiver and Shake'; 'Shake Dog Shake'; 'One Hundred Years'; 'Just Like Heaven'; 'Push'; 'Fascination Street'; 'Open'; 'High'; 'From the Edge of the Deep Green Sea'; 'Disintegration'; and 'End.'"

"Fascinating."

"The encore was 'Friday I'm in Love'; 'Three Imaginary Boys'; 'It's Not You'; 'Boys Don't Cry'; 'Fire in Cairo'; and 'A Forest.'"

"Neal, your nostalgia is not going to get you this shirt."

"What *will* get me the shirt?"

Hmmm . . . *brainwave.*

"Neal, I want you to shag **LACEY**. That way I can take the moral high road and dump her for cheating on me."

"I don't know, Ray. **LACEY**'s technically shaggable, but it's just hard to see pictures of her and me together in my head. And I mean, she's also just emerged from an epic fuckfest with you. She's likely worn out."

I reached down and rubbed my stomach. "My, this shirt is in amazing condition considering it's two decades old. It's vintage, not a reproduction. It was probably left here by some Kiwi missionary with retro musical taste and a hankering for life's finer things."

Neal's lips quivered. "Okay, Ray, I'll shag her."

"Good. I'm glad you've come to your senses."

"Now give me the shirt, please."

"Not until the deed is done. And there's one more thing."

Neal's eyes became cold slits. "Yes?"

"I want that piece of red plastic that was hanging from the outdoor eaves back at the grocery store."

"You fucking *bastard*!"

"So I'm a fucking bastard. Big fucking deal."

Suddenly Neal had me face-mushed-down on the kitchen's rattan mat, twisting my arms behind my back.

"You fucking pig!" I yelled. "Let go of me now or I'll bleed all over your precious shirt. I've been known to trigger nosebleeds by willpower alone."

"I agreed to shag **LACEY**, but no, Raymond Gunt got *greedy*."

"Fuck off and die, Neal. My price is my price."

There was a noise in a back hallway, and when Neal turned to see what it was, he gave me enough room to wiggle free and grab a white plastic trash vortex chair.

I whacked him in the face, making his nose fountain with blood.

"I'll fucking *kill* you, Gunt."

"No, you won't, Neal, because if you get blood on this garment, it's officially not collectible anymore, and neither you nor nobody else will ever want it."

Checkmate.

I stepped back. "Now hand me that piece of red plastic and I will hand you your T-shirt. I won't even make you fuck **LACEY** first."

"You are a cruel bargainer, Raymond Gunt."

"Just piss off and give me the plastic."

I removed the shirt while gazing into a salt-crusted old mirror that sat beside the room's principal decoration: an orange and black NO SMOKING sign. I was as red all over as a Halloween devil.

That was when we heard shrieks coming from outside. Neal and I forgot our trade transaction and went to look. A collection of villagers had circled the hotel, armed with baseball bats, car antennas, coconuts and coral chunks. A woman wailed, "*Vakubati! Vakubati!*"

I stormed out to confront them. "Now just one fucking minute!" I yelled. "You have some nerve to try to blame me for the problems of this wretched fucking world."

They chanted: "*Vakubati*, take your dreadful fuck-people and leave our gracious islands now!"

"You have *got* to be kidding."

From behind the angry villagers, I saw two more forms of wrath incarnate emerge: Fiona, dressed as if for tea at Wimbledon, and **LACEY**, still dishevelled after hours of God only knows what unspeakable things we'd done together.

Fiona shouted, "Thanks a fucking lot, Raymond! We finally get to visit Eden, and you get us all kicked out!"

"I did no such thing. These doughy-ankled lagoon rats are living in some ancient era before science or rationality."

Fiona used the same X-ray face she had used when she figured out it was me who'd caused Matt Bradley's death. Her eyes screwed up intensely. "I don't know how, Raymond, but I know, in some way I'm unable to fathom, that it really *was* you who started this nuclear war."

"Fi, are you totally fucking crazy? And how the fuck can you side with these oily trolls at a moment like this?"

"*Did* you, Raymond?"

"Did I what? Start a nuclear war? What the hell is wrong with you?"

"You're not answering my question."

"I don't believe this."

At this point, **LACEY** interjected, "Fi, how did the two of you meet, anyway?"

"How did we meet? Raymond threw an empty lager can at me."

35

Well, then.

We've all been in a pickle at least once in our lives, haven't we? One is born, one grows up. One gets in a pickle. The pickle is resolved and then one dies. *Snap!*

At that point, the Zodiac that had brought Neal to shore offloaded another wave of crew to retrieve their belongings from the hotel, and of course *Stuart* would have to show up just then, Sarah at his side.

"Herry Potter, you asshole—now we have to leave the island because of your fuckheadedness."

"Oh, hello, *Stuart*. I'll thank you not to swear; there are ladies present."

"I'll deal with *you* later," Stuart threatened. "Everyone grab your things and get on the bus to the dock. We're headed to location, and the yacht leaves in one hour!"

As if in a zombie movie, the show's production staff converged around from all directions, thus defusing our confrontation with the locals.

Fiona passed by me, snarling. "Trust me, Raymond, I *will* find out how you started the war."

"I love you, too, Fi."

"Come along, **LACEY**. You can help me pack."

LACEY went past, sniffling. "Raymond, I did things with you that I wouldn't even do with the Russian guys who run the airport limousine service."

Then Sarah approached, her face grave. "Raymond, I heard all about your erotic holiday with **LACEY**. I think it's terrific that you're finding love. You richly deserve it." She sounded like a gracious yet saddened contest loser. *Fuck.* Any chance I might have had with her was out the window. How to undo this mess?

I pleaded my case: "No, Sarah, it wasn't an erotic holiday at all."

Cue the chanting natives: "Dreadful *vakubati*, take your fuckpeople and leave our gracious island, now!"

Sarah made a brave face. "I have to get my things, Raymond."

Being possessionless—I'd long since lost track of whatever I'd brought on this deranged odyssey—I waited out front while people packed. The natives surveyed my every move, brandishing their crude weapons at me. Then I heard a whisper from the front door. It was Sarah. "Raymond, come help me with this."

This turned out to be a wheelbarrow-load of Spam-like tinned meats from China. The images on the labels reminded me of, say, the creatures from the Burgess Shale, magically brought back to life only to be slathered in salted goat gelatin and ruthlessly resealed into rectangular tins.

Oh Christ . . .

I was caught in a Spam spiral: that mystical state of mind where one's brain becomes entirely absorbed by trying to analyze the contents of Spam and/or Spam-like products.

I thought of nipples—the nipples of all races—pressure-packed into convenient 5.5-ounce tins of—

"Raymond?"

"Whuzzat? Oh, sorry, Sarah. I was stuck in a Spam spiral."

"Oh, I've had that happen too. It's awful, but it always goes away."

I stared at the barrow-load of tinned meat. "Sarah, are you sure you want to take this Spam-like food product with us?"

"We'll be needing this. There probably won't be another supply ship for months, if ever." She smiled at me with her heart-melting Sarah smile. "That **LACEY** is one lucky girl. I wish I'd made my move when you were still available."

"**LACEY** and I aren't a couple!" I insisted.

"It's okay. Fiona told me all about your fear of commitment, Raymond. There's no possible doubt in my mind that you and **LACEY** are together for the long haul. I wouldn't dream of doing anything that might derail your tender, newly born love."

There was no doubt in *my* mind: **LACEY** must die.

....

The Burgess Shale Formation, located in the Canadian Rocky Mountains, is one of the world's most celebrated fossil fields. At 505 million years old, it is one of the earliest fossil beds containing the imprints of soft tissue. Many of the animals present in the shale have bizarre anatomical features and bear only the slightest resemblance to other known animals. Examples include *Opabinia,* which had five eyes and a snout like a vacuum cleaner hose; *Nectocaris*, which was either a crustacean with fins or a vertebrate with a shell; and *Hallucigenia*, which walked on bilaterally symmetrical spines. Stephen Jay Gould's book *Wonderful Life* (1989), brought the Burgess Shale fossils to the public's attention. He suggested that the extraordinary diversity of fossils indicates that life forms at the time were much more diverse than those surviving today, and that many of the unique creatures were evolutionary experiments that became extinct.

If we ever wonder what life might look like on other planets, this is where we can see it.

....

"First thing we should do is cover the cans so that the natives don't steal them."

"You're so clever." Sarah grabbed some laundry from a line and gently wrapped the tins. I couldn't help envisioning her swaddling our first child. "There," she said, "Snug as a bug in a rug."

My heart continued to melt.

"Look, there's our shuttle bus."

We walked busward through the protesting carb magnets, with Sarah attempting to bring peace along the way. "Such a lovely place, and your hygiene practices are so refreshing *and* planet-friendly. The ocean really *does* know what to do with poo, doesn't it?"

Safely at the bus, we stowed the entire Spam barrow in a rear luggage compartment, then hopped on.

Fiona was already settled at the back of the bus, deeply engrossed in her iPad screen. Good.

Stuart, still outside, was barking into a military phone: "What do you mean the president wants his Cure T-shirt back? Are these people insane?" He poked a button at the bottom of the phone and hopped inside the bus. He glowered at me. "Oh. I see that Herry Potter is here."

"Yes, yes, yes, Stuart, whatever."

His attention migrated elsewhere. "Cheryl! Where's the shot list for tomorrow morning?"

Sarah was smiling. "It's so sweet to watch you two act like little boys."

"How long have you and Stuart been together?"

"Three years now. Sometimes I wonder where it's all going. He can't seem to make his mind up about things."

The bus was nearly full.

"There are days when I'd really like to maybe start fresh with some new guy, but . . ."

She looked infinitely sad. I took her hand and held it tightly in mine. "Don't worry, Sarah. Things'll all be good in the end."

She started to cry—a brave little tear, one that nearly drowned my soul.

Huh?

What was that?

A tear that nearly drowned my soul?

That was poetry! Real fucking *poetry* coming from me, Raymond Gunt! A total raging poet, like in some crap basement club surrounded by starving unfuckables speaking in tongues. Me! A fountain of poetic shit!

Oi!

So . . .

I made a vow then and there to do anything it took to make Sarah mine.

To the west, out the window, what might possibly have been the airborne remains of Seoul created the most delightful sunset imaginable.

Life is good.

36

Now . . .

I like to think of myself as a kind person. And what is so wrong with being kind? I go through my days trying to do nothing but dispense sweetness and light. Shine, shine, shine! *That Raymond Gunt's a giving soul!* And yet what do I get for my kindness?

There I was, on the bus, off to hook up with the network yacht—easy-peasy—when some troll from catering whisked Sarah away from me to discuss provisioning. Neal came and sat beside me and, as the bus took off, we started discussing the philosophy of love.

"You know, Ray, a real man is not one who can bed ten thousand women but he who can bed one woman ten thousand times."

"Neal, if you're going to mouth inane platitudes like that, I request that you move your endildoed arse to some other seat."

"I just thought it would sound good, like a man on the telly promoting fancy biscuits because . . . because . . . because . . ."

Because just then, the slightly aged but quite amply endowed blonde in front of us removed a shawl to reveal a profoundly unignorable cocoa-coloured skin tag projecting from her shoulder. It was perhaps an inch long, somewhat meaty, with small but distinct little horns on it, shaped like New Zealand's North Island.

"Ray, are you seeing what I'm seeing?"

"Yes, Neal. Yes, I am."

"It's like a nipple gone horribly, horribly wrong."

"Christ, Neal, the last thing I need in my life right now is to have nipples de-eroticized. And yet I can't stop looking."

"But, Ray, its colour, its texture . . ."

Neal was correct: the skin tag indeed resembled a teat of sorts, not entirely Caucasian—perhaps Vietnamese or octoroon? A tiny chocolate filament sprouted from Auckland and glinted in the end-of-day magic light.

"Ray, it's like a biological toggle switch."

"Neal, could you stop making your inner dialogue an outer dialogue?"

"Why don't you flip the toggle switch, Ray?"

"What?"

"Go on, Ray, give it a tickle."

"Neal, are you fucking *mad*?"

"I'll bet you it's one of her erotic fantasies, having a stud muffin like yourself flip her switch a few times in the glow of a Polynesian sunset. I'm a good judge of these things, Ray. I swear, you'd be helping her fulfill her deepest needs."

"Neal, there is no conceivable way that tiny squib is in any way erotic." Staring at the skin tag was rather like being caught in a Spam spiral, except instead of ruining my appetite it was ruining my sex drive. And frankly, it was also deeply creeping me out. It was as if the skin tag had achieved sentience and was staring back at me, plotting my demise.

"Ray, tell you what: if you flip the toggle, I'll give you my piece of red plastic."

"Why don't you just do it yourself, Neal?"

"Because I think *you're* the one who needs some sexual healing, Ray, after your epic fuckfest with **LACEY**. Touching the skin tag will stabilize you."

The skin tag continued to stare at me, cunningly, coldly—trawling through my mind for points of weakness with which to attack me.

Neal continued. "Between you and this sadly disfigured lady in front of us, it's a yawning vortex of sexual neediness."

"Okay. You have a point. But promise me this isn't some sick voyeuristic thing you get off on?"

"I promise."

"No tricks, either—I flip the switch a few times, and that plastic is mine, no catches or further conditions. And I'm still wearing the Cure T-shirt, so you really do want to stay in my good books."

"On my word."

....

An **acrochordon**, also known as a **skin tag** or **fibroepithelial polyp**, is a small benign tumour that develops primarily in areas where the skin forms creases, such as the neck, armpit and groin. Acrochorda are harmless and typically painless, and do not grow or change over time. Tags are typically the size of a grain of rice.

The surface of an acrochordon may be smooth or irregular and is often raised from the surface of the skin on a fleshy stalk called a peduncle.

Skin tags are more common in people who are overweight and in pregnant women. Acrochorda have been reported to occur in forty-six percent of the general population.

Because tags are benign, treatment is unnecessary unless the tags become irritated or present a cosmetic concern. If removal is desired or warranted, a dermatologist or similarly trained professional may use cauterization, cryosurgery, surgical ligation or excision to remove the acrochorda.

They're gross.

....

The way things turned out, you'd think I'd single-handedly gang-raped the woman with the skin tag—Shelley, it turned out her name was. These Americans and their puritanical fucking fussiness. I mean, it's not like I was getting any jollies out of reaching towards the infinitely menacing, cruel and unforgiving incubus of mottled skin that was feeding on her shoulder. And, given the force of evil that was embedded within the vile wattle, it took some guts to do what I did. *And* I might *also* add that I was helping Shelley fulfill a sexual fantasy at the same time. Yes, give, give, give. That's me, Raymond Gunt.

Eventually, with utmost fortitude, I clamped my right thumb and forefinger on Shelley's skin tag just at the moment our bus driver chose to run over a drunken Samoan, who quickly came to reside behind the bus's front right tire. There was a catastrophic bump, and in the blink of an eye, Shelley's skin tag ripped away from her shoulder, prompting her to shriek like a smoke detector. Dazzling Carrie-esque crimson fountains geysered upward. Shelley dashed for the door, as did our driver. I looked at my hand: in the shock of it all, my finger and thumb had seized up, leaving me unable to drop my newly liberated satanic flesh nubbin.

Neal yanked me away from the appalling mess on Shelley's seat back: "Ray, for God's sake, don't get any blood on the Cure shirt."

Shelley was out on the roadside shrieking, as was our driver, who then quickly fled on foot.

The TV production staff couldn't wait to see the carcass beneath us and quickly left the bus like Muppets vacating a vaudeville stage. Fortunately, everyone assumed Shelley had a nosebleed or some other form of collateral damage from the collision and completely ignored her.

Neal whispered, "Ray, maybe Miss Skin Tag doesn't remember what happened—you know—post-traumatic shock from our bus having run over a Samoan."

Beneath the bus, the corpse had an almost cartoon-like dusty tire tread overtop his kidneys and lower back.

"He's a goner, he is," said Neal. "Saw lots of accidents like this back in my paramedic days—mostly after sunset at the end of bank holidays."

"Isn't there anything you can do for him, Neal?"

"Nope. Can't comfort him, because he's dead."

The crew was now photographing the scene with their iPhones. Shelley, thank Christ, had stopped shrieking and joined the rubbernecking crowd, her right hand clamped to the wound on her left shoulder.

Fiona, now out of the bus, dragged her attention away from her phone and was also staring at our dusty, motionless, unfortunate speed bump. She looked towards me, made an *ugh* noise and then went over to Shelley. "You: what happened to your shoulder?"

"I—I used to have a skin tag there, and now it's gone. I've no idea what happened."

"You lost a skin tag in the accident?"

I glanced ever so casually Shelley's way and Fiona caught me. "Raymond Gunt, you come over here right now."

I thought, *You festering twat*, yet I couldn't help but obey.

"What do you know about this woman's shoulder?"

"I beg your pardon?"

Fiona X-rayed my soul. "This woman here—"

"My name is Shelley," Shelley said.

"Shelley here lost a skin tag during the accident, and you were sitting directly behind her."

I played it cool. "I'm sorry to hear that. Nothing too painful, I hope. Nasty things, skin tags. The devil's doorbells."

Shelley stared at me. From within her pain-cramped face, recognition emerged. "Raymond Gunt? *Ray?*"

I was baffled. "Um, yes . . .?"

"It's me, Shelley."

"Shelley . . ." I scoured my memory banks.

"Kodak Shelley. Los Angeles Airport. 1985."

Dear *God* . . . This was the Shelley I'd banged in the executive lounge's men's lav at LAX back in 1985. "Shelley! Yes, Kodak Shelley. Lovely to see you again. How are you?" I was desperately trying to remember that 1985 shag and whether there was anything iffy about it.

"You two know each other?" Fi asked.

"Intimately," said Shelley. "And not only that, after he had his way with me in the airport lounge toilet at LAX, Raymond here stole a set of wide-angle lenses from my display case. I had to replace them, and it cost me eight hundred bucks, and I almost lost my job, too." Shelley's eyes had become snaky and vengeful.

"That was *swag*, for Christ's sake," I protested. "Nobody ever pays for fucking *swag* at conventions. You should have put it on the entertainment tab the way everyone else does."

Shelley raised her bloody hand to slap me, and I reflexively extended my own hand to ward off the blow. My fingers unclenched, revealing the skin tag pasted onto the meat of my thumb. Shelley screamed. "You monster! You stole my goddamn skin tag! I don't believe it!"

Fiona smiled. "I knew it: good old Raymond, wrecking everything again."

Sarah raced over to us as Shelley continued to scream. "Good lord, Shelley, you're hurt—you're bleeding!" She placed a comforting hand on Shelley's unsoiled other shoulder, vibrating with concern. (*Oh! My Sarah! What an angel!*)

Shelley attacked, clawing at me with her warty she-talons. "You fricking ghoul—stealing body parts! What the hell is wrong with a person like you?"

"Jesus, Shelley, I did you a favour."

"What the hell?"

"I removed a piece of possibly carcinogenic tissue from your shoulder. I most likely saved your life, and what do I get from you? Nothing but shit. I'm a hero. I saved you from getting cancer, Shelley, that's right—*cancer!*"

Neal leapt to my defence then, containing her flailing arms in a bear hug. "Best remove that shirt right now, Ray. I can't stop this ticking time bomb forever, and I want my shirt in mint condition."

"Right." I doffed it and handed it to Sarah, who, sensing the need for a collective gear change, said, "Look! Brave and kind Raymond is removing his shirt so he can crawl under the bus and remove the victim!" She smiled at me. "You are a wonder, Raymond Gunt. **LACEY** must be so proud of you."

On cue, **LACEY** entered our charmed circle. "Gallant, isn't he?" She picked up a small chunk of coral and threw it at my chest. "You go, hero boy. Save our day, *vakubati*."

Shelley spat at me: "You *prick*."

Sarah looked at Shelley. "Calm down, Shelley. I'll have my personal assistant, Scott, bring you some pre-moistened towelettes so you can clean yourself up." She pulled a small walkie-talkie from her purse. "Scott, can you bring me the tub of baby wipes right now?"

Scott was five feet away. "Roger." He walked three steps towards us and removed the plastic tub of wipes from his knapsack. He handed them to Shelley.

Sarah said, "Sweetie, don't worry too much about the tropical parasites that sleep inside the fecal dust along the roadside. What matters most is that you feel fresh and comparatively safe."

....

Lymphatic filariasis
Dengue virus type 4
Soil-transmitted helminth infection
Parastrongylus cantonensis
Plasmodium berghei
Trypanosoma cruzi
Leishmaniasis
Schistosomiasis
Multidrug-resistant falciparum
Simulium (Gomphostilbia) palauense

Stuart approached. "Gunt, get that goddamn corpse out from under the bus or we're never going to get to the fricking dock before it's totally dark out."

Suddenly all eyes were on me. For better or worse, I had to lug the barbecue-grade carcass out from under the bus. Christ, it was like trying to drag a concrete-filled grand piano across a sandy beach. But after a sweat-soaked few minutes, the job was done.

Stuart barked, "Okay, everyone back in the bus."

Sarah held up her hand. She said, "Scott, write a note to the authorities and attach it to the body with gaffer tape. His family will want to know what happened."

"And serve him for dinner, too," I added.

Sarah giggled. "You're such an imp, Raymond. And possibly correct."

Scott's note:

We ran over him by accident.
We will file incident report with local authorities
*   later.*
Have an awesome day.
Scott
☺

He taped it onto the speed bump's chest, and then we hopped onto the bus.

I must say, I never paid too much attention in history class when they taught about the fight for civil rights in Mississippi in the 1960s, but for the first time in my life, I was able to sense how a black man might have felt accidentally walking into a ballroom cotillion of virginal, creamy white Daughters of the Confederacy[3] in Tupelo, Mississippi, in 1961. As I got onto the bus, my busmates silently simmered at me.

Shelley led the attack: "I can't believe you stole my skin tag. That is so disgusting. Why would anyone even *do* that?"

I glanced at my thumb, where it remained, stuck with blood. I peeled it away—it felt like masking tape—and discreetly dropped it on the floor.

"You are the worst human being I have ever met," Shelley went on. "The. Worst. Person. Ever. And what in hell's name are you even doing on our production bus? Don't tell me you're involved in this show!"

Stuart piped up, "He's a B-unit cameraman."

"Where is he slated to stay?"

A guy with a clipboard volunteered, "South island camera camp B."

"Wrong. He's staying on the yacht," said Shelley.

Stuart was taken aback. "The yacht?"

"Yes. In room seventeen."

"Ahhh . . ." Stuart smiled. "Perfect. Oh, and by the way, people, this is also the pinhead who spelled the 'Harry' in 'Harry Potter' with an 'e'."

"I can't believe anyone could be that stupid," Shelley said.

A chant began: "Pot-*ter*. Pot-*ter*. Pot-*ter*."

Scott was in the driver's seat and the bus belched forward. Fuck these people. I was sick of them and hungry, too. "Neal, we never had a proper dinner in the end. Is there anything to eat on this fucking bus?"

---

3. *I'm sure these days they're now called something horrible like* "U.S. Power Tweens."

Always prepared, our Neal. He tossed me a cardboard meal box that contained a vacuum-wrapped cheese block manufactured 60,000 miles away in a Republican cheese factory in Nebraska, a cellophane packet of saltine crackers, an unripe banana and a—dear-fucking-God, surely not. My brain couldn't absorb what I had just seen—and once seen, it could never be unseen. There in the box was a . . .

. . . .

A **knork** (the "k" is silent) is a hybrid form of cutlery that combines the cutting capability of a knife with the spearing capability of a fork in a single powerful utensil. The word "knork" is a portmanteau of "knife" and "fork." Typically, one or both of the outer edges of a knork are sharpened to allow the user to cut food.

An advantage of the knork is that people with one arm can use it easily. It is also sometimes known as a Nelson fork, after Horatio Nelson, who used this type of cutlery after losing his right arm in 1797.

. . . .

"Look, Ray—it's a knork!"

I was speechless.

Neal prattled on, "I've always wanted to see one in real life. It's sister cutlery to the spork, and it's sometimes called a Nelson fork, after Horatio Nelson, who used this type of cutlery after losing his right arm in 1797."

"Fuck me with a power tool, I *would* end up saddled with a living Wikipedia."

"Nothing wrong with displaying a bit of knork spirit, Ray."

I could feel my eyes bulging from my skull. "Neal, for fuck sake, if you keep on discussing hybrid cutlery, I'll have you ball-gagged and tossed off the yacht like a Belarussian hooker."

"I'm just saying, Horatio Nelson was a smart man, Ray. But okay, then, seeing as you're being ungrateful about your snack pack, maybe you'd like some trail mix instead." He took my box and handed me a foil packet.

"That's very gracious of you, Neal."

I grabbed the bag, ripped it open and chugged its entire contents, having only millionths of a second to think the two fateful words that mar my life on earth: *macadamia nuts*.

"Whoops!" said Neal. "My mistake. Sweet dreams and do try to be a bit nicer to me when you wake up."

Blackness.

37

When I oozed my way back into consciousness, I felt a rotating motion gently scrubbing my gentleman's region. *God bless the South Seas!*

The warm, smooth finger teased its way towards my mangina—*ahhhh*. My eyelids squidged open a bit, and the truth was revealed: Billy, Fiona's assistant, last seen the previous week in her Covent Garden offices, was giving me a sponge bath wearing rubber gloves and using a foam scrub brush with an extended handle like they use in prison kitchens filled with all those rapey-looking cooks.

"What the fuck! Billy, get your hands off my nether bits!" My head felt like two train cars colliding.

"Oh. Good morning, Raymond. I'd like to point out that my hands aren't touching you. All the tea in China couldn't—well, whatever. Not to worry. Fiona and I drew straws, and I got the shorty, so here I am playing Nurse Jackie. Had a nice little coma, did we?"

"How long have I been out of it?"

"Maybe two days."

"Where am I?"

"The luxurious TV network yacht, obviously."

I tried to reach for a towel to cover my nether bits, but an IV line got in the way. "Jesus, Billy, why are you washing me?"

"If you must know, darling, you gave birth to a bowling ball of fecal matter a few hours back, and its odour got into the ventilator shaft and began to . . . *infuse* the racquetball court next door. People were retching."

"There's a racquetball court next door? A yacht has a racquetball court?"

"That's just the start of it. Anyway, your close personal friend, Stuart—what on earth did you do to him to make him so nasty about you? Anyway, Stuart demanded it be dealt with, so here I am." He rinsed his scrub brush into a plastic bucket.

"Jesus, stop touching me, Billy."

"You'll notice that when I absolutely have to make contact with my hands, I'm touching you with the outsides of my fingers, not the insides."

"There's a difference?"

"Science has shown that it is impossible to be sexually aroused by outside-finger stimulus. Homeland Security requires all their airport security inspectors to use only the outsides."

I couldn't believe the mess my body had made. "Christ, can't they have a slave or a poor person do the shit jobs like this?"

I got a face from Billy. "Darling, we are now in a place with neither law nor order. And with the global nuclear kerfuffle, all the local help have jumped ship and are headed back to Bonriki, though heaven only knows why. My theory is that in a life or death crisis, one must find one's local tribal chief, whoever he may be, and make him happy. In my case, this means Stuart, so to please *him*, I am cleaning up *you*. Truly marvellous—except for this room, here: seventeen. Not the best room, really."

I looked down at myself. *Christ.*

Billy said, "What did you eat, Raymond Gunt? Iron filings? Superglue? Higgs bosons? Nineteenth-century German furniture?"

"Do you have to be such a ripping cumfart about my situation? I'm not the one on hands and knees in Hampstead Heath baying for boy cherry."

Billy looked insulted. "First of all, *ick*, and second of all, I'll have you know I am a bear and prefer people who are age-appropriate, and third, if *anyone* around here is into age-inappropriate nookie, it would be *you*. It must be awful knowing that you're breaking all human taboos every time you get a hard-on."

"A bear? What's a bear?"

Billy lost his temper. "Raymond, enough! Let me finish up here and we'll go our separate ways."

I could feel flakes of peeling skin on my sunburned face. "Christ. Hand me a mirror."

Billy rummaged in his aubergine murse and pulled out a compact. "Take one look and you'll see that in your current state you'd be lucky to bang a goat, let alone a human being, Raymond."

A goat? *Uh-oh* . . . "Have you been spending time with Neal?"

"Neal? No, but I can dream." He lifted my leg. "Just let me do a final bit of mopping up here." He scrubbed me until I stung, then vigorously rinsed his brush. "But Neal's people did leave you a note. Here it is."

Neal's *people?*

Billy handed me page 6 of the daily shooting script, on the back of which Neal had written:

Ray,

Oh. My. Fucking. God.
     I'm stationed in the North Island camp, but we
call it Thong Kong. Ray, honestly, pussy grows on trees
here. I don't know how the crew gets anything done in a
day. You have to make it over here as soon as possible.

Your pal,
Neal

PS: How was your nap? ;)

I was desperate. "Billy, how do I get myself over to this Thong Kong place?"

"Oh. So you want a favour now, do you?" He performed a Dita Von Teese move while removing his rubber gloves. "I think not."

"Oh, come on, Billy, you know we're pals."

Billy turned his back on me and started bagging all of his cleansing equipment in a black bin liner. He then paused to inspect the IV drip in my right hand.

"Come on, Billy, we've known each other such a long time. Take me to the North Island."

"You're barely out of your coma. And I have to think about my image. I can't be seen to be hanging out with the uncool kid." With this, he finished bagging his gear. "Ciao, darling. Wiping up after you even once is more than enough for a lifetime." He closed the door, taking with him the bag filled with my toxic waste.

I climbed off the gurney, feeling a bit wobbly, and looked around the room. Private single bunk on the port side. A small window with a pleasant tropical view. In the sky above were clouds reminiscent of exquisite, flawless, snow-drivenly pure, fluffy white peekaboo panties.

Ahhh . . . the South Pacific.

Thumps on the other side of the wall above me snapped me out of my reverie. The racquetball court? I removed my IV and took a quick shower in a bathroom roughly the size of a piece of carry-on luggage, and then chugged a gallon of warm water from the tap. Fortunately, the chap who'd inhabited my room before me had left behind a trove of garments of reasonable enough taste. Unfortunately, he was twenty-five percent larger than me, so that once togged up I resembled a sort of serial killer version of the Scarecrow from *The Wizard of Oz.*

As suddenly as an earthquake, the most gut-snarlingly terrifying engine kicked into gear above my head. What the fuck?

Wait—room seventeen. Maybe this was why nobody wanted it. Well, I was going to put a stop to whatever maniac was using an industrial gravel crusher directly above my room. I headed out. As my door clicked shut, I realized I had no key. *Crap.*

I inspected my new neighbourhood, and it was like a hotel, really: creamy wool carpeting, light coming from sources recessed into walls, and framed photographs of TV network plutocrats holding up jumbo marlins. My room was alone on the port side. The other rooms, to starboard, were luxurious and spacious to judge from the generous gaps between the doors.

The noise from the gravel smasher above me grew in its anger. Fucking hell. I found a staircase and climbed it. Pushing open a door, I saw a row of industrial-sized washing machines—huge honkers that could easily accommodate your next-door neighbour's Fiat, let alone a boatload of beshatted sheets. I wasn't in there for five seconds before a Samoan cheerfully passed me, headed out the door; he threw me a fob with several keys as he went. "This laundry room now be your shit job, not mine. You have a happy and gracious apocalypse."

"Thank you very much."

The door closed behind him. This was my chance to find clothes that might fit me better. I pushed an OFF button and opened the door to what turned out to be a dryer holding a load of laundry mixed in with kitchen trays, cafeteria-sized cans of Heinz ketchup and beans and, well, just about anything one might find unbolted on a glamorous TV network yacht. Good on my Samoan friend for getting a bit of fun out of his sack-of-shit life situation.

What now? I went back down to my floor. None of the keys worked in my door, so I embarked on a fishing expedition along the hallways to see if any of the keys worked in any of the doors, and I was richly rewarded. At the front of the boat, I entered a stunningly designed glassed-in area that stopped me with its beauty: perhaps Brad Pitt and Angelina Jolie might live in a place like this. Rare woods and sleek crystal light fixtures, exotic potted ferns and expensive-looking canvases on every wall. A tray rested on a polished marble side table, and on it sat several bottles of chilled Sauvignon Blanc and six glasses. *Time for a toast to myself*, I quite reasonably thought, for having navigated yet another level of the TV network lifestyle.

Raymond, you're a survivor, you are.

Why, thank you, Raymond, I was just thinking that myself.

Delicious wine, isn't it, Raymond?

Why, yes it is, Raymond, yes it is.

I think we all need quiet little moments like this to remind ourselves of how far we've come in life. The moment didn't last long, however. An American male voice came from beyond a set of glass doors to a patio area on the deck, intruding on my almost religious state of bliss.

38

"Oh, fuck me ragged!" A squash racquet narrowly missed my wineglass. "Herry Fuckbuddy Potter, what the *hell* are *you* doing in my suite? And dressed like the Hillside Strangler. Get out *now*, before I call security. How did you get in here?"

"Stuart, calm down. The door over there was open," I lied. "I'm just doing some reconnaissance. A mutinous Samoan has just trashed the ship's laundry. I wanted to make sure he didn't go further."

"He *what*?"

"Stuart? Stuart, honey? Who's that?" Sarah's voice.

I called out, "It's just me, making sure the ship is all shipshape."

Sarah came in through the glass doors, magnificent in a knit bikini, her limbs glistening from a recent application of tanning oil. "You're on your legs again! I'm so glad. Have a glass of wine with us."

"Sarah, what do you possibly see in this pathetic English gimp?"

Sarah stared sternly at her loathsome boyfriend.

"Raymond has rescued me twice from dangerous situations with highly menacing men. You should give him a handshake, Stuart, not your scary outdoor shoo-the-raccoons-away voice."

Stuart could only acquiesce to his goddess. "Right. Pour yourself a fucking drink and then leave." He stalked out, vibrating with rage. My wineglass became a goblet filled with my enemy's tears.

"Just ignore him," Sarah said soothingly. "He's in a state because so many of the locals have abandoned ship and the production. We'll never get the series shot at this rate. But at least the cast arrived, although your ex-wife had to go back and find some replacements."

It was most unlikely that Fi would screw up on her job, the one thing that meant anything to her. "Were some of the contestants unfu—*inappropriate*?"

"No, she did a great job, but a bunch of them caught a wicked strain of norovirus in the LAX waiting lounge while it was shut down.

I'd forgotten the nuclear war. "Right, right—nuclear war—how's all that going?"

"Nothing new, just all these countries being childish."
She topped up my glass.
Ahhhh . . .

I felt statesmanlike discussing important current affairs with Sarah. I wondered how far this magic moment would take us until . . . fucking hell, I remembered waking up to **LACEY** in the fuck hut beside that ghastly poo-ous lagoon, the woman's eyes like two drainholes sucking everything good and joyous from the world.

Sarah chose that moment to add to my pain. "You'll be happy to hear that your **LACEY** is fine. She's in the

South Island camp. You must be aching to see her." She
sipped her drink. Were her eyes actually filled with regret?
She raised a glass. "To you and **LACEY** and a future of
perfect sex and happiness together with no one else except
just the two of you, forever and ever and ever and ever."

"Uh, it really wasn't like that at all, Sarah. In fact,
I don't remember what happened."

"Just a minute, Raymond. I'm buzzing." Sarah removed
the tiniest and slenderest mobile phone from her lady's
region. "Hmmm. Right. Okay. Not to worry. See you in
five." She hung up. "Raymond, want to come with me to
the North Island camp?"

O.

M.

F.

G.

Thong Kong.

"Why, um, yes. Neal's over there, isn't he?"

"Indeed he is, poor fellow."

"Poor fellow?"

"Sprained his ankle. It must hurt like the dickens.
Come on. We have to meet the Zodiac right away. Chug
the rest of your drink and we're off."

I chugged, then grabbed the bottle.

39

A minute later we were climbing into the Zodiac bound for the North Island—me!—a man of the world on a speedboat, squiring such a glorious humpcrumpet as Sarah to a turquoise lagoon populated by TV industry bigwigs and Neal's own personal sex ranch. *Yessiree, nothing could possibly go wrong on a beautiful day like today.*

And then we landed and . . . nothing went wrong!

The North Island camp was largely empty. Fiona had delivered the replacement contestants, and shooting had begun on the South Island.

Sarah vanished to do her urgent business, leaving me to search for Neal.

Hmmmm. If Neal had injured his ankle, he couldn't be working on the shoot. Wait a second: Neal had no actual *job* here on the island. *I* was the one the network had hired.

I looked up a small hill (elevation: 3 feet above sea level) and noticed a lovely little bungalow in the Bahamian style: solid typhoon-proof construction tastefully camouflaged in turquoise paint with pink storm shutters, graced by butterfly palms and a zoo of flowering plants. A chill ran down my spine: *That fucker.*

I stormed up the rise and banged on the door. "Neal, I know you're in there. Don't try to pretend you aren't. This is me, Raymond."

The door was opened by some lopsided gronk who I could tell immediately was a cameraman.

"Yes?" The gronk's burliness shielded the house from my entry.

"I'm Raymond Gunt. Tell Neal I want to speak with him."

The cameraman called over his shoulder. "Some guy here says his name is Raymond Cunt. He wants to talk to you." There came a muffled reply, and he turned back to me. "Right. You can come in."

I entered the most beautiful house I've ever seen. Cut flowers, sofas upholstered with the hides of near-extinct animals, marble floors. The walls dripped with paintings of Tahitian birds offering you their melon breasts on a plate along with hibiscuses and mango wedges. But by far the most overwhelmingly desirable aspect of this house was the utterly silent and stunningly effective air conditioning. Fuck *me.* This was heaven.

I headed off in the direction from which I'd heard Neal's voice. I found him in a room at the back. The sun-proof shades on the windows were drawn, and the room was rather dark. Neal was in striped pajamas adrift on a duvet surrounded by massive pillows while a muted TV set displayed a compilation of Australian rugby brawls. On his bedside were magnums of undrunk champagne and platters of sliced cold cuts and French cheeses.

"Raymond. You finally made it."

"Neal, good God. What's happened to you?"

"A bit of a sprain in my ankle, I'm afraid."

"That's all?"

"You know, Ray, you could have a little empathy for a friend in a bad situation."

"How is this bad, Neal? You're ensconced in a tableau that's a cross between a *Hello!* Magazine home visit and Prince Harry's trip to Las Vegas." I plucked some capicola from his snack platter, along with a slab of wonderfully ripe Camembert. "But where the fuck is all the pussy you were talking about?"

"Oh, that."

"What do you mean, '*Oh, that*'?"

"It's not just the ankle, Ray."

"Oh?" Suddenly I felt like a bit of a shit as I poker-facedly waited for Neal to tell me he had inoperable leprosy or one of those no-hoper diseases with its own dedicated coloured lapel ribbon. "Go on."

"I've got pussy fatigue, Ray."

My eyeballs exploded.

"It's what happens when you have too much sex too quickly, Ray. Surely you've had it before."

"I have never in my life even heard of pussy fatigue, Neal, and I seriously doubt it exists. You have no idea how hard I worked to get here to Thong Kong from the yacht, and now you tell me you're *pussied out?*"

"It's a real condition. Google it."

"You know darn well there's no Internet because of the nuclear war. You just don't want to share."

"That's a bit harsh, Ray. I'd be happy to share, except the ladies have all gone off on a healing retreat this afternoon."

I was so stricken by this news that tiny convulsed dinosaur noises emerged from my choked larynx.

Neal went on. "I don't think they had dick fatigue— I think it's more of a spiritual cleansing. Glorious girls, though. So giving. So concerned about my pleasure, never theirs. And their energy! Boundless. When they're not servicing me, they're off in the kitchen making me snacks or giving me foot rubs to get me through the worst of my sprained ankle. Oh, look." He pointed to the TV screen, which displayed the messy aftermath of a particularly forceful brawl. "You can see the bone sticking out of that bloke's leg there. Poor fucker. Good thing he's not in Bonriki, though. He'd be on the spit in seconds. Care for some champagne, Ray?"

....

Vitamin Supplement for Pussy Fatigue

Below are pussy fatigue–related alternative medicine supplements and vitamins. Also explore information on treatment with, health benefits of and side effects from pussy fatigue products. Uses vary, but may include boostiing energy, enhancing immune function, and increasing stamina. All are non-FDA-reviewed or –approved, natural alternatives to use for fatigue and vitamin deficiency.

Energane
Anti-Fatigue Formula (120 caps)

Super Zeaxanthin with Lutein Meso-zeaxanthin
Life Extension (60 softgels)

Fatigued to Fantastic! Adrenal Stress-End
Enzymatic Therapy (60 caps)

This is real.

40

"Well, Neal, you certainly seem to have landed on your feet here, even with a sprained ankle. How, exactly, did you sprain it, anyway?"

"Come on, Ray, don't be a dick. You could even move in, if you wanted. There's a nice little hut out back I use as a storeroom. It's a bit small, and you'd have to move some tinned goods and a deep-freeze to fit in a cot, but it's a big step up from one of the tents in the crew village. Those tents give me the chills. Hermit crabs'll come in at night and eat your face off."

I remained disgusted. "How the *fuck* did you manage to become Boss Hogg here? How the *fuck* do you manage to bag the only decent air-conditioned accommodation between Guam and Bora Bora?"

"This house is a legacy of the people's princess, it is. Brings a tear to my eye."

My attention was temporarily sidelined by some truly astonishing Brie and a mound of pâté, while Neal fast-forwarded through the DVD. The sight of so many Australians rankled me. "Fucking Aussies. Fucking Kiwis.

Smug, smug, smug. *We're so violent! Look at us! Fight fight fight! We have vibrant little economies shielded from pollution and immigration, and our restaurants are really good.* Fucking Kiwis. Fucking Aussies."

"Mind your language, Ray."

"Have you turned into a fucking American?"

"Ray, we're in *Princess Di*'s house."

"What?"

"This was going to be Princess Di's sanctuary from the world. One of her many rich boyfriends built it just for her. The most perfect house on the planet, as far away as it is geographically possible to be from intrusive cameramen."

I looked at Neal with my coldest death-ray eyes. "Neal, are you rubbishing my occupation? My very way of making a living?"

"Ray, I'm not saying it was you *in particular* who murdered Diana."

"Thank you. Thank you very much. I'm glad you hold me in such high esteem."

"But every time I make love in here, I can't help feeling a pang in my heart. She was so young. So good. Murdered by the media."

"Neal, I hate to break the news to you, but you don't have pussy fatigue. You have displaced royal bang syndrome."

Neal stared at me goggle-eyed.

"I'll explain it to you: you live in a cardboard Samsung box in a West London alley and yet you *really* want to get it on with some rich titled piece. Except you can't— you live in a cardboard fucking box—so instead you bang every restaurant hostess from Heathrow to Shepherd's

Bush who takes pity on you. But it's not the same. Is it? *Is it,* Neal?"

Neal, of course, was now bawling. "You're right, Ray. It's not. I don't want to fuck non-royals. Not in my heart."

"No, you don't."

"No. I want to fuck the people's princess. Except she's gone. It's like since 1997 I've been adrift on an asteroid, being bombarded by non-royal pussy at every turn, and it's driving me mad! *Mad,* I say."

"Excellent." I rubbed my hands. "We're making progress here."

Right then Sarah walked in. Christ, just what I needed: Sarah to see Neal all vulnerable and needy in precisely the way women find irresistible.

"Neal, how's your ankle?"

"Oh, hi, Sarah," said Neal from within his silk sheets, looking nauseatingly like a puppy. "I'm getting by, I suppose."

Sarah glanced at me, her expression saying, *Is there something I need to know?*

I shrugged. "Neal here is mourning Princess Diana."

"Oh, Neal," Sarah gently remonstrated. "That was so long ago. She needs peace now. She really does. And we all need to move on . . . individually and as a society."

"You think so?"

"I *know* so, Neal."

Neal wore a face of profound sadness. "You're American, Sarah, so you'll never know what it was like to have Diana as your princess . . . your *very own* princess."

"But I *do* read magazines—at least, I used to, before the Internet. And if Di's wedge-cut hairdo didn't change the way the women in my hometown looked at both themselves and at royalty, then nothing did. She was a force of nature."

"Seriously? In the United States, too? Her hair was her trademark, you know."

"Oh, I know. People think Americans are morbidly obese Wal-Mart shoppers who willfully undereducate their young people just so they can save a few extra dollars to pay for their five-ton recreational vehicles, but Americans are *more* than that, Neal."

"Really?"

"Yes, *really*. Americans are . . ."

I swear that if real life could ever break into a song and dance number, that would have been the moment.

"Americans are . . ."

Neal was staring at Sarah wide-eyed, as if waiting for her to confirm whether fairies were real.

"Americans are . . . basically Englishmen with the English part removed."

"Yes?" Neal sat up on the bed, clearly still in suspense. "What else?"

Sarah paused to think. "Americans are . . ."

Needy glances were exchanged in all directions.

Her face brightened. "Americans are the people who watch the TV show we are currently producing on this very island! Isn't that something?"

Silence. Neal slumped back on his pillows.

Sarah looked crushed by her failure—and touchingly demure. "I don't know what to say about Americans, Neal. They'll do anything for no reason whatsoever and go down in flames smiling at the TV camera while doing it. It's kind of awesome, but it worked much better when there were only a few million of us instead of 350 million. There's not much left to consume. In fifteen years, we turn into India. We're a catastrophe in the making."

Neal looked unutterably sad—and sympathetic. Sarah looked like she was melting. Ho. Ly. Fuck. Neal and Sarah were having a moment of real connection. This was intolerable.

"Neal, about my Cure T-shirt . . ."

"What about it, Ray?"

"May I please have it?"

"I don't have your shirt, Ray."

"Now, now, don't be coy. Just tell me where it is, and I'll fetch it and pretend you never brazenly lied to me like you just did."

"I didn't take your shirt, Ray. You gave it to Sarah, remember?"

"Oh. Right. I did." *Fuck*.

"And I gave it to Fiona," said Sarah. "I hope that's okay. She looked so sad, having to jet back to do the recasting. I thought the shirt would be a nice pick-me-up, although I had to Google the Cure to find out who they were."

"*I*—" I was livid, but couldn't let on.

"Fiona's back," said Neal. "She'll probably be resting up in the tent city."

"You should go visit her, Raymond. I know she still has strong feelings for you," Sarah said.

"I'm sure she does."

Mental images of Fiona's warty face quickly made me remember why I was really there on the North Island:

Thong Kong and the promise of unlimited pussy. I felt conflicted because I had genuine feelings for Sarah, yet I also still wanted a full-on highly lubricated orgy. I sighed. Life does throw us these cruel existential puzzles.

Sarah had to leave. "Bye, fellas. I'm off to tame the beast!"

I was unsure what she meant, but whoever the beast was, I would love to be him, being tamed by Sarah.

41

"Sarah's a nice girl, Ray. You sweet on her?"

"Neal, I came here for Thong Kong, and I want it now! I want acres of throbbing, needy cocktail-bunny quim. I want—wait—I think I *am* sweet on Sarah."

"Well, she's a keeper, she is. Just like that **LACEY** of yours."

"**LACEY** is not *mine*, Neal. Why on earth does everyone think we're life partners?"

"*You're* the one who had the epic fuckfest with her."

"Neal, there's just something not right in the head with **LACEY**. The only thing you can do to fix a girl like her is go back in time to the age of fourteen, or whenever it was, and unmolest her or whatever it was that happened to her—but you can't really do that, so instead we end up with a world of **LACEY**s, wasting valuable food and oxygen and causing massive problems within the service industry."

"I hear there's a sacrificial rock nearby. Want to go see it? I need to exercise a bit to help the sprain. Could be fun—a small hike, nature, coconuts . . ."

"Neal, you're trying to change the subject. I want a pussy blizzard and instead you offer me a field trip to see a *rock*?"

"Touch of culture never hurt anyone."

"And how did they ever get a rock onto this island anyway? The whole place is made of coral."

"See, Ray—makes you want to investigate, doesn't it?"

I sighed. "I suppose so. Get out your cane and we'll go see this magical stone."

Neal quickly donned another of Arnaud du Puis's linen outfits. "Some people say the rock was delivered here by space aliens, Ray."

"You have got to be fucking kidding me."

We headed out the door into the perpetually hot, wet terry towel of a day. The idea of a sacred rock made me think of Stonehenge and alien theories about it. "Stonehenge being designed by aliens is crap, Neal. Think about it: aliens establish contact with earthlings and instead of giving us something useful, like mathematics, wheels or the power of flight, they decide instead to give us *large rocks*?"

"Never thought of it that way, Ray."

We rounded a corner. Neal's face lit up. "We're here!"

I looked at the rock. It was a rock. I hated it. "You lead me to believe we're off to see Stonehenge, and instead all I see is *this*?"

"Ray, I think you oversold it to yourself. I only said it was a rock. Even still, it's sort of awe-inspiring. Reminds us that we're all made of stars."

"It's a fucking rock!" I kicked it, which was a stupid idea. I hopped about for a bit on one foot, shrieking.

"The gods are punishing you for mocking their sacred rock."

I literally screamed at Neal, "I don't fucking care about some fucking rock!"

"Temper, temper. Come back to the house and I'll find you some painkillers."

I felt a rare pang of remorse for screaming at Neal.

"Some painkillers might be rather nice."

Back at the house, Elspeth and Tabs greeted us at the front door, dressed in Playboy Bunny costumes. At last, the gods were smiling on me.

Then I remembered: didn't Neal owe me that piece of red plastic? *That fucker.*

....

Stonehenge is a prehistoric monument located in the English county of Wiltshire. It is composed of two rings of standing stones set within the earth. The site is surrounded by hundreds of burial mounds, known as barrows.

The smaller, inner circle was built between 2400 and 2200 BC. Some of its original stones have been removed, some have fallen over and other missing stones have been cut up and used for other construction purposes by subsequent generations. The stones weigh up to 4 tons each and were quarried around 230 miles away in the Preseli Hills of southern Wales.

The larger, outer circle is estimated to be about five hundred years younger than the inner ring. Its stones weigh up to 50 tons each. They are sandstone erratics, which can be found scattered all over the English chalk downs. They are likely to have been transported to the site from the neighbouring Marlborough Downs, 25 miles to the north.

Stonehenge was completed around 1500 BC. It had fallen into a state of obscurity and disrepair, and in 1982 was slated to be torn down to make way for a housing subdivision until the stone grouping was repopularized by the beloved 1984 cult film *This Is Spinal Tap*.

I decided I'd be gentlemanly in front of the ladies. I said, "Hello, ladies."

"Hello to you, too, Raymond," Tabs said. "Is Neal filling you in on the excitement of island life?" She had become slutty perfection indeed. My, how quickly that doe-eyed, fresh-faced thing had gone native.

"Yes, I suppose he is."

Neal's face was childlike. "We went to visit the sacrificial rock."

Elspeth squeaked, "No! You shouldn't be up and about." Her eyes were moist and wide, as though she were worried about a wounded kitten.

"Thanks, Elspeth. But a short walk is good for a sprain. I didn't want the blood pooling."

"Neal," I said, "there's just one thing. A few days ago, back on the bus, we made a deal about that piece of red plastic."

"Indeed we did, Ray."

"Excellent. So hand it over and I'll consider us square."

"Oh, um . . . you see." Neal and the girls exchanged guilty looks. "Your piece of red plastic. Right."

"So you *do* acknowledge that it rightfully belongs to me."

"Oh, no question, Ray. You earned it fair and square for removing Shelley's skin tag, bloodbath and all."

We lapsed into awkward silence. As I am known to be debonair at times, I thought I'd say something witty. "Come on, then, you didn't do something stupid and stuff it up your arse, did you?"

Hydraulic jackhammers couldn't have roused the trio more quickly. "*Who told you!?*"

"Ha, ha. Yes, yes. Good fun. Good fun. Give me my plastic, Neal."

They stared at me. It was sinking in: Neal actually *had* stuck my sacred plastic up his arse.

"Neal, tell me this isn't true."

"Now, Ray, you need to know—"

"Know what? What could explain this?"

"Here's the thing, Ray. I didn't stick it up my arse to *keep* it from you. I stuck it up my arse because . . ."

"Yes?"

"Because Elspeth thought it was just the right size and shape for a ripping good prostate massage."

"She *what?!*"

"Really did the trick, too, I must say." Neal winked at the blushing Elspeth.

I was speechless. Who wouldn't be?

"And then it got stuck in there sideways and, as you know, I developed pussy fatigue. I might be able to remove it, but the rectal trauma could be horrific. I believe I should leave it there until it vacates the premises naturally."

"Neal, you are going to take a pair of giant forceps, right here and now, and pry my much-deserved treasure from your butt."

Everyone giggled.

"Just what is so funny?"

Elspeth said, "Just sounded sort of gay is all—you prying your treasure from Neal's bumhole."

"I'm so glad I was able to lighten the mood."

Neal looked at me with sad eyes. "Doctor's orders. I'll keep you posted, Ray."

Fucker.

And that's when things stopped being merely bad and became catastrophic.

* * *

Dear The Gods,

Yes, it's me! Yes, that's right, Raymond Gunt. Hope you've been well lately, causing a few storms, frightening the occasional simple village folk . . . life's great when you're The Gods. Thunder! Lightning! Fucking irreparably with Raymond Gunt's life! Whoops . . . did that slip out? Sorry. Feeling a bit emotional is all, but I was wondering, now that we're having a small chat, could you focus your attentions on the people around me, rather than on me? Not that I want others to suffer. More like I, myself, would just like to live in a bit of comfort. If that means a lessened quality of life for those around me, so be it. As you can see, I am a reasonable man.

Yours,
Raymond Gunt

* * *

42

So, here's the thing.

Having adjusted somewhat to the fate of my red plastic, I was going about my day, having adventures like any of us do—in this case, contemplating a not unpleasant *ménage à trois* with Elspeth and Tabs (*Hooray! Finally! Took long enough!*)—when a sound from the tent area, and from my deepest memories, ripped through my soul like an industrial meat slicer.

"Raymond Gunt? Raymond, are you here? I know you are. I can smell fear in the air." It was a woman's voice, crusty and loveless, seasoned by a lifetime trapped on a conveyor belt of fags and discount booze.

Neal, Tabs and Elspeth stared at me with raised eyebrows. All colour must surely have drained out of my face, sunburned or not.

The voice continued, "Or should I say Herry Potter? How the fuck could anyone be stupid enough to spell 'Harry Potter' with an 'e'?"

"Anyone you know?" said Neal.

"You feeling okay, Ray?" asked Elspeth.

From around a coconut bush appeared the testicle-congealing slag known as my mother, dressed in the shabbiest of high-street summer style, smoking two cigarettes, her pair of bingo wings flapping, looking for all the world as though she'd just popped out the front door ready for a day of shoplifting with her best friend, Sheila.

"There you are, Raymond. Fiona said you'd be here."

Fucking hell. This is just the sort of thing Fiona would do, the miserable bitch.

Neal and the two girls wore the innocent but entitled expressions of car passengers whose half-hour delay in stalled traffic has earned them a good long gawp at the blood-soaked crash that interrupted their journey.

"Hello, Mother. Welcome to Kiribati."

"Look at you, Raymond, all dressed up like a pervy version of the Scarecrow from *The Wizard of Oz*."

"Mother, this is Neal, Elspeth and Tabitha."

Mother stared at the trio like a grifter assessing fresh marks. "Hello, then."

"Has Fiona set you up in nice digs?"

"She's done more for me in one day than you've done in a lifetime, useless son that you are. Brought me down here for a holiday, out of the kindness of her heart."

"That's Fiona, all right—give, give, give."

Mother glowered at me. "Are you taking the piss?"

"Yes, Mother. I'm taking the piss."

I heard Neal whisper, "The apple doesn't fall far from the tree, does it?"

"Okay, then, Mother, if you're finished . . ."

I could tell she was about to launch into one of her

invectives in which politics and religion and utterly ambiguous personal foibles coalesce to create a sort of satanic meatball of misinformation. "I am *not* finished. By changing one vowel in the name 'Harry,' you desecrated the imagination of every child and of every child-grooming pedophile who ever entered the Potter universe of mugwumps and pixie-wixies or whatever else that that billionaire woman is always writing about. Childhood is sacred, Raymond, *sacred.*"

"Mother, that made no fucking sense. What do you want?"

"Fiona very kindly invited me down here for a leisurely South Pacific vacation, and all I've found so far is tinned luncheon meat and some ghastly fungus that has turned my minge into a Halloween house of horrors. I want my holiday, and I want it *now.*" She dropped her two dead cigarettes onto some highly endangered plant and crushed them with her heel.

Silence.

"Well, Mother, you certainly know how to win over a crowd."

"Raymond Gunt, you are a bad, bad son. I rue the day I ever dreamed of bearing offspring."

"Do you?"

"I do."

"Well then, guess who is about to stop making payments on your breast enlargement surgery."

"You wouldn't!"

"*Wouldn't* I?"

Neal said, "Ray, really? You paid for your mum's implants? You're a good son, you are."

"Thank you, Neal."

Mother was running scared. "Raymond, they can't take my implants away, can they? They're already inside of me."

"Yes, Mother, yes they can. If I don't keep paying, they will systematically hunt you down wherever you try to hide. They will pounce on you from behind, armed with Stanley knives, and they will rip you open right there on the cobblestones."

Mother burst into tears.

"Christ, don't bawl."

"I love my breasts, Raymond! They're the only things of mine withstanding the horrible hand of time!"

Though it went against all my instincts, I walked over and put my arm around her, causing my entire musculature to involuntarily shudder. "There, there. I promise to continue making the payments."

She honked an oyster of phlegm into the coral dust. "Oh, Raymond, I take it all back—you *are* a good son. I'm just so stressed out from travel. Oh Lord, now I've farted—and my nose is running. I need a tissue."

Elspeth gave up the Playboy Bunny fluff ball attached to her tender rump. Mother honked a cargo of deep-sea creatures into its pristine softness.

Elspeth, Neal and Tabs stood transfixed.

"Why you and Fiona never had children is beyond me, Raymond. You'd have made a fine father."

"Thank you, Mother, but Fi's not really the nurturing type."

"You just never gave her a chance."

"Mrs. Gunt," said Neal. "Why don't you stay with me in a proper house? You'll like it very much."

"Really? Neal, is that your name? Thank you very

much. They put me up in a tent, without even a telly to keep my mind off my woeful situation. A house would be lovely."

"Neal," I interjected, "I thought *I* was supposed to be moving into the house."

"No, you're staying *behind* the house in the hut, Ray. Your mother can stay in the business centre, on a beautiful sofa bed, with an ensuite bathroom and a big-screen colour telly."

I was suddenly invisible to my own mother, as she suction-cupped her right tentacle onto Neal's left buttock. I was livid. It was time to find Fiona and figure out just what sort of master plan she had in mind for me.

To get her attention, I shouted, "Mother, would you be so good as to tell me where the delightful Fiona is . . . perhaps honing her talons on a massive medieval granite knife-sharpening wheel?"

"She's in the big red tent, I believe, Ray. But don't go barging in. She's getting a massage from one of those ladies who likes ladies, if you know what I mean."

"Charming."

"The masseuse has skin like the back seat of Grand-dad's old Vauxhall. And she's probably got a clit like a golf ball."

"Yes, Mother. Delightful."

A Siberian wind blew through my heart at the thought of Fiona being pounded like so much bread dough by some careerist bull moose. But I needed to find out the scope of Fi's treachery. What else could she have in store for me?

43

Indeed, I found Fiona in the red tent getting pounded by what looked like a lorry driver with tits. When I opened the tent flap, the masseuse looked up at me like I was the devil. Beneath her mitts lay Fiona, like so much bread dough. I said, "Oh, hello, darling."

"Oh, it's *you*." Fiona craned her neck around to make eye contact with her lorry driver. "He's harmless. Raymond, this is Chaz."

"Lovely to meet you, Chaz."

Fiona screamed at me, "Stop staring at Chaz's tits—she's a dyke, you simpleton! And I don't even want to know how you ended up in your ridiculous outfit."

Chaz grunted and reached for a towel to wipe lotion from her hands. "Want me to call security?"

"No, thank you, Chaz, dear. This is my ex-husband."

Chaz froze in mid-motion. "Seriously?"

"Don't act so shocked, Chaz. He didn't *always* resemble a pemmican scarecrow. In fact, there were a few moments—not many, mind you—where he was passably okay-looking."

The stupid bitch was trying to butter me up, but I was having none of it. "Darling, I'm here on a fact hunt."

"A big fact hunt?"

"Yes, an enormous fact hunt."

"A heaving, pulsating, throbbing fact hunt?"

"No, more of an oozing, quivering, tender fact hunt."

"Is this fact hunt needy and desperate and looking for someone to teach it the ways of the world?"

"Indeed. *Naughty* fact hunt. *Bad* little fact hunt."

There it was—the old magic between me and Fi, happening again.

Chaz threw down her towel and stormed out. "You people are *sick*."

"If you say so."

I threw Fiona a shirt. "Did you really have to drag Mother into whatever your game is?"

"Your mother deserves a holiday, Raymond. She's had a long hard life."

"She's had no such thing. She's been a benefits scrounger as long as I can remember. What she doesn't scrounge, she wheedles or steals, as you very well know."

Fi sat up and attempted to take on her domineering stance. "A bit of compassion for the woman, Raymond. Come with me to the production trailers. You may as well see where you're working."

We left the tent and followed a path towards a trio of rusted-out trailers like the ones you see in American horror movies in which a family of four is brutally bludgeoned to death, their carcasses picked clean by wild animals and insects, only to be found years later by hillbilly meth makers who use the bones as doorstops while converting the remains of the trailer into an incestuous copulation den filled with smashed beer bottles, fag ends, misspelled graffiti and bullet holes.

"You still haven't answered my question, Fi. Why did you bring Mother down here?"

"Oh, very well, Raymond. I did it to torture you. Satisfied?"

"Really? You brought her down here just to annoy me?"

"Yes, Raymond. Yes, I did."

My heart melted. "That is, in a weird way, kind of sweet, Fi."

"I'm not a total monster, you know."

I could see some of the show's staffers milling about outside the trailers, like the dodgy-looking people you find on Google once you remove "safe search"—not that I've ever done that. Many of them were carrying empty plastic cola bottles filled with something resembling dirt. I stopped one particularly slaggy-looking production assistant to ask what was in the bottles.

"These? We're gathering insects for the bug-eating challenge this afternoon."

I shuddered. "Bug-eating? Really?"

"Yup. It's one of our favourite contestant challenges. Unless team members eat a plate of live bugs, they don't get to read letters from their loved ones back home—or some other prize equally stupid."

I looked into the PA's face, hard and sunburned, scoured clean by a lifetime of putting out. I figured this one's done list must have been at least ten thousand blokes long.

Fiona cut into my reverie. "Raymond, stop ogling her tits and come along."

I suddenly felt, of all things, *married*.

We entered one of the trailers and found a production

team seated on stools staring at a wall covered with screens displaying multiple camera feeds. I felt like I was in a home away from home. Then I heard some familiar voices: "Ray! Welcome to paradise!"

It was Tony and Eli, two cameramen I'd last seen in Damascus when we set fire to cars because we were on deadline and badly needed footage.

"Tony! Eli! I hope you brought the petrol!"

"Ray! You're just in time. It's bug-eating day!" Eli exclaimed. He and Tony were delighted to see me.

"So I hear."

Fiona seemed furious that I had actual acquaintances on set. Through the simmering mirage-like heat waves rising from her inflamed body, I could tell she was planning some sort of accidental-seeming death for both Tony and Eli. Poor fellows.

I said, "Tell me more about bug-eating day."

Christmas morning glee shone from their eyes. Eli, the older one, filled me in. "Everyone on staff goes out with buckets and bottles and collects as many terrifying insects as they can. Anything will do: grubs, spiders, millipedes, mostly anything you find beneath a stump."

Tony took it from there. "Stumps are actually the best place to find things, Ray. Things with five hundred legs, six eyes . . ." He picked up a blue plastic tub. "Think about it. If you saw a prawn walking across your living room floor, you'd shoot it with a handgun, but find one in a Pacific net? *Bon appétit*." He removed the blue lid from the tub to show me a hairy black spider the size of a Sunday roast. "Look at the hair on this fucker."

I cooed my approval.

"Not much protein in hair, though. Hair is a bran-like fibre. But in the legs and thoraxes of spiders lie pockets of protein not unlike those found in lobster claws. If this thing lived in the ocean, we'd be making chowder from it in ten minutes. People are dietary hypocrites. Land equals evil. Sea equals good."

"Beats what you find in a Honolulu vending machine. Any of these things toxic?"

"Oh, probably," Tony said. "We lost our entomology textbook in transit, and the Internet's down, so we can't look them up."

"Do contestants eat them whole or smoothied?"

"Depends. We start out with live bugs, but if everyone balks, we smoothie a few handfuls and throw some live ones on top as a garnish. Whoever eats the least amount of bugs is kicked off the show and loses their chance to earn a million bucks."

I was greatly impressed. "Pure genius."

"Come along then, you two—we're just about to leave for the big event."

I could tell this suggestion came at the wrong moment for whatever Fiona had on her agenda for me. But watching a group of brain-dead Americans eating bird-sized insects trumped any plot against me she might have had in the works.

"Sure, let's all go," she said. "And Raymond, afterwards you and I can talk. I miss having someone intelligent to banter with."

Moi?

Intelligent?

Here's the thing about Fiona: when she's nice to you, everyone else on earth vanishes and you feel like you're melting under a beam of sweetness that erases your memory of, say, the time she used your Visa and PIN number to buy two dozen dildos and had them delivered to a daycare centre in your name.

In any event, earlier, while Fi was temporarily distracted searching for some clothes to put on after her massage, I *did* notice a plastic bag containing my Cure T-shirt peeking out from beneath a stack of modelling headshots in her tent. I pinched it and reached outside and slid it beneath the tent's front corner. Tonight I planned to return and reclaim my treasure.

Raymond Gunt: 1; The Gods: 0

....

Florida Man Collapses and Dies After Winning a Friday Night "Midnight Madness" Insect-Eating Competition
October 12, 2012

Floridian Edward Archbold, 32, died after consuming 60 grams of meal worms, thirty-five 3-inch-long "super worms" and a bucket of 1-inch-long South American cockroaches in an effort to win a "Midnight Madness" insect-eating contest held at Ben Siegel Reptiles, 40 miles north of Miami in Deerfield Beach.

Having eaten more insects than thirty other contestants, Archbold's first-place prize was a live python. However, soon after winning, he began vomiting. The Broward County Sheriff's Office reports that Archbold collapsed outside the event venue and was soon pronounced dead at a local hospital. Legal representatives of the store have told the press that roaches are sold as reptile feed, are raised in sterile containers from hatching onward, and are safe for human consumption. As well, all bug-eating contestants had signed waivers that acknowledged they understood the risk of illness and injury associated with eating massive amounts of live insects.

Lydia Wellstrom, Director of Parasitology at Baltimore's Johns Hopkins University, says that eating cockroaches is not harmful to one's health per se, but that insects do contain many allergens. "Even so, anaphylactic shock was probably not the cause here. Outside the industrialized West, insects are a dietary staple, cherished both as a staple for daily meals and as highly anticipated snacks."

A Ben Siegel Reptiles store rep said the prize python, worth $850, will go to Archbold's heirs.

....

44

Given the fuss involved in getting to this wretched island from London, I'd largely forgotten that there was a TV show we all had to yank out of our collective arse. After driving in a wheezing golf cart through a forest of Venus flytraps, we arrived at a barren patch of land on which rested a dozen picnic tables painted in bright clownish colours. Seated at them were twenty people who all looked, to Fi's credit, highly fuckable. "My hat goes off to you, Fiona. This is a truly . . . *enjoyable* cast you've assembled. At the last moment, no less. Bravo."

At that instant, a brunette with a single rubber band around her breasts and another one bisecting her crotch area vomited onto the white dust behind her. A pigeon-like flock of Pringle-sized winged insects descended on the puddle, while Scott, Sarah's production assistant, shouted through a bullhorn, "Shovel! Shovel! Shovel of dirt to table seven! Quickly. The bug wagon just arrived!"

An acne-faced pleb ran to shovel grit over the puke.

Fiona, Eli, Tony and I found a vantage point on some small shaded bleachers outside of a predetermined series

of established camera angles. While a PA handed us lem-
onades, I asked Tony and Eli when their shift started.

"We're on sunset-to-dawn beginning tomorrow. Join
us? I can put your name on the roster."

"Please do."

"Oh look!" said Tony, pointing to a jumbo plastic
Diet Pepsi bottle full of millipedes being emptied into
tiki-style bowls. "The games are about to begin!"

Sigh.

Sometimes life is good.

....

Entomophagy is the consumption of insects as food by
humans. Human insect eating is common in cultures in many
parts of the world; over one thousand insects are known to be
eaten in eighty percent of the world's nations. Insect eating is
rare in the developed world.

....

A bowl full of millipedes, as long as they're not
actually writhing, is a not untasty-looking sight, something like a cross between Kellogg's Coco Pops cereal
and a spicy Indonesian bami goreng. In my enthusiasm,
I called out, "Garnish them with a sprig of parsley!" and
was roundly admonished to shush up: nobody wanted to
hear my voice on tape. I blushed for my lapse in professional standards. I mean I *really* blushed: what the hell
was I thinking, breaking the fourth wall? Christ. My
mother's voice from early childhood sprang to mind: *For
fuck sake, Raymond, doing random shit like you do is
why you're never going to be allowed to have fancy
things in your life. Now nip down to the chip shop and
swipe me some fags. If Mr. Bradbury catches you, just
blow him. He's not picky. Just make sure I get my*

*Rothmans at the end of it. Don't stand there like your
arse is full of bowling balls, boy. Move it!*

Ahhh . . . precious childhood memories.

You'd think I could just sit there for a few hours and
watch some wildly attractive semi-naked people eat
millipedes, but no—and why? Because from behind the
bleachers, in a wail no sound technician on earth could
ever scrub from a sound track, I heard my mother head-
ing my way.

"Raymond? Is that you in them seats? Move over,
because I'm coming up." She clumped her way up the
rows to settle beside me, Fiona, Eli and Tony.

"Hello, Fiona dear. Hello, boys. You two are Yanks?
Good on you. We put out for you something special
back in World War II, we did. Shove over, Raymond."

"So, how was your gourmet meal, as prepared by
Tabs and Elspeth?" I inquired.

"Gourmet food means nothing to me at this point,
Raymond. I've got me a dead colon. May as well ask me
to digest a concrete lawn ornament."

"Lovely."

"Don't be such a prig, son. I spent half your childhood trying to coax a poo from you. My God. I may as
well have been trying to pry a hooker's tit from your
father's claws. The way he'd lay into a woman? Jesus
and Mary, it was like a peregrine falcon making off
with a fluffy little duckling while its mum screams from
the reeds. Mind you, that kind of manhandling has its
merits—or *you* wouldn't be here today! Har, har har!"
Mother coughed up a fetal pig and horked it off the
bleachers into some crabgrass. "Oh, look at me and you,
Raymond, a million years later on a glamorous South

Seas island, like two peas in a pod. Nothing like family, I say, *nothing.*"

We all stared down at the contestants. At the purple-coloured picnic table, Tammy [Dental Hygienist, Texas] was about to guzzle a soup bowl full of hostile earwigs—who could object to watching that? Tammy furtively held a wriggling horned thingy up to her starving lips, and suddenly Mother went ballistic, shouting, "Oh, my dear God, Jesus, no! Stop!"

Everybody stared at her as she carried on screaming. "Good God, girl, what are you thinking, putting those nasty creatures down your throat?"

"Mother—"

"This is all part of America's undeclared war on science! I can tell!"

Time stopped as we all tried to figure out what she was on about.

"Mother, that makes absolutely no sense. The insects here are delicious and protein-rich, raised in hygienic farm-like environments."

"Eco-friendly and green," added Tony.

"When Tammy or whatever her name is eats them, she's actually receiving all the EU-sanctioned daily dietary recommendations," I said.

Mother looked fed up with me. "Raymond, she's a ho eating a fucking bowl of bugs. Don't you talk down to me, son. I'm just saying that the Americans don't like science anymore and are trying to get rid of it as quickly as they can. That young woman eating bugs over there would have been an astrophysicist if her country hadn't shipped their entire economy to China. Her life could have had dignity; instead, she's eating worms to pay for an endless string of abortions."

(You'll note that Fiona stayed silent during all this. And that my mother knew the word "astrophysicist"— who would have guessed?)

"Well, whatever, Mother. This is a TV show. It has endless minutes that need to be filled with endless amounts of footage. If you make any further outbursts, the PAs will drag you off to some forgotten lagoon where those people I mentioned a while back who gave you your brand-new tits will take them back with carpet knives as they squeal with glee."

"You can't blackmail me over my implants anymore. Tabitha told me while I was eating that once your implants are in, they're in forever and can never be removed no matter what, like a band of travellers taking over your backyard while you're at church."

"Mother, you've never been to church in your life except to pilfer sedatives from the purses of those Presbyterian women who run the thrift sales."

Stuart stalked over to us. *Fuck.*

"Potter, what the fuck is going on here?"

"Just chatting with my mum is all, having a lovely time watching some attractive young people eat insects."

"Can you tell your mother to please keep her fucking voice down?"

"How dare you swear at my mother!" As though tasered by some unseen force of filial duty, I dove off the bleachers head first at Stuart and knocked him to the ground. "Nobody talks to my mother like that!"

45

If you've ever seen a fight erupt in public, you'll know
that nobody ever dashes in right away to stop things—
even nuns and vicars want a dab of free blood. So there
I am hammering away on Stuart, with him hammering
away on me, with grit in our eyes and countless dozens
of entertained eyeballs staring at us, cast and crew yell-
ing encouragement, when in my blurred peripheral vision
I see Mother crabwalk down the bleachers, screaming,
"Kill him, Raymond! Kill that nasty fucker who swore
at me! Kick him in the teeth! Kick him in the bollocks!
Kill that fucker! *Kill! Kill!*" I have to admit, I felt just
the tiniest whiff—just a kitten fart, really—of love for
the old woman.

Fiona was also on her feet, chanting, "Get him!" I had
no idea whom she was supporting.

And then, when we had started to slow down a bit, a
couple of the more burly PAs pulled the two of us apart
to Mother's chorus of "Fucking pussies. Fucking he-puss-
ies is what you are!"

Stuart pulled free of his PA and started brushing the

coral dust from his khaki trousers. "Potter, you are FIRED from this show."

Tony and Eli grabbed me so that I didn't lunge at him again. "Fine. Like I *care*. And by the way, while we're all here, Stuart, how can someone who's a big shot TV network guy like you be so incredibly fucking cheap that he actually seeks out free bootleg CDs of a children's movie? I mean, how can anyone be that fucking cheap, Stuart?"

Victory! I could see everyone thinking: *Well, yes, this Gunt does have a point. Why couldn't a flunky have bought one for you? You couldn't just get it off Apple TV or Netflix? You really had to save a few bucks by having someone import a bootleg?*

Nailed you, you *fucker*.

"Actually, the CDs weren't for me, you selfish dickhead. They were for the children's hospice in Bonriki."

Hospice? *Uh-oh*.

"That's right, a hospice! For children dying of cancer. Yes, you heard that right, *cancer*."

I could feel audience sympathy drifting Stuart's way.

"The trans-Pacific Internet connection went down, and the children really wanted to see *Harry Potter*, like it was a final wish, so I thought that I, Stuart, would make a difference. So excuse me if helping some dying children get their final wish is cheap. I guess we should all follow *your* fine example and retreat to a lagoon-side fuck hut while the rest of the world goes to hell."

I could then see an idea entering Stuart's mind, and I sensed I wouldn't like it one bit. "Yes, well, Herry," he said calmly. "I'm not a total asshole, and I apologize to your mother for swearing at her." He looked at Mother, who was just then shaking dandruff flakes from her hair. "Sorry about that."

"Not to worry, whoever you are."

Stuart turned back to me. "Okay, here's the deal. Just to show you how magnanimous I am, I'll set you a challenge. If you can eat a full bowl of bugs, you can have your job back."

"Really? You're not just fucking with me?"

"In front of everyone I give you my word: one bowl of insect medley and you are not just a B-unit cameraman again, but you officially become an A-unit cameraman, with a hike in pay."

I had to admit, being an A-unit cameraman has always been a career dream of mine. How hard could it be to eat some bugs? What was the catch? I nodded.

Stuart called out, "Okay, fifteen-minute break for everyone while Raymond here eats a bowl of mixed insects. Gather close!"

Cast members and crew bustled in to form a circle around me. Moments later, Scott appeared with a writhing bowl of . . . well, nature's medley: grubs, spiders, centipedes, millipedes, encyclopedias, mumps, cysts and whatever other unholy spawn the crew had managed to find beneath the island's logs.

But here's the thing: the show's contestants were actually starving, whereas *I* had had a delightful meal of cheeses and cold cuts in Neal's palace. There was barely room for a Mars bar inside me.

If Sarah were there, she would have stopped Stuart from being such a twat. What did she see in him?

"Okay, Herry, every single bug down the hatch and fully swallowed. Puke and you're out—unless you choose to ingest the puke, but I don't credit you with that level of commitment."

"Fine, Stuart, I understand."

Me, an A-unit cameraman!

"Good. Now let's get some cameras rolling—I want to document this train wreck."

Mother nuzzled in beside Stuart and began brown-nosing. "You should see his refrigerator back home, a cold and godless place it is. Ooh, look at that little bugger there—he's got to be a six-incher, and all those tiny legs—it makes you marvel at the universe."

Chili Cicadas with Rice

A beloved Mexican classic—and a sure-fire
family-pleaser for those special occasions.

½ onion
3 tablespoons olive oil
¾ cup cicadas
1 12-ounce can navy beans, drained
1 6-oz can tomato paste
3 teaspoons chili powder
1 clove garlic, minced

Dice the onion and sauté in olive oil. After a minute or
so, add the cicadas and cook until both onions and
insects are translucent. Yes, that is correct: *translucent*.
Add the remaining ingredients and simmer on low heat
until flavours have melded together—at least one hour.
Ladle onto brown rice.
Be sure to serve it more than once every
seventeen years . . . *Olé!*

The flavours came in waves: a pecan-like crunch, followed by an avocado smoothness, followed by a glob of something chowdery and phlegmy. Next? A clump of larvae, tasting something like chanterelle mushrooms.

Did all of the wriggling and writhing disturb me, you ask? Fuck no. That's why God gave us jaws. Added bonus? Live bugs were better than anything you'd find in a Honolulu Airport vending machine. I ploughed through my bowl like it was so much bar mix, with supportive chanting from all around.

"Shells for texture; guts for flavour!"

"The vitamins are in the legs, Ray, the legs!"

Scott offered, "If it tastes sour, it's probably an ant."

"All that formic acid," another PA added.

Halfway through my bowl, I spat out a thorax of some sort to ask for a glass of water, but Stuart scotched that idea. "You should have thought of that beforehand, Gunt! And pick up that thorax you just spat out and eat it, too."

Fuck him.

Crunch.

I don't know if you've ever eaten a bowl of insects. Perhaps you enjoy them regularly—and good for you! So you know that bug eating is all about mind over matter. Something crickety tasted prawn-like, and I couldn't help but wonder what most things in the bowl might have tasted like with some peanut oil and a bouillon cube in a good hot wok.

By now Stuart was looking thoroughly pissed. Fuck him. He'd shortly have to rehire me on as an A-unit cameraman. *Ha!*

Within a very jumbled minute or so, everything from the bowl was gone, except a huge pink millipede. For the first time I couldn't use mind over matter. Its two rows of little pincers were fluttering in waves along its length, and I couldn't imagine eating anything so utterly disgusting.

Stuart could sense that I'd lost my momentum. "Just look at it, Gunt: if that thing crawled into your tent at night, it'd chew your dick off. But you still have to *eat* it."

"No need for colour commentary, Stuart."

"No, I want you to know *exactly* what you're eating: it's the most vile insect ever known to man, repulsive and ready to explode with guts and stingers."

"Stuart, just fuck right off."

I steeled myself for the final mouthful. *Raymond, you've probably eaten far worse things at a kebab take-away. So just do it.* I threw the bug in my mouth and was just about to crunch down on its middle when my mother shouted, "Raymond, just think of that thing as a giant pussy with teeth!"

I promptly hurled out every single organism I'd just ingested in one glistening Niagara of mangled coffee-coloured protein.

46

The next thing I knew, I was being lifted off the ground and onto a wheezing golf cart driven by Eli, and we were chugging back through the forest of vile Venus fly-traps. I then fuzzed out of consciousness and came to with my head on a foam pad and a freezer's dull thrum in my ears: Neal's storeroom. A nice calm place, really. Private. Quiet.

Out of nowhere I needed to wank. Seems simple enough, you'd think, but from some damaged corner of my brain came a slew of political thoughts—possible nuclear war and all—and suddenly my innocent desire to self-pleasure took on a charged new meaning. Before the nuclear war, my thinking had been along the lines of, "Sure, right now I'm wanking, though it's just a pale substitute for the genuine action I hope to have in the near future." But when your future no longer feels infinite, the sterility and pointlessness of wanking is hard to overcome. Instead of feeling sexy and tingly, it felt useless, like recycling plastics or registering to vote. I called the whole thing off.

A person listening to this tale might be thinking, "Oh, woe is poor Raymond." But what happened next might well surprise that listener. I stood up and felt a little rumble in my tummy. I spotted a door beside the deep-freeze that opened on that most prized of luxuries in the tropics: a fully functional flush toilet, its cistern groaning from an abundant load of name-brand loo roll. I stepped inside and began to take what I honestly considered to be a dump of the gods.

After I was finished, I ambled over to Neal's. It was nearing sunset, and he was behind his bar in a smoking jacket, finishing a fag and holding the glasses up to the sunset-drenched window to check for dishwasher spots.

"Where are the girls?"

"Oh hello, Ray! Gave me a start, you did. They're off getting pedicures. Fancy a cocktail?"

"Please. Vodka martini, straight up, dirty with two olives."

Neal, being a good friend, really (and no longer my slave), prepared my martini without mentioning my disgrace at the purple picnic table.

I sat at the bar. "By the by, where's your bouncer chap who answered the front door the first time I was here?"

"Eamon? He's working in the herb garden I've started out back. I was inspired by the herb garden outside your flat in London. Nothing like fresh herbs to make the meal—they add a bit of love to the menu."

"Neal, you take back that last thought or I will justifiably vomit yet again, this time all over your bar."

"Sorry, Ray. Just trying to be gracious."

Neal handed me the martini—it was perfection. I felt like Noel Coward or James Bond or one of the great debonairs of all time, greeting the early evening with style. I exhaled and took stock of my day. In one of my more philosophical moods, I asked, "Neal, have you ever taken a large and satisfying shit, only to look in the bowl afterwards to find . . . *nothing*?"

"Phantom shit, Ray. Happens all the time."

"Nonsense, Neal."

"Let me guess: afterwards little to no wiping required."

"Why . . . that is correct. None, really. A shame with all that five-star loo paper available."

"Perhaps it's interdimensional leakage, Ray. That could explain it."

"Interdimensional leakage? What is *wrong* with you? I shit in the real world, Neal. My shit does not enter a parallel universe or time stream."

"You're the one who spoke the words 'parallel universe' and 'time stream,' not me."

"Meaning what?"

"Meaning that even *you* believe there are unsolved mysteries in this universe."

"I grudgingly concede the point."

Neal handed me another well-deserved drink. "I watched your bug-eating challenge on the show's website. Great stuff, Ray. Bold."

"The entire planet has no Internet except here on Arsefuck Island? How does that happen?"

"Calm down, Ray. They've got some smart young kids on the show, with solid IT skills. They set up a very robust LAN, with a rewards program where you can get discount car rentals for—"

My overtaxed brain shot sideways from both ears.

"*Car rentals?* Your driver's licence expired the day Nirvana taped *MTV Unplugged in New York*—and there are no cars to rent. They've all been melted by nuclear war."

"No war just yet, and who knows—diplomatic talks might stave it off."

"Neal, if you keep spouting this naive claptrap, I'm afraid I'll have to stop having my philosophical discussions with you."

"That's not fair, Ray. I'm trying to keep our spirits up."

"Another martini. Please." *So delicious.*

....

A **martini** is a cocktail made with gin and vermouth, garnished with an olive or a lemon twist. Until the 1950s, the standard proportion was one part vermouth to three or three and a half parts gin. In recent years, martinis made with vodka rather than gin have become much more fashionable. Many people have martini shakers in their homes—either received as wedding gifts or purchased in an ironic retro mood. They never get used. They're kind of like the fedora hat of the beverage world.

....

I looked around. "Where's Mother's room?"

"Down the hall. She's watching some telly and eating crisps."

I pointed at a set of French doors. "What's out there?"

"The infinity pool."

Fucker.

Neal looked around as if to make sure nobody else was near. "Ray . . ."

"Yes, Neal? Smashing martinis, by the way."

"Ray, do you feel slightly, I don't know—*guilty*—for starting the nuclear crisis?"

"Guilty? Why should I feel guilty?"

"Well, I mean, we could have crashed the plane and prevented that atomic bomb from going off."

"Neal, you're thinking like a little girl. The planet is choking—choking on a continent-sized lump of plastics, and Lieutenant Jennifer whatever-the-fuck-her-name-was, in her heart of hearts, thought she was doing the right thing. We should commend her."

Neal looked genuinely distraught. "But I keep asking myself what a better person might have done. The world's going to end because of you and me. Not only that, we can't get a trans-Pacific Internet connection and the ladies at Kum Guzzling Traktor Sluts were going to do a special Skype performance just for me today. They call it 'The Missile Silo'—a part of their ongoing celebration of the Cold War's end. Pretty ironic, given that we've gone and started it all over again."

"Neal, Neal, Neal, Neal, Neal, Neal, Neal. Come over here."

Neal came close and I slapped him, one-two. "Stop that line of thinking right now. Jason Bourne would have done exactly what I did—"

"Kack his trousers?"

"Not my proudest moment, Neal, but yes, Jason Bourne would have shat his pants, given the situation."

"Really, Ray?"

"Yes, Neal, *really*. The thing about Jason Bourne is that he only really shines when he's being chased. Without the forces of evil pursuing him, Jason Bourne is basically council house trash living on KFC and the proceeds of his illegal Polish and Romanian girlfriends who'll toss you off for a tenner at the local lottery ticket kiosk."

"So Jason Bourne is almost just like you and me."

"Or," I clarified, "*I am basically Jason Bourne.* Simple logic."

"What about James Bond, then—would he have tried to stop the bomb dropping?"

"He'd have been at the back of the plane fucking a goat. Again, pure logic."

"I never studied logic, Ray."

"Well, Neal, I'm not one to lord it over people, but yes—I *did* study logic."

"Fancy prep school?"

"No. A fucking hellhole."[4]

I swallowed an olive and changed the subject. "So. How is my piece of red plastic coming along?"

Neal gave a weary sigh. "To be honest, I wish it would come along a bit quicker. It's hard going through life with a persistent prostate massage. I hope Mother Nature will soon take her course."

My suave, contemplative mood continued, well into my third martini. "Neal, I truly think that wormy-fleshed canker I call my ex-wife is up to something sinister. Any ideas what it could be?"

---

4. *I did have a scholarship to a fancy place, but Mum spent it on a Benidorm holiday with her best friend Sheila. I only learned of this decades later. I was on a TV shoot about pedophiles in the private school system, and this bloke we were filming looks up at me while we're changing batteries and says, "Gunt? That sounds just like 'cunt,'" and I say, "Yeah. I get a lot of that." And so he says, "You're Raymond Gunt?" and I say, "Yup. That's me." And he says, "Why ever didn't you accept that scholarship we gave you?" and I say, "Scholarship?" Yes, that's how I found out about it. At least I escaped a decade of arse-rapings, but still, it would have been nice to be more posh, you know, using all the magic fancy words that leave Pippa Middleton all moist and gagging for it.*

"Fi? Not that I can think of. Maybe she wants to . . .
dunno . . . get back together with you."

"Highly unlikely, Neal. Oh, by the way, I found where
she hid the Cure T-shirt, so I pinched it and hid it beneath
her tent. We can get it later."

"You're the greatest, Ray."

Then the doorbell rang and Neal went to answer it. It
was Billy, of all people. He and Neal hugged like old friends.

"Billy, fancy a drink?" Neal said.

"I do. How's your pussy fatigue coming along?"

"I think I've rounded a corner and will make a full
recovery."

"And your ankle?"

"Ditto. Raymond—look who's here!"

"Hello, Billy."

"Hello, Raymond."

"You two sound like you need more alcohol. What'll
you have, Billy?"

"A greyhound, please."

"Perfect. We have fresh pink grapefruits from the tree
out back. Why, what's this we have here?" From beneath
the bar Neal produced a professional juice squeezer.
"One greyhound, coming up!"

....

A **greyhound** is a cocktail composed of vodka and grapefruit
juice. For some reason, it's just kind of gay.

....

While Neal pulped the grapefruits, Billy and I regarded
each other with deep suspicion.

"So, Billy," I finally said, "tell me, what's the deal
with being gay?"

"Huh?"

"I mean, I look at a gay situation, as it were, and nothing the least bit sexual happens."

"Right."

"So, what happens with *you*?" I was drunk enough that the question was sincere.

Billy picked up on this, and looked thoughtful. "Well, imagine you lived on a planet where people got sexual stimulation almost entirely from their ears, and everywhere you looked advertisers were using slick airbrushed photos of ears to sell cars and soft drinks, and all the people on this planet wanted to do was to sit in their bedrooms rubbing their ears together and sticking their fingers in each other's ears for hours and hours and hours. That's what it's like for me when I look at straight people having sex . . ."

I was all ears, so to speak. "And?"

"Wait a second," said Billy. "You're not getting off on this conversation, are you? Fiona said you could be weird about this kind of thing. Were you seriously considering fucking goats in Bonriki?"

"Neal! You told Fiona about our discussion?"

Neal put a mint sprig in Billy's greyhound and handed it to him. "Nothing wrong with exploring other modes of being, Ray. And remember, you didn't really fuck a goat. You only fucked a goat *in your heart*."

"I was doing no such thing! I seem to remember us talking more about fucking sheep in the end."

"Well," said Billy, "haven't *I* stepped onto a minefield?"

I reached for a paper napkin and knocked over a drink I hadn't seen beside a plate of garnishes. "Oops. Sorry, Neal."

"Not to worry. Just some coconut milk and sugar I was going to turn into an energy drink. You all right?"

"I got it all over my pants, but give me a damp cloth and I can wipe it off." I looked up. "Billy, why are you even here? Shouldn't you be out kidnapping toddlers for Fiona to char-broil for dinner?"

"I'm actually here on Fiona business."

"Go on."

"She has a surprise for you."

I knew it! My eyes narrowed into thin, snaky slits as I stared at him.

"She does. And she wants me to bring you to see it."

"Do you know what this surprise is?"

"Yes, I do."

"Will it involve public humiliation?"

"Definitely not."

"So it's a *good* surprise, then?"

"Definitely."

"If you're lying, I get to make you my slave for one week."

"Slave? I'm not fucking any goats for you, but if Fiona's surprise is anything less than splendid, I'll be happy to be your personal assistant for a week."

I sighed. How far the once mighty human race has fallen—from the majesty and glory of slavery down to the sterile, joyless realm of the personal assistant.

Well, a personal assistant is better than nothing. "Okay. Let's go."

47

It was dark out, but you'd never know it by the temperature. As we left Neal's *casa*, I was instantly homesick for its kickass air conditioning. Weather reports never mention mugginess, do they? No. No, they don't. They only show little suns or clouds. If I ran the weather service, I'd invent new icons for South Pacific swelter: tiny gas chambers or tiny dishwashers with their doors wide open and chokingly hot steam billowing out.

Fucking heat.

I said, "So, Billy, can you give me a hint about Fiona's special surprise?"

"No."

"Come on."

"*No.*"

"Has she located a patch of quicksand for me to investigate? A flock of sleeping HIV-infected bats she wants me to startle awake with a foghorn? Or perhaps she wants to feed me a pudding made from time-expired dairy products?"

"Raymond, I'm not telling you anything. Neal, how's your ankle on this sandy path?"

"I'll make it okay, Billy. Thanks for asking."

I was incensed. "*I'll make it okay?* Neal, for fuck sake, you're talking like you've lost a limb in Afghanistan."

"Leave him alone, Raymond. A sprained ankle is nothing to laugh about."

"Okay, how much farther to go, Billy?"

"Just around the corner."

At the tent city, the evening shift change was in progress. Since I had been fired, I didn't have to worry about it. Scurrying around us were men and women in cargo pants and T-shirts, carrying clipboards and camera gear, their belt loops jammed with gaffer tape, flashlights, Swiss Army knives and all the other equipment one needs at a moment's notice. One thing that was odd, though, was that nobody seemed to notice me or make eye contact with me. *Hmmm.*

Just then Stuart walked by. "Fuck me with a chainsaw. *Gunt*—what are *you* still doing here? You've been cast off the island. Go. Leave. Now."

"Yes, Stuart. I'll hop the next British Airways jumbo leaving from Arsefuck Island International Airport."

"Well, you can't stay in our camp, eat our food or use any of our infrastructure. I've also told all staff members that anyone caught communicating with you will be fired. Have a nice life."

". . ." (The sound of me having no stinging, witty retort at hand. Fucking Stuart.)

"Potter. Out of here. Go. Now." Stuart walked away.

I turned to Neal. "Well, isn't *this* just ducky? So what now—I find a little island and make a lean-to from palm fronds? Maybe play a ukulele until I die of old age?"

"Think of yourself as a DNA stockpile ready to

repopulate a post-nuclear society badly in need of quality genetic material, Ray."

Billy cut in, "Kids, can we stay on topic? We are headed to Fiona's surprise."

Neal put a hand on my shoulder. "Don't worry, Ray. I'm not a staff member, so nobody can fire me if I talk to you. You stay on in the hut. If I see anyone from the show coming by, I'll send you a signal so you can crawl behind the deep-freeze until they go away."

"Oh. My. God. It's come to this, has it?"

"I'd let you stay in the business centre, but your mum's in there and I have to think of her health."

"Neal, my mother will outlive cockroaches in the post-nuclear era. She is unkillable. Have *her* bunk beside the deep-freeze."

"I can't change her room now that she's settled in. Besides, she said she'd make me egg and chips for breakfast tomorrow."

From my left came an "Ahem!" The enchanting Billy.

"Oh, all right—lead me to Fiona's surprise."

Billy pulled a walkie-talkie from his belt and whispered into it. We passed through some coconut shrubs and emerged into what resembled a children's playground painted in garish colours.

"This is actually the site of the contestants' next challenge."

"What is it?"

"To quote the tent full of producers I overheard, the challenge is 'to show as much jiggling side boob as is legally permissible.'" Billy stopped us. "Right then, here we go." He made a small flourish, then bowed and said, "Raymond Gunt, may I please present to you your ex-wife, Fiona, and your very own mother, Chantelle Brittany Gunt."

The unholy duo emerged from behind a huge cable spool painted bright orange. "Surprise!" they shouted.

My mind began to spin as it considered the treacheries these two had cooked up. And then my legs were . . . itching? What the fuck? I looked down to see my entire lower body covered in a cloud of angry winged Pringles.

"Raymond!" shouted Neal. "Your entire lower body is covered in angry winged beetles. Good lord! I think they have teeth!"

I'm not proud of it, but I shrieked. "Get them off of me, Neal! Get them off me!"

"They're attracted to the coconut milk he spilled on his lap," said Billy. "Sugar in concentration makes Pringles even angrier than they normally are."

Neal shouted, "They don't have teeth, Ray!"

"I don't give a fucking shit—get them off of me." I was doing frantic jumping jacks.

"Ray, what I *meant* to say is that instead of teeth they've got pincers! Like those shears you use to trim hedges!"

I screamed some more, then fell to the ground and rolled over and over, squishing hundreds of the nasty fuckers—which, in turn, seemed to attract even more furious Pringles.

Finally Neal managed to strip the pants off me, and with them, the rest of the Pringles. I lay there panting, and looked up to see Fiona and Mother staring at me, mouths agawp, their stunned silence interrupted only by Mother taking a lusty drag from her filter-tipped cigarette while she simultaneously ate the very last of a package of crisps. She dropped the bag onto the ground, where it was immediately enveloped in its own cloud of angry winged Pringles.

Fiona said, "Jesus, Raymond, I've never seen you look worse in all the years I've known you. I'm actually in awe of your ability to hit new lows."

"Thank you, Fiona."

Mother sized me up. "Son, you look like the pavement beside Mr. Chandra's kebab shop at three a.m. on a Saturday night. You're a living puddle of sick, is what you are."

"Yes, well. Moving forward, why don't you tell me why you brought me here tonight."

The two women looked at each other. Mother squealed, "I can't wait anymore, Fi!"

"Okay, fair enough," said Fiona. "I'd hoped the scene would be a touch more dignified—and sanitary—than this, but here goes. Raymond Gunt, I'd like you to meet . . ." She made a what-the-hell gesture.

Drum roll

"Your biological son and daughter!"

From behind the orange cable spools emerged a boy and a girl—they were sixteen, maybe.

"Nice to meet you," said the young man.

This kid . . . he was—he was *me* with a chin.

"Father!" said the girl. She was like Fiona, except beautiful.

Unfortunately, at that moment, I burped and a Pringle flew out of my esophagus. I passed out.

* * *

"Is he dead?"

I heard a young woman's concerned voice, but I was unsure who she was. I was in that weird state where one awakens but can't remember what room, or even what city, one is in. Only gradually does one's situation become clear.

"Oh dear," the voice continued. "He's got blood and bites all over his groin region."

I opened my eyes a tiny bit and saw the most astonishingly luscious barely legal bird I'd ever laid eyes on.

"Mum," the girl said. "Can I help out here? I took a first-aid course last semester."

Mum?

Fiona said, "I'm sure your father would love that."

Fiona? Father?

The girl's voice again. "Kyle, can you hand me those pants over there?"

"These ones?" Kyle, whoever he was, held up a pair of pants covered in what looked like the remains of a large Mexican dinner.

"Yes, I think that leg has the least amount of bug splat on it."

Who is this girl? And who is this Kyle?

Wait, wait, wait . . . he's my son.

My son! And my daughter! But hold on! Why is my gentleman's region feeling warm and pleasurable . . . oh, dear God . . .

"No! Please! Stop!"

I gently removed my daughter's assisting hands. "It's okay! I'll clean myself off, but thank you. Thank you."

The age of consent is the minimum age at which a person is considered to be legally competent to consent to sexual acts. Most jurisdictions set the age of consent at fourteen to eighteen.

In some jurisdictions—the Mexican state of Nayarit, as well as in Bolivia—there is no fixed age of consent. Instead, sex is allowed between people who are pubescent or post-pubescent. The same applies in Yemen, but only between married partners.

The age of consent in Kiribati is fifteen. In Vatican City, it is twelve, although some claim it to be fourteen.

Fiona gave me an uncertain look. "Raymond, your daughter's name is Emma, and your son is named Kyle."

All I could do was stare. The pair of them were radiant with health and resembled nothing so much as Nazi catalogue models from the 1930s. How was this even possible? My own DNA is about as viable and sturdy as a strip of dead cassette tape tossed into the brambles alongside a motorway. And Fiona's DNA must be like something extracted with tongs from the Pacific Trash Vortex.

Mother was in tears. "My own blood! Grandkids! Fi, you are a miracle worker, you are." She grabbed Kyle in one arm, Emma in the other, and pulled them towards her chest like Nautilus equipment. She gave them each teary, fruity, mucusy kisses that left yellow nicotine moons on their foreheads. I hope they both checked to make sure they had their wallets afterward.

"Fiona, what the fucking hell? You can't be serious."

"Raymond, remember that abortion holiday I went on back in 1997?"

"The one where you told me you'd gone lesbian and didn't come home for a year?" The penny dropped. "You didn't go lesbian after all! You were too busy not aborting Kyle and Emma!"

"It would appear so. I was hoping they'd never have to meet you. But the nuclear crisis was upon us, and I didn't want them vaporized if England gets nuked."

My mother butted in. "Kyle's the spitting image of you at this age, Raymond! That is, if you had a chin, a manly jawline, curly golden locks and a ripped musculature."

Emma stared at me with radiant daughterly pride. "Mother's told us so much about you, Father. Oh! I want to hug you to pieces like a teddy bear!"

She hurled herself onto me where I lay, and she certainly smelled terrific and—Christ, I mean, how do people manage not to shag their own kids? The temptation . . . well, best not to venture down that road. I extricated myself from Emma's slender, supple, lightly tanned arms from around me. Her skin was heavenly. She was Tabs without any mileage at all. None.

Meanwhile, Kyle was documenting our meeting on his phone, saving a cherished memory. Then I heard him say to Fiona, "If the crew likes it, they said they'd put it up on the island's website. Apparently, they're lacking in the heartwarming department, and this footage could be download magic. My first big break. I wonder if I can digitally remove the Pringles in the background."

Emma was now hugging Fiona. "Isn't Dad dreamy, Mum?"

Fiona looked at me and mouthed, "*She's still a virgin,*" followed by, "*Don't even think about it.*"

Neal, long silent, cried out rather tearily, "A celebration is called for! Back to the house for a feast!"

48

Dear Reader,

I suppose you're a respectable person who tries to act like children are a miracle whenever the subject comes up, but let's be honest: ugh. All they do is waste your money and suck up your time, and when they get a bit older, they go off and start fucking utterly inappropriate human beings and mocking you behind your back—all the while draining your bank account. Hmmm. Seems like a description of my marriage to Fiona.

So, you ask me how I felt upon discovering I had sired offspring? At least I never had to deal with shitty nappies, or waking up early, or outdoor football practice, or helping them cheat on homework, or instructing them on how to torch a car. Thank fucking Christ. As for Kyle and Emma, they seemed so different from me that I might as well have sired aliens from Betelgeuse—which, in turn, made me feel weird about myself. You know, big picture questions like

*Why am I here? What is life about? What is it to be
part of the chain of life? And really, I mean, who the
fuck needs any of that?*

*Questions like that just lead to misery. You'd get
a lot more value out of being alive if you put your
spiritual energy into doing the daily jumble puzzle
or speculating on the size, colour and texture of the
nipples of the women on the Oscar red carpet.*

Yours,
Raymond Gunt

* * *

We returned to Neal's in time to catch Tabs, Elspeth
and six shockingly hot lady friends headed out the front
door, all of them doubtlessly harbouring lady-boners
barely concealed by the skimpiest of thongs. One of them
was carrying a rattan picnic hamper, which she dropped
on the front stoop when we arrived, causing a miniature
avalanche of dildos, bottles of different flavours of lube,
a gimp's hood, ten vials of poppers and a small portable
stereo system. For one billionth of a second, but certainly
no longer, I felt a fatherly twinge that Emma and Kyle
should see such wicked things, but once that billionth of
a second passed, I thought, *Fuck it.*

"Oops!" said the butterfingered fuckmuppet. "I'll just
gather all of this up."

"I'll help," said Emma. "What is all this stuff, anyway?"

The fuckmuppet paused briefly, assessed Emma's level of
cluelessness and said, "Just some chew toys. You know—
dogs will be dogs. Ha, ha, ha."

"Lucky dogs to have such a wide and colourful selection of toys to choose from! But I hear it's not good for dogs to be in the tropics—you know, heartworm and ringworm."

Kyle seemed as clueless, dutifully filming the dildo spill for a possible segment on Arsefuck Island TV. He asked, "Can I meet your dogs tomorrow? I can mix them into my news segment using Final Cut. It's all in the editing, you know."

Fiona actually snickered at her son's naïveté. Mother was too preoccupied lighting her next few cigarettes to notice anything. Billy was staring at his iPhone, doubtless trawling for fuckbuddies with some unholy gay app. Neal was already inside the house. And me? I was livid, watching my only chance to enjoy the full spectrum of Thong Kong vanish into the night in a slipstream of pheromones and coconut tanning oil.

Neal came back out, saw the rage in my eyes and said, "Ray, don't worry. There'll be other opportunities."

I refused to be mollified.

"But I have to admit, I've never seen the girls so ready for it in all my time on the island. Fortunately for me, I still have a touch of pussy fatigue and am not as sorely tempted as I might normally be. But forget about pussy—let's celebrate your new family!"

What a comedown.

"Look," shouted Emma. "Your lady friends left one of their dog toys at the bar. I'll run and take it to them." She paused and studied the contraption in her hands. "Funny-looking thing, isn't it? It's like three bicycle handles welded together. You'd certainly only want to give this one to a big dog." She ran away down the path to return the toy. I was proud of her willingness to help strangers, but stunned that a sixteen-year-old could be so naive.

Kyle was inside, shooting footage of Neal's living room. He caught me looking at him and said, "This could be a possible lifestyle segment." He'd obviously inherited the Gunt genius for camerawork, but considering everything he'd just seen, you'd think he'd go wank for an hour.

I pulled Fiona to one side. "What nunnery did these kids grow up in?"

"Kyle and Emma were raised in a small village in the North of England with no Internet connection, satellite dish or even basic telly. If you do anything to corrupt them, I will kill you. You know I'll do it, so don't even think of so much as offering them a beer or revealing to them anything that goes on inside your diseased mind."

"Right."

"Emma is an especially sweet girl. I want her to stay that way."

"Okay. Where is this morality explosion coming from, if I may be so bold as to ask?"

Fiona sighed. "Raymond, these kids don't even know what swearing is. They think it's *French*."

"Fuck *me*."

"These kids can be better versions of you and me, versions who'll never get fucked over by the universe."

"Why didn't you tell me about them?"

"Because that would have somehow ended up with them being fucked over by the universe. Your karma is dreadful, Raymond. It's a fact." Fi's nose got sniffly. "It *is* sort of magic, though—you and me being parents and all.

And we'll never have to worry about organ donors ever again. We've always known that liver of yours won't be long for this world."

"It does get me a bit teary-eyed thinking about it. But tell me, does Kyle ever stop filming things?"

"He just discovered digital cameras and the Internet last week. Billy's been teaching him."

"Billy's been *what*?"

"Raymond, relax."

"One minute Billy's teaching Kyle about email. The next minute Kyle's got a fist up his arse."

"It's fine, Raymond. Really. Billy's not into twinks. And Kyle does have camerawork in his genes."

I stood there trying my hardest to feel fatherly, but I was coming up short. I tried figuring out the math of the past week. London . . . LA . . . Honolulu . . . macadamia-induced comas . . . the hunt for fuckable contestants . . . Wake Island . . . I couldn't quite under-stand Fiona's timeline. "Fiona, how did you get Kyle and Emma from the north of England to this island so fast? Haven't all the airports been shut down?"

Fiona put on her guilty face, something I've only ever seen a handful of times. "Some were, some weren't."

"Oh. My. God. You stole them, didn't you!"

"What was I supposed to do, Raymond? Let them die of radiation poisoning in some pathetic hick town? Besides, do you think they are even remotely traumatized? No, you don't, because in my own way I'm a terrific mother."

Across the room, my own mother was chugging a 26-ouncer of vodka. She belched and then ravaged Neal's bowl of cocktail garnishes like a circus elephant.

"So who raised them?"

"Some goody-goodies I found during my abortion holi-day. Talk about dull. But at least Emma's not pulling a train at some party that's being house-wrecked by a Facebook flash mob, and Kyle's not carjacking pensioners for fish and chip money. Come on. Let's sit down. I'm as tired as you."

We sat in the *Hello!* magazine spread of a living room. Emma rushed back through the door, dildo mission accomplished. She came up to me from behind, put her hands down the back of my shirt and started administer-ing a backrub.

"Father, you must be tired after working so hard on this television show. Let me give you a deep-tissue mas-sage like the ones I give our border collies after a long day of sheep herding. It will leave you ever so relaxed."

Neal, Fiona and Mother all cocked eyebrows in our direction.

"Perhaps not right now, Emma," I said. "Maybe Neal can offer you a nutritious snack. Neal! Do you have something nutritious to feed my, um, child?"

"Eamon's cooking up a feast as we speak."

Next Kyle came over. "Father, can we go online and check out the island's website?"

His expression was so earnest I couldn't bring myself to tell him to fuck off. "Sure, why not. Neal, how do we go online?"

"In Grandmum's room."

A minute later we were trudging through dunes of crisp wrappers, cigarette packaging and tissues soiled in various earth tones. There, on the desk, was a Mac monitor covered with Mother's grotesque old-lady undergarments. I used a ballpoint pen to punt them off the desktop, and touched the spacebar to activate the machine. I clicked on the browser and up came **Survival: a website dedicated to smiles here on Survival Island.**

"Click on it, Dad!"

I clicked on ENTER only to find . . .

Please take a moment to register!
It's easy and fun!

Choose a user name and a quick password and you're off!

Password must be fourteen or more characters long.
Passwords are case-sensitive.
Must contain one upper case and one lower case letter.
Must contain at least one numeral.
Must contain one non-alphanumeric character.
Must not contain a space.
Must not contain invalid characters tabs or letters using non–North American English diacritical or orthographical marks, e.g., ü, é, ę, œ, å, ī.
Must not contain forward or reverse fragments of five or more characters of your first name, middle name or last name, regardless of the case (upper or lower) of the letter.
Must not cannot contain forward or reverse fragments of five or more characters of your NetID/EnterpriseID, regardless of the case (upper or lower) of the letter.
Must not contain forward or reverse alphabetic sequences of five or more letters, regardless of the case (upper or lower) of the letter.
Non-alphanumeric characters must not be arranged in "emoticon" format, e.g., :), ;), <3.
Must not contain repeated characters in groups of three or more, e.g., aaa, 1111
Must not contain more than two sequential characters of user's account name.
Must not contain more than two sequential characters of log-in ID.
Must not contain more than two sequential characters of email address.
Must not contain more than two sequential characters of initials.

Must not contain more than two sequential characters of first, last or middle name.

Must not contain more than three sequential numbers of user's birth year.

Must not contain more than three sequential characters of user's birthdate in dd/mm/yyyy or mm/dd/yyyy format.

Must not contain any common words or proper names of five or more characters, regardless of the case (upper or lower) of the letters.

Password must be changed every five calendar days.

After two consecutive unsuccessful password attempts, the account will be revoked.

Passwords deemed not robust enough by the site's algorithm will be rejected.

Never, ever give away your password information to anyone, spouse included.

"Fuck me. There is no way I'm registering on some useless fucking website. Any password I give them they're just going to put into some Nigerian scam engine."

"No way, Dad—it only takes a second. Here, I'll get you started."

Username = %Wor7dsbe5tdAd$
Password = 7My.Da6isS<per!

Cheesy little emotional blackmailing fucker . . .

"Why, thank you, Kyle. I'm genuinely touched."

"Let's look at you and your fecal trauma clip. Don't worry. Growing up on a farm, we learned that feces are a natural part of all ecosystems."

"Whuzzat?"

Blink

Suddenly there I was, slathered in poo, being scrubbed into consciousness by Billy, as viewed by a grainy ceiling nanny cam.

So.

Fucking.

Humiliating.

"Dad, you've got the most popular clip on the site. Look at all the hits. Seventeen unique visitors!"

Christ. "What else is on here?"

"We can check out the contestants on the show. Here . . ." he clicked on a link. "Here's a gallery of the headshots. It sort of makes you want to choose which one of them you'd like to have as a friend, and who you think might not be a good friend. Or who would be a real enemy."

"I actually helped your mother choose the contestants for the show."

"Really?"

Fiona coughed from the doorway and gave me an icy stare.

"Absolutely. There are so many characteristics you need to look out for when choosing. Are they sociable? Do they feel awkward in front of cameras? Are they, ummm . . . highly *photogenic*? It's a very long list."

"Wow. I'd never have thought choosing contestants was such hard work. I think working in television would be a dream job."

Another cough. "No, Kyle," said Fiona. "With a brain like yours? You should go into philosophy. Or sciences. Yes, definitely sciences. Any science. Actually, anything at all except for television. Never the telly. Never ever, ever, ever, ever."

"Tell me, Kyle, how did you get from the north of England to this lovely island here?" (More dagger eyes from Fi.)

"I got a phone call from Fiona—Mum. We receive a Christmas card from her each year."

Fiona shot me a triumphant glance to the effect that she was Mother of the Fucking Year.

"Anyway, on the phone she said she would like to take us shopping at Harrods in London. We were thrilled. She even paid for our train tickets. But after we said hello to her at the station and had some quick fizzy drinks, I guess the train trip was so soothing that both Emma and I fell asleep, and when we woke up we were in a private jet somewhere over the Pacific Ocean. Talk about a treat!"

"I'm sure your parents must be thrilled for you."

A final set of dagger eyes from Fi.

"We tried calling them after we got here, but it's difficult at the moment. I'm sure Fiona—Mum—made sure everything was all right with our parents."

"No doubt she did." At least I now understood all Fi's impromptu flights and the mysterious cash drop-off I witnessed at Bonriki International Airport.

Suddenly we heard shouts from the front door. Then Eli and Tony burst in, to tell us that the luxurious TV network yacht had sunk.

"What the fuck? Did it hit a reef?"

"No. Someone bashed a hole in it. No idea who."

"The debris washing ashore is amazing: small bales of U.S. twenties, Tupperware containers filled with cocaine . . . It's ungodly what TV networks keep on their yachts. It's absolutely the best Easter egg hunt of all time on the beach. And by international salvage laws, it's finders keepers."

It had been ages since I'd done some serious power looting: Beirut in the 1990s, shooting for BBC2. A bomb went off and an entire upscale shopping precinct was evacuated. Nicked myself fifteen thousand quid worth of Rolexes. And then my blood froze—wait: "Is Sarah okay?"

"I saw her on the beach, so I guess she is."

Neal jumped in. "I used to be a paramedic. Maybe I can help."

Kyle and Emma were practically squeaking with excitement. Emma said, "I've been waiting to administer the breath of life to drowning sailors for ever so long. Just think of the number of men I can revive!"

Neal pulled me aside and whispered in my ear, "*Zodiac.*"

"Neal, what the fuck are you talking about?"

"Zodiacs. Now that the yacht is gone, the Zodiacs are the only way to get from anywhere to anywhere. If we find one for ourselves, we'll be one-eyed kings in a totally blind country."

"Neal, for a street-tard, you are totally fucking brilliant. What should we do?"

"First, let's get to the beach. During my convalescence, I've been going over maps of the entire region. Lots of little islands here—perfect for stashing a whole cruise liner, let alone a small inflatable boat."

I let Neal's grotesque abuse of the word "convalescence" pass and followed him to the main beach with plunder in my heart.

49

First off, no sign of Sarah, but I knew she was safe. The bonus good news was that the first thing I found at the high tide line, all tangled in the kelp, was the cold, lifeless body of **LACEY**. Not that I wished her any ill, but really, the world was a much better place without her. Personal upside? Sarah would no longer perceive me as being "taken." Such an honourable girl, my Sarah; she'd never steal another woman's man. The planet could certainly use a big dose of Sarah's spirit—there'd be no more wars, no misery, just peace, peace and more lovely peace. Now, if only that fucktard Stuart were dead. No sign of *his* corpse.

A brilliant full moon added a festive Polynesian dimension to our exploits. Pretty much everything on the beach was tangled up in everything else. At the south end, an improvised morgue was being established, but by whom, and for what reason, I couldn't imagine. Chop them all up and use them for crab bait, as far as I was concerned. On that note, crabs were already scampering up from the waters in pursuit of a feast. Neal also said to watch out for what he called "necropickpocketers."

"A rare breed of thief, the necro."

"Neal, there is no possible fucking way such a tiny category of street riff-raff exists."

"Deny it if you will, Ray, but I've seen them myself at crime scenes, plying their trade. They usually work with someone else to act as a distraction—quite often a clown making twisty balloon animals. You've got everyone squealing, 'Whee! It's a little bunny!' and meanwhile your necro is right in there with the corpse, taking the stuffing out of the goose. Chilling, it is."

"Let's just find ourselves a Zodiac to steal."

Down the beach, I saw my daughter administering the kiss of life to what was most likely a cameraman pretending to be waterlogged. Part of me was hoping that one of her patients would come on to her, thus giving me a reason to go over and crush him. Fatherhood!

Kyle had put away his camera and was helping arrange bodies into neat rows. How on earth did I sire two such virtuous beings? And where was their sense of larceny? Could they not understand that reckless amounts of drugs and cash were a desirable thing to have in one's life?

To be honest, Neal and I were at first slightly diverted from hunting for a Zodiac, both looking for bales of money and tubs of cocaine, and about three-quarters of the way down the sand, we caught each other with the exact same miracle-expecting beachcomber's expression and had a good old-fashioned laugh at our mutual weakness.

"Ray, just think of shitloads of money, all yours, for free! For doing fuck all!"

"Or a brick of coke merely for being in the right place at the right time."

"Okay, okay, I know . . . still, we've got to focus. Steal a Zodiac and be kings of this small empire."

"Thank you, Neal."

"You're welcome, Ray."

"Look there," said Neal, pointing to a Zodiac temporarily beached at the high tide line. "That one is going to be ours."

"Right. Let's just saunter over and slip away before anyone gets huffy."

Neal and I did a dum-dee-dum-dee-dum walk in the boat's direction. At one point, I tripped over a dead producer, but Neal said, "Ignore him, Ray, it's too late."

I felt like I was on a battlefield—and winning—because I was alive and all these dumb fuckers were dead.

Just then our plan became more complex: on the strip of packed wet sand near the water, we spotted Stuart running towards the Zodiac. He was carrying some boxes labelled EMERGENCY MEDICAL SUPPLIES and wore the smug expression of someone who spends his life waiting for the world to turn to shit so he can jump in and be a hero and make everyone like him.

Neal and I picked up our pace, and we arrived on opposite sides of the boat at the same time. It was bigger than I remembered, and somewhat like a bouncy castle with a big-arse engine attached.

"Potter? What the *fuck* are you doing here?" Stuart yelled. "Helping? I find that hard to believe."

I winked at Neal. "Of course I'm helping, Stuart. Neal is an ex-paramedic, and I do happen to care deeply about humanity in crisis. Just tell us what to do and we'll cheerfully be your slaves."

Stuart gave me a moral X-ray, which he clearly found

inconclusive. Still, he said, "Okay, then. Get in the boat and come with me. There are some people clinging to the reef who need to get to shore."

"Bob's your uncle." God, this was going to be easy.

We were about halfway between the shore and the reef when I said, "Stuart! Stop the boat a second." I pointed urgently over the side.

He did so.

"I think it's . . . a . . . a drowning woman . . . and she's holding a child!"

"Seriously?" He left the engine on idle and got up to look at my fictitious victim, at which point Neal whacked him on the back with an oar, sending him off into the churn. I took over the tiller and—ta-da! We were out of there, leaving Stuart dog-paddling and screaming unspeakable things at us. He was, pardon my French, *totalement fucké.*

I looked at my watch: it was midnight. "Now let's go find Sarah."

50

"I must say, Neal, being a pirate is a total fucking rush."
I was at the Zodiac's prow, feeling like the king of the world.

"I see its attraction, Ray."

"Plunder and killing!"

"Swagger and pillaging!"

Neal had taken over the driving, and he was making foamy, lusty figure eights in the Zodiac, all overseen by stars as bright as a drunken Piccadilly night. Our short-term plan was to stash the boat in a small cove Neal knew of a few miles away, but then we found a bale of cash about the size of a loaf of bread inside a jumbo plastic Ziploc bag—finally, a decent reason to not want a nuclear war. "About time I got properly pimped out in some new threads on Jermyn Street. And just imagine the cardboard box you can buy with all this, Neal!"

I was in such a good mood that I even forgot about Neal's unwillingness to shit out my piece of red plastic, and then it hit me: *the Cure T-shirt*.

Fuck.

"Neal, we're going to have to go back to the tent city."

"Whyzzat, Ray?"

"The Cure T-shirt."

Neal took on the look of someone who's just been shot. "Where is it?"

"I told you. It's hidden under a corner of Fiona's tent."

"Is it clean and bagged?"

"It is."

"All right, I have a plan."

Neal having a plan is about as complex as Neal finding a parking spot.

"We'll hide the boat in these mangrove roots," he said, "and then we'll sneak in and get it."

I stared at him in silence. "That's it? That's your plan?"

"Do you want the shirt or not, Ray?"

"Let's not dilly-dally, then."

After we camouflaged the Zodiac among the mangroves, we entered some palmetto scrub. It was maybe a ten-minute walk to the tent city, and we were unsure of what our reception would be there. I didn't think Stuart would have drowned, but a loudmouth like him would probably make a big deal out of our whacking him out of the boat. Fuck it: it was our word against his. He fell out of the boat. End of story.

Neal hissed, "Ray, look at this."

I glanced down to where he pointed: a creature in a shell was plodding across the sand.

"What's that?"

"It's a hermit crab of the superfamily Paguroidea."

"I've heard of the Paguroidea family. Almost 1,100 subspecies in it."

"Indeed there are. They have an asymmetrical abdomen concealed in an empty signature gastropod shell."

"Remarkable."

"Indeed. And now look up at the sky."

I did so.

"Orion's Belt. It's very clear tonight."

"You mean those three stars in a row? Tell me more about Orion's Belt, Neal."

"Certainly. The Belt of Orion is what is called a small 'asterism' in the constellation Orion. It consists of the three bright stars Alnitak, Alnilam and Mintaka. These stars are more or less evenly spaced in a straight line, and so can be visualized as the belt of the hunter's clothing. In the northern hemisphere, they are most visible in the early night sky during the winter, in particular during the month of January at around nine p.m."

"The natural world really is amazing, isn't it, Neal?"

"It certainly is, Ray."

"I find it relaxing to observe the small things that we, in our hectic lives, tend to overlook." I pointed out a shrub. "That's the *Coccoloba uvifera*, more commonly known as the sea grape. It's a species of flowering plant in the buckwheat family, of all things."

"Really?"

"Oh yes. It's native to coastal beaches throughout the Americas. I suspect this specimen here was introduced as an ornamental."

"You have to watch it with introduced species, Ray. They can wreak havoc on an ecosystem."

"Most people underestimate the fragility of marine landscapes."

Suddenly it became hard to see—and then I couldn't see anything, at which point I felt a searing bolt of pain on my forehead. Fuck me ragged—had I passed out again? I hadn't eaten a fucking thing in hours.

"Ray? Ray? You okay?" Neal was looming over me, backlit by stars. "You banged your head on a palm tree."

"Fucking hell. I had the most ghastly dream while I was passed out there. A nightmare—a delusion? Whatever you want to call it. You and me were walking along and talking about plants and stars, and it was so fucking boring. I mean, *me* talking about *plants*?"

"Never want that to actually happen."

"You said it. How far are we from the tent city?"

"It's just ahead."

Neal helped me to my feet. We found a small path and tiptoed along it, ending up just a few tents down from Fi's. Brilliant. A handful of people were to-ing and fro-ing, their eyes glued to iPhones.

"Perfect. Everyone's too busy to notice us."

"Okay, Ray, you go out and get the T-shirt."

"Me? Why me?"

"Because you know where it is, whereas I'd probably fuck up if I went."

"Fair enough."

"Hurry."

So I did. I looked at a piece of wood as though it were an iPhone—one of those weird tricks of modern living that makes a person totally invisible. When I reached Fiona's tent, as quick as a hawk, I swooped down and lifted the corner. The shirt was gone. *Crap.*

And that's when I was clubbed on the head, but this time I didn't pass out. I turned around to find Fiona, livid, holding a tiki log in her right hand, my T-shirt in its bag in her left.

"Raymond, I can't believe you shoved Stuart out of the boat!"

"We did no such thing."

"Don't even bother pretending otherwise; I saw you do it." She whacked me on the shoulder.

"What the fuck! Fiona, stop!"

"Where's the boat, Raymond?"

I turned to face her. "*Ahhh*. So now I've got something you want, right?"

"You tool. In about thirteen minutes, every person on this island is going to realize that, with the network boat sunk, there are only a finite number of calories, almost no water, and way too many people here. I do not want to be a part of that scenario. You've got a boat. It's a big advantage."

"So . . ."

"So right now, you, me and our two children go to Neal's house and ransack it for food. And then we take our hoard to some other, safer, hidden island. There are lots of them. And then we stay alive while everyone else dies a hideous, most likely cannibalistic death. After that, I have no further plans."

She was right.

"And don't even *think* of kicking me out of that boat, Raymond. You're a family man now and you will live up to your responsibilities."

"Neal has to come too."

"Fair enough. At least he has genuine skills that could come in handy."

"*And* he gets the Cure T-shirt as a reward."

Fiona thought this over for longer than one might imagine, and then she heaved a sigh. "You're right. Where is he?"

"I'm right here." He was behind us.

"Good. You'll have heard all this, then. We have to go clean out your place immediately."

Poor Neal looked crestfallen. "It was such a perfect kingdom while it lasted. But I do see your point. I'll go bring the boat around to the mangrove patch nearest the house."

* * *

I was expecting to find Neal's place looted already but when we looked in the windows, things were untouched. "Fiona, people are so fucking stupid." Then I had a thought that sank my mood: "Christ. What about Mother?"

"I need to discuss that with you. Rumour has it she's in Neal's business centre having a fuckfest with Eamon."

"Oh *him*. Well, they deserve each other. And honestly, shagging her brains out is a much more desirable way for Mother to go than sitting around with us feeling guilty because she may have to dine on a family member. Let's keep her out of our plan."

"Excellent idea."

Just then Kyle and Emma showed up. Fiona briefed them, ending with, "And remember, make no noise whatsoever inside Uncle Neal's house. We want Grandmum to enjoy her time giving Mr. Eamon his medically approved therapeutic shiatsu massage."

"No problem," said Kyle. "I can hear them already. It sounds like it's going very well."

"Gosh, this is exciting!" added Emma.

"Okay, let's go do our thing."

51

"What shall we steal next, Dad?"

Ah, families . . . nasty, dreadful, toxic things, but in those rare moments when they work, they can be something that approaches fun.

"We've nicked all the tinned goods, Kyle. Now go through the cutlery drawers for the basics, and for fuck sake—I mean for God's sake—*Yay God!*—make sure we have a tin opener. Your mum is just about through loading up her golf cart."

"I'm on it." And off went Kyle.

Emma and I went to the hut out back. As we were pilfering the last of the bug sprays and medical supplies, we had one of those father-daughter moments that money can't buy. We were about to walk out of the hut, talking as we went . . .

"I must say, Dad, Grandmum's shiatsu client is having a terrific time. But is it natural to scream whenever . . ." Emma stopped and looked at the loo door at the same moment I did. We both realized the same thing at the exact same time.

"Dad, this could be the last time we experience a flush toilet for the rest of our lives."

We were frozen to the spot. I felt as if we were all headed off to war. "Emma, why don't you have, ummm, a farewell flush."

"Thanks, Dad. I'll always remember this."

So Emma went to say farewell to civilization as I packed the last items on my golf cart, whistling "The Angry Dance" theme from *Billy Elliot*. I got to thinking of that crazy day on Wake Island and how it already felt like another historical era. And then I heard an echo of my song—it was Neal, joining in, doing a little Billy Elliot jig while carrying a full 10-gallon gasoline can in each hand.

"Ah, Billy the little poofter," said Neal fondly, ending his jig with a small plié. "Dance your brains out, you gay little mite. Just don't get caught in a bareback fourgy in the airport loo."

Emma rejoined us then, carrying medical supplies and a twenty-four-pack of Andrex Bright & Bold tissue. "It's more as a souvenir than for wiping, really," she said, balancing it on the cart atop a box of shotgun shells.

"She is a chip off the old block, isn't she, Ray? Shall we go? I can hear people approaching."

"You and Emma go ahead, Neal. I have something I need to do."

"But, Ray, it sounds like a lot of people."

"This is important, Neal. It's the Last Flush."

Emma quickly shushed him, bless her. And I went for my final dump in the modern world.

....

Andrex is a British brand of toilet roll owned by the American company Kimberly-Clark. Its mascot is the Andrex Puppy, a Labrador retriever puppy that appears on the brand's television advertising. It is sold in the U.S., Canada and Australia as Kleenex Cottonelle. In Australia, the puppy is known as the Kleenex Puppy. Kleenex is a partner and supporter of Guide Dogs Australia.

The name "Andrex" comes from St. Andrew Mills in Walthamstow, where the toilet tissue was first made in 1942. Its concept of two-ply luxury paper was conceived by Ronald Keith Kent, who also named the product. It was inspired by the two-ply facial tissues Kent had seen American women using.

Until 2004, it's oddly pervy slogan was *"Soft, Strong and Very, Very Long."* This slogan was replaced by *"Be Kind to Your Behind."*

....

For once the gods delivered: large, well-formed, structurally sound cylinders came flowing out of my arse like it was a kielbasa sausage factory. And not phantom shits, either. These were real, visible and tangible. As I reached for the Andrex, I felt a small tear in my eye. Before I knew it, it was time for the Last Flush. I was just about to depress the handle when my Spidey sense began to tingle.

From the voices I could discern that a group had descended on Neal's house. But it wasn't an angry mob in pursuit of non-perishables. It was that roving fuckfest called Thong Kong—finally landing right on my doorstep.

52

Dear Reader,

I know you're probably thinking, Oh, poor Raymond! He finally encounters Thong Kong, and now surely something is about to go horribly, horribly wrong. But strangely, after flushing, I walked out onto Neal's immaculately manicured lawn, where—how does one even begin to explain? An orgy like something out of the Scandinavian pre-condom porn era had converted his grounds into a carnal petting zoo. The girls were so mind-meltingly hot— and largely unclad except for those wearing the remains of Japanese schoolgirl outfits. Somewhere to the right I heard canisters of whipped cream being deployed, and then a hand grabbed me by the collar and hurled me into a tengy. What is a tengy? It is a fourgy with six more people added. That is correct. I, Raymond Gunt, took part in a tengy. How many of you can say that?

Yours,
Raymond Gunt

* * *

Okay, so there I was in the tengy, but at first, because it was dark out, I couldn't tell whose body parts were rubbing me—but isn't exploration a big part of the charm? Then, in light from one of several tiki torches lit over by the infinity pool, I saw what were possibly the most melon-like breasts of my life, coming towards me in a trajectory of unmistakable lust, and I thought, "Life is good, isn't it, Ray?" at which point my lower abdomen cramped like a Ford Fiesta slamming into a brick wall. Mother of God, the pain! I rolled over and went fetal in the hope that it was a one-off sensation, but then I cramped again and realized that my last flush was, actually, not *the* Last Flush. I ran back to the throne with no time to spare and proceeded to fire shit out my arse like a space cruiser entering hyperspace, all the while listening to the moaning, simpering, taunting soundtrack of Thong Kong.

Fucking hell.

After I emptied my thruster of all remaining fuel, I ran out onto the lawn to enter what was, by that point, a fifteengy. Then a woman's voice (Who? No idea) said, "Uh, uh-*uhhh* . . . rules are you have to wash your winky before entering the fun. Pool's over there."

I am not an unreasonable man, and could, in fact, understand why a bit of hygiene might make the world a better place. So I scampered over to the infinity pool, hopped in and gave myself a Puerto Rican enema, then ran back to the cluster, by then a twentygy.

I heard another woman's voice—it was Tabs!—saying, "Hi, Raymond. The girls and I have all decided that we are going to collectively give you the most intense hours of sex ever imagined in the history of humanity. Right, girls?"

Giggles and taunts of *What are we waiting for, then?*

Tabs led me over to the sacred rock, which was now covered with a foam mattress. Around it, vanilla-scented tea candles had been arranged, and there was also a towel to the right on which were laid out anal beads, a buggy whip and a selection of masks, feathers and silk scarves of just the right length for binding limbs.

Tabs said, "Lie down, Raymond, and get ready for ultimate tantric pleasure."

I thought my brain was going to explode. Tabs and ten other women formed a circle around me, and Tabs said, "Let the massage begin."

Dear God, it began, and it was heaven.

Ahhh . . .

Yes . . .

Mmmm. Perfect.

The smell of Naugahyde.

Something musky . . .

Ahhh . . .

I heard a large crunching noise. What the fuck? I looked up, and behind Tabs loomed Mother, wearing her hideous tarpaulin-like underwear. Her face was blank as she ate cheddar cheese crisps, one by one, taking time to lick her fingers thoroughly after each one. She caught me staring.

"Oh, don't mind me. I'm just watching. Raymond? Is that you in there? Dear God!"

She approached the rock and inserted herself into my coven of erotic masseuses. Her repulsive Toby mug face. Her skin—oh God, it was the most disgusting thing I'd ever seen—like folds of vanilla cake batter dotted with the occasional chocolate chip and raisin. Colourless. Dead. Life-sucking.

"Mother, what the fuck!"

"I haven't seen your willy, Raymond, since I caught you wanking in the loo at Sheila's abortion party."

"Get the fuck out of here!"

"No need to take that tone with me, son. Last time I looked, this was a free island."

My dick shrank to the size of a raisin, and my reptile cortex yanked my balls deep inside me. The girls were giggling now, and the mood was totally shattered.

"Okay, Raymond, don't worry," Mother said. "I'm a modern woman. You girls go right ahead and pleasure my son. You just pretend I'm not here, even though I am." She looked into her left bra cup. "Fucking hell, I'm out of crisps."

53

Dear The Gods,

*Was any of that really necessary? Mother? Crisps? The
memory of Sheila's dismal abortion party where there was
no food and where the only wankable image available was
a Jenny Craig weight loss brochure sent to Sheila by woe-
fully misinformed postal gods? Fucking hell! I went from
James Bond to Mr. Bean in two fucking seconds. Really,
The Gods—no, really: would keeping Mother away from
the sacred rock have been all that difficult for you?*

*You wanted a battle? You've got one. This means war.
Throw me your worst, motherfuckers.*

*Yours with some displeasure,
Raymond Gunt*

* * *

With as much dignity as I could muster, I grabbed my pile
of scarecrow togs and scuttled along the trail to where the

Zodiac was stashed. I was feeling sorry for myself, which is something I almost never do.

How much time had passed since Thong Kong had arrived? An hour? Two? Christ, I hadn't even bothered to think about everyone at the Zodiac, waiting for me, wondering what was going on. Well, fuck 'em. I hoped they'd waited.

I was just about to start snivelling when I heard my name. "Raymond?"

I froze.

A woman's voice. "Raymond!" she called again.

"Yes?"

From behind a coconut shrub emerged Sarah—Sarah! "Raymond, are you alone?"

I looked around me. "Ummm, yes. Yes, I am."

She grabbed hold of me and gave me a massive, tongue-filled kiss. When she pulled away, she looked me deeply in the eyes and said, "I've got it all figured out."

"What?"

"Our plan."

"*Our* plan?"

"Yes, you silly goose, *our* plan."

Our plan?

Skyrockets!

Roman candles!

Confetti!

Lots of people in ethnic garb dancing!

Cumshot compilations!

So *this* was what love felt like. Nothing else felt like it. Nothing. Not even the week-long coke binge Fi and I did at some record producer's compound in Honduras.

There, on that lonely path in the middle of the Pacific

Ocean, Sarah could have commanded me to die on a battlefield, but such is love: Sarah's wish was my command.

"I've got a Zodiac," she said, "and enough Spam to last us a year."

I was speechless.

"I've also brought along ten hot pieces of swimwear *and* my entire lingerie collection."

All I could muster was a noise like randomly typed letters on a keyboard: "*Bfnlhfliahelf fhslfv dsfhelfel.*"

"Oh, you silly thing. Let's hurry. The others will figure this out soon enough. The boat's down here." She pulled me towards a path that led in a different direction from where Neal and I had our Zodiac stashed. So this was the moment of choice; one of life's literal forks in the road.

"Raymond?"

"*Nvnd phwqpg pgeh eljfdl.*"

"You feel for me the way I feel for you, Raymond, right?"

"*Mfbrigueobf.*" I slowed down a little and managed, "Of course."

"Then let your heart be your guide."

I followed her down her path, my pulse beating so forcefully that my head felt like a tom-tom. When we reached the water, Sarah said, "Think of it as *The Love Boat*, Raymond—just you and me."

There was precious little Spam in the boat. "Are you sure this is enough for a year, Sarah?"

She was undoing some ropes. "You silly! This is but a fraction of it. I've been stockpiling our island hideaway all week. It's like a supermarket. You'll see."

I was just about to hop in when I heard, "Goodbye, then, Raymond."

Neal's voice. I froze.

"Don't worry, Ray. I'm not going to stop you."

"It's not what it looks like, Neal."

"Raymond, I'm on your side here."

"Meaning?"

"I want you to be happy with Sarah."

"What about Fiona and my . . ." The word did not come naturally to me. ". . . kids?"

"Fi's pissed off, but she'll survive. She has to keep her language clean because of the wee ones. It's funny, actually."

I was once again speechless.

"Before you go, I want to give you two things, Ray."

I was feeling a bit wary now.

"First of all, the Cure T-shirt." He pulled it over his head and held it out. "You deserve it. Not just because you found it to begin with, making it technically yours, but because you have my respect, Ray. This is my way of showing it."

"I—I have your respect?"

"Yes, you do. And here's one more thing." He reached into his pocket and removed something red. The piece of red plastic. "It wasn't really stuck up my arse all week. I've been carving it into a gift I wanted you to have for rescuing me and giving me one of the most exciting lives a man can lead." He handed it over. God bless him. From the piece of red plastic, he'd carved me my own knoon.

. . . .

A **knoon** (the "k" is silent) is a hybrid form of cutlery that combines the cutting capability of a knife with the containment
capability of a spoon in a single powerful utensil. The word
"knoon" is a portmanteau of "knife" and "spoon." Typically,
one or both of the outer edges of the spoon-like utensil are
sharpened to allow the user to cut food.

. . . .

54

Dawn was rising as Sarah and I pulled the boat into a tiny cove protected by a sandbar. Passing by, you'd never know the island was there; a genius location, lost to the world. I saw a thousand minnows in the water as we pulled up on the white coral sand beach. Sarah tied the boat to some sort of gnarled saltwater tree thingy and said, "Come here, Raymond—let me show you our new home."

She held my hand and we walked through flowers and coconut shrubs and came to a sensational ultra-high-tech tent like the kind you'd use on the moon.

"It's fucking beautiful," I said.

"Isn't it? And out back . . ." Holding my hand, she brought me around behind the tent, where three sub-tents were set up. "We have Spam, water, fuel and every other sort of supply you can imagine."

"Sarah, I am in awe. How did you manage to get all this out here?"

"You've noticed I've not been around much the past few days, right?"

"Well, yes. But I thought it was just that you and Stuart were screwing each other's brains . . . I mean, that you were having private time together."

"Nonsense. Stuart's a workaholic. But because he's high enough up the food chain, nobody questions me about anything, so I can do whatever I want. Now let's go and . . ." She became coy and took my hand, and we scampered to some blankets spread before a fire that was ready to light. There was a silver bucket with a bottle of bubbly and some fresh fruit and cheeses. She knelt and put a match to the kindling. *Whoosh.*

"Sarah, this is heaven!"

"I'm so glad we're finally together. Since the moment we met, I've been dreaming of this." She pulled me down onto the blankets, and we began to make out like teenagers. And sometime during all this foreplay, a little voice ran through my mind—it was my voice, of course, but one I don't use too often. It was my *nice* voice, and it said, *Well, Raymond, good things come to all good people who wait. You've got your Cure T-shirt and a custom-carved red plastic knoon. You've got a year's supply of Spam and booze, and you've got Sarah. Life doesn't get better than this, Ray, it really doesn't—so enjoy it all!*

I was enjoying it, by God, and we finally got down to the real business there on the blankets. Sarah's singlet was gone and then her bikini top and then her pants. I could barely keep myself together.

Wait—was I hallucinating?

Wait—what the hell?

Wait—*what the fuck?*

I jumped back about five feet, and a pickaxe of pain dug into my forehead and skull. I felt like I was burning up. Sarah looked at me, giggled and said, "Now, Raymond, are you telling me that nobody told you . . . that you didn't know?"

"I . . . I . . . I . . ."

"Oh, Raymond, this is truly, truly funny. You mean you really didn't know that I'm a man?"

55

"I figured you'd probably be out here."

"Yes, well, whatever."

Fiona was in the Zodiac on the foaming sea, along with Kyle and Emma, both of whom were delighted to find me perched on a coral cluster on the north side of Sarah's island. The kids obviously had no clue of what had happened to me and, with Fiona in charge, most likely never would.

Emma shouted, "Come for a ride, Dad! It's so much fun!"

Kyle added, "We've seen a barracuda and everything."

Fi looked at me pointedly. "Seen any barracudas lately, Raymond?"

"*Fu*—ha, ha, ha."

"I've made sandwiches," Emma cajoled. "And we have some delicious lemonade. It's a sea picnic. Climb in, Dad."

"You may as well get in the boat, Raymond," Fiona offered.

Bloated hag. "Well, okay."

I climbed in and Kyle asked, "What's that amulet you have around your neck?" He was referring to the knoon, which I had made into an amulet with a piece of nylon netting I found snagged on the coral. "Can I see it?"

I handed it to Kyle. Meanwhile, Fiona was her usual bullying self. "Raymond, you take that Cure T-shirt off right now and put it on top of your head. Your scalp's so red you look like a preemie baby."

"Okay, okay. Probably not a bad idea, even if it does make me look like a Gumby."

"What's a Gumby?" asked Emma.

"Just a character from an old TV show, sweetie," said Fi. "But don't worry, you'll never have to watch it, or any other TV show, because TV is crap and the people in it are dreadful and I will work myself to the bone to ensure that both you and Kyle find careers as far away from TV as is possible within the constraints of civilization."

"Okay, Mum, sounds reasonable."

"Speaking of civilization, Raymond," said Fi, "you'll be happy to hear the nuclear crisis is over."

"It is?"

"And not one city blown up in the end."

"Great." I couldn't find the energy to muster any vitriol for my idiot species.

Emma piped up, "Shall we have some sandwiches now, Mum?"

"Excellent idea, Emma. Get them out of the cooler."

Emma opened the cooler, removed the sandwiches and let out a small gasp.

"What is it, Emma?"

"Oh, Mum. I forgot to cut the crusts off. I'm terribly, terribly sorry."

"No problem, sweetie. Hand them to your father. Kyle, give your father back the red spoony-knifey thingy."

"Yes, Mum."

"Raymond, please use your red plastic thingy and cut the crusts off the sandwiches."

I looked at her and she looked at me.

Fucking hell.

"Yes, Mother." And so I trimmed off the crusts.

Douglas Coupland (pronounced KOHP-lend) (born December 30, 1961) is a Canadian writer, designer and visual artist. His first novel was the 1991 international bestseller *Generation X: Tales for an Accelerated Culture*. He has published fourteen novels, two collections of short stories, seven non-fiction books and a number of dramatic and comedic works for stage, film and TV. In June 2014, Coupland will have his first solo exhibition at the Vancouver Art Gallery, after which the exhibition will tour internationally.

Coupland is left-handed, is allergic to sulfa antibiotics and has never purchased anything from a duty-free store or eaten a peanut butter sandwich. Being born on the second-last day of the year, Coupland was always the youngest in his school classes, and until he turned thirty he was painfully skinny, which is why there are so few photos of him between the ages of eighteen and thirty. He now looks back on those few photos that exist and wishes he'd taken more, as he was, for a short window of time in the mid-1980s, technically hot.

Does he have any regrets about his twenties? Oh sure, everyone does. Coupland wishes he hadn't worried so much and had relaxed a little. But, like most people with this mindset, he believes that his life would have gone nowhere had he not worried so much, and that it was the worrying itself that got him out into the world, hustling his ass and doing stuff. Coupland is quite certain, however, that he had a protective coating of youthful cluelessness that allowed him to make life decisions that, upon mature reflection, are utterly horrifying. For example, attending art school and then, in the few years afterwards, having made a modest go of things in the visual world, discovering writing and deciding to become a writer. Talk about a surefire career path! And yet it all kind of worked out in the end, and we must thank nature specifically for loaning us all a protective coating of cluelessness in our youth.